FALL LINE

Also by Joe Samuel Starnes

Calling

FALL
LINE

A NOVEL BY

JOE SAMUEL STARNES

NEWSOUTH BOOKS
Montgomery

NewSouth Books
105 S. Court Street
Montgomery, AL 36104

Library of Congress Cataloging-in-Publication Data

Starnes, Joe Samuel.
Fall line : a novel / by Joe Samuel Starnes.

p. cm.

ISBN-13: 978-1-58838-265-8
ISBN-10: 1-58838-265-6

I. Title.
PS3619.T375F35 2011
813'.6—dc23

2011033089

Design by Randall Williams

Printed in the United States of America by
Sheridan Books

CONTENTS

Morning

This dog Percy is there when the dawn breaks, running beside the river and then turning away, through the woods and up the hill, leaves crushing under his feet, his path worn more than ten years, stopping to smell the holes where the chipmunks burrow out of sight when he trots by. His fur is black and his paws black and even his tongue black, the blackest of all chows, but he is only half chow and half mutt like the backwoods country dogs that roam the woods around the old lady's home. His black eyes are steady and see the earth up close in the bridge between light and darkness enshrouded in a cool mist from the Oogasula. Drops of dew sparkle on the evergreens and silvery and bluish reflections dance on the clear water gurgling on the banks and streaming in the middle, small white caps breaking in the slow bend of the river.

He runs up through the woods, farther away from the smell of the cold river water and through the lower hardwoods and into the pine thicket up the hill where the new shortleaf pines begin, growing every day, a few feet each year, their rough bark trunks shooting out of the red clay and yearning for the blue sky. He noses the fresh pine needles that cover the ground like a blanket before he crosses back into the hardwoods and digs in the old stumps, sniffing for the chipmunks down in their holes. He imagines their brown fur with the black stripe punctuated with white dots curled into a tight dusty ball. He can smell the chipmunks clearly, can hear their pitched little grunts and squeals. He growls softly at them, his fangs showing. He runs on and smells the scent of rabbits and a possum and the big hole where the groundhog nests. He is on the lookout for squirrels, the flying one in particular, but they are nowhere to be seen. The old man had taught him when he was a pup to stay after the squirrels and to tree them and to bark and point up with his nose, until he could come along with his shotgun. The old man had become more and more wrinkled until he was carried off in a box a long time ago, and had missed a lot of squirrels Percy had scared up. Percy runs on, keeping his nose to the ground but his eyes look up in case the squirrels appear along the break of blue sky between the pines and oaks and yellow poplars. The image of the flying squirrel coasting like a bird from tree limb to tree limb with his four paws spread and his fur like a cape is etched in Percy's mind. He watches for the squirrel and dreams about him when he naps.

He crosses into an open field, the land that had been the forest before men with roaring saws cleared the trees, sawing them down to stumps and hauling off the wood down the narrow logging roads. He stops and pees on the stump where the possum hides and then runs over and sprays another stream on the holes burrowed by the chipmunks. He sniffs the fresh sap, hardening in the dry sun, and runs off from the cleared land and up a hill covered in hardwoods.

The woods on the hill still have salt licks where a few deer used to gather this time of year, but he knows only to go there when he can't smell metal and gunsmoke and the drift of cigarettes or hear the slow deep voices of men, hunched in deer stands they nailed up with makeshift ladders, rungs made of small boards hammered onto the bark of the tree trunks. He sniffs the ground and smells where deer have been out in the early morning, their urine and feces fresh in the dew-covered brown leaves. He darts his eyes around but the whitetails are nowhere to be seen.

Percy pauses. There are no woodsmen out today, a good day for hunting, unseasonably warm and dry, but no hunters have been out for at least a month, not since the trees in the wide valley were cut. There are no lowing cows to listen for either. When he was younger he often crossed the hill into the pastures and chased the cows, scaring the clumsy herd into fits of mooing and clomping. He had heard the cows up until a month ago, but the sound of the herd and the farmers and their dogs are long gone from the low fields farther down the bend of the river. In days past when chasing cows he might fight with the farm dogs, a pack of lab mixes that were big and strong but soft and scared of him, two of them no match for his chow anger. He had put his teeth in their clean hides many times and he had picked up a few wounds from them. He'd twice caught a little birdshot from the farmer's .410, the second time enough to keep him away from the dumb cows and the domesticated dogs for good, even if the man was using a shotgun he'd seen only little boys carry.

At the end of his romps he goes down to the river and runs along its edge, sniffing out the water and scaring frogs off the bank, their long legs slingshotting them out with a splash. He'd eaten a small frog when he was a pup and got sick and felt the legs kicking and moving all the way down his throat and into his belly. He was ill for three days. But he still likes to sniff out the frogs and scare them into the water, sometimes jumping in after them and paddling with his head above the surface, his black eyes alive with the chase, the smell of river water, the cool breaking of it on his fur, his paws paddling against and across the current. Also in summer he looks for snakes in the flat shoals and tries to catch them, snatching their long bodies up with his teeth, getting one right in the middle lengthwise and shaking it ferociously, all fur and fury and growling, beating it on the ground wildly until it quits hissing and wriggling. Once he had seen a dog that used to run with him get bit on the nose by a rattler. The dog's head swelled up and it went back in a briar patch and took three days to die, moaning and whimpering in the tangled vines. Percy has never been bitten by a snake and still tries to catch them. He has lashed many cottonmouths to death, although he has not caught one this year and now it is too late, the warm season passed and the frogs and snakes all sleeping in their holes until the days get longer and warmer. Even so, he checks the riverbank every day for snakes and frogs. The cold-blooded creatures are sneaky and he looks out for them year-round.

He expects the old lady to come out into the woods with him like she does once a year about this time and cut down a red cedar and drag it back to the house and dress it up with ribbons and gold balls and then feed him ham, but lately all she has done is sit on the porch and gaze out across the woods, muttering to herself. It seems there will be no decorated tree in the house this season, but he watches for her in the woods every day. He still misses the old man, pocket full of treats, rubbing Percy's belly until his back paws twitched this way and that.

He ends his route as he does every morning, with a traipse along about half a mile of river, backtracking his early run, eyes alert for beavers or water rats along the bank and spying the water for a fish or turtle at which he could bark. He doesn't run as hard or bark as loud or growl as ferociously as he once did. After his run he goes home and curls up under the porch and nestles there with his paws in the air and rubs his back on the ground, and then drifts off into a nap. He kicks his legs in his sleep, dreaming of the flying squirrel and snakes and chasing deer, the whitetails flashing as they splash into the river, the river he has known all his life.

ELMER BLIZZARD GAZED ACROSS the land he might be the last to ever see. He took a long drag on a cigarette and flipped the butt onto the ground and stamped it under his heel. Up the hill from the river in a clearing used for a cow pasture stood an ancient oak, its bare branches stretching high into the clear sky like they were reaching for something, hopeful even after hundreds of years of nothing, while waiting in the cresting field. Sherman himself had stopped for a smoke under that tree when the Yankees burned a swath through here ninety-one years ago. Wouldn't be long till the lake would come and that old tree would be nothing but deadwood where catfish would gather if Georgia Power and the government's plan played out correctly.

He reached into the back of his britches and pulled out his .38 revolver and aimed at a bobtail squirrel in the neck of a tree, pulling back on the trigger and firing three times at the varmint. It shrieked and scurried down the trunk and across the ground. Elmer pulled the trigger a fourth time but he had used his last bullet so the empty chamber clicked hollowly. He put the gun back in his britches and scowled at the squirrel as it dashed away.

He turned to take in the landscape. Down the slope the river streamed through the gully, narrow but deeper in the cut of red clay between gently rolling hills. Pulpwooders had clear-

cut all the pines where the lake would go, leaving only a field
of stumps, but most of the hardwoods they left behind. Across
the river and further up, sapling pines took over and stretched
a long way back, the new trees courtesy of the Georgia-Pacific
Plywood Company. Lake must not be going that high over
there, Elmer figured, and that'll be beyond the shoreline.

It was December but the sun was warm and the brown
grass rustled in the easy wind. The road where he'd parked
curved down toward the Oogasula and ran parallel and close
to the water for about fifty yards before it veered back the other
direction in a lazy curve, a mirror image of the river's course.
He ambled down to the water's edge where he stood in plain
view of old Mrs. McNulty's house, the little shack across the
road from the kudzu-covered junkyard situated in a flat low
spot at the bend in the river. From about a hundred yards away
he could see her, squatting on her porch by an antique bathtub,
fooling with something under it, her back to him. She was a
big-boned woman who carried herself proud, her posture like
that of an old Indian chief, her hair dark despite her age. She'd
been living in the house without electricity or running water
as long as he could remember, that tub sitting out front the
whole time. A black chow came hesitantly out from under the
porch and stood next to her, his wide tongue hanging from his
mouth. The dog looked at Elmer and then back at her.

Elmer turned to face the river, unzipped his fly, pulled it out
and peed into the current. "Big water's coming," Elmer said.
A long golden stream arched through the air and glittered in
the sunlight before splashing in the water. "Yep," he continued,
looking back at Mrs. McNulty's shack, not opening his lips
very wide when he spoke but still speaking loudly in a scratchy
drawl, "the power company gonna flood you out, honey pie."

He zipped up and spat, the little white gob floating on the

surface like a water bug until it submerged in a riffle about twenty feet away. "Big water's sure nuff coming."

Mrs. McNulty didn't turn to look at Elmer until he was up on the top step, the board creaking like it always had. He was a little man, wiry, 150 pounds at most, so it didn't squeak much. Wasn't any point in fixing it now, that old step, all those years of being loose. She'd let all those things go when Ralph died. Ralph never was a finisher anyhow. He had been promising to do something about the bathtub he had brought home and abandoned on the porch a generation ago. The tub was chipped and dirty and it was packed full of rags and shoeboxes containing car parts, mainly door handles and hood ornaments. All the things Ralph had left behind.

"Hey, Elmer," she said, regarding him cautiously but friendly—she'd heard stories and knew he wasn't a deputy anymore. "What you shooting at over there?"

"Hey . . . Mrs. McNulty. Aw, just an old squirrel. I figure I'd get him 'fore he drowns."

"My old dog here is scared to death of guns. Didn't you hear him whining?"

Elmer looked at the dog, sitting next to Mrs. McNulty.

"No, ma'am. He looks all right to me. I know he's seen guns before."

"But that don't mean he likes 'em."

"Well, I'm sorry if I disturbed him."

He glanced around her yard and then down toward the river. "What you still doing out here? They want everybody out today. Paper said you got to clear out by sunset."

"Yeah, I know it." She was still squatting by the tub. "I'm just trying to figure how I can get the feet off this thing."

"You worried it's gonna up and run away?" He spat off

the porch into one of the wild hydrangeas alongside Mrs. McNulty's steps.

"Now that I'd like to see," she said. "Who knows what's gonna happen when that water comes? This old tub just might try to run."

She laughed, a hacking chuckle, and continued, gesturing across the road to the vine-choked junkyard.

"Man from the state said all these cars will make this part of the lake one of the best fishing spots in the whole mess. Sumpin' about the fish wanting somewheres to hide."

"Yeah, I reckon they right," Elmer said, turning to look at the leaf-covered old cars dating back to the beginning of automobiles—Model A's and T's and old trucks, a tractor here and there, a Stanley Steamer, all rusting away. "How long ago did Mr. McNulty start hauling vehicles out here?"

"It's been near forty years, I guess."

"Yeah, I wonder what he'd think of this. I guess this part of the lake'll be fifty feet deep down here in the gully. And I bet the top of that old oak tree will be sticking up through the surface of the water."

"I wonder why they didn't cut it down, like they did all those pines?"

"Ain't no telling," Elmer said.

Mrs. McNulty put her hand on the tub and looked toward the river beyond the junkyard.

"You think that dam is really gonna fill up the land, like they say it is?"

Elmer spat again. Her hydrangeas were getting wet.

"Aw . . . hell, naw," he said. "I don't think those damn fools know what they're doing." Elmer spat one more time. "You think it's gonna take, this big lake here?"

"I don't know, Elmer. I don't know. The first I heard about

it a few years back, it didn't make a dadgum bit of sense to me. I thought they was all talk. Then, last year, they came around with a five-hundred-dollar check and court papers. Didn't give me no choice. It was then I started to believe. They say it's progress. I guess you can't stop it . . ."

"Shit," Elmer said, not caring if he cussed in front of her. He knew she'd heard uglier, all but two of her children either in prison or the crazy house or dead or worse—run off up north. She put her hands on the end of the tub and stood up out of her crouch. At her full height she was six inches taller than him. She brushed her black bangs from her forehead.

"Progress," Elmer said, taking a step back. "Monkeying with the land God made ain't progress. It's just plain craziness if you ask me. God didn't build no lake here."

"Old Percy and I here would tend to agree with you." The dog's fur was thick and dusty, and she leaned down and scratched under his chin. "Don't we, boy?" She patted him on the head and looked up at Elmer.

"What brings you out this way?"

"Aw, I'm working for the sumbitches. The power company. On their scout crew. They want to find anything of value they can sell before it ends up on the bottom of the lake."

"Well, I guess I better get these claw feet off and take 'em with me before you do."

"Shoot. I ain't gonna take 'em from you. They ain't worth that much. But I'll help you get 'em off. You're going to have to flip this thing over if you ever gonna get 'em loose."

"Yeah. I reckon you're right."

She picked up several of the shoeboxes full of car parts stored in the tub and set them against the wall of the house. Her gray robe fell open and he was glad to see she had a housedress on under it. Elmer helped her clean out the tub, dumping rags in a pile. When it was empty, she moved around to the end and gripped the lip of the tub with one hand on the side and one on the end.

"Elmer, you get the other side there and we'll flip it this way," she said, gesturing toward the house.

He nodded but looked unsure.

"This thing is cast iron, ain't it?"

"Yeah, but we can get it."

She weighed at least fifty pounds more than he did and had strong arms and legs and a sturdy back from years of hauling things around a junkyard.

"Got it?" she said.

"Yep."

They turned it over. The rusty tub lay on its rim like a dead pig, belly up, its claw feet extending stiffly into the air. Elmer studied the bottom of the tub, caked with spider webs and dirt. Each foot had a screw hidden in the soles.

"All you need now is a screwdriver to get the bolts loose," Elmer said.

"Lemmee see where it is. Come help me look."

He followed her into the front room of the shack. The house was as messy as any he had ever seen, and he remembered his mama talking about the McNultys being good people but sorry housekeepers. Car parts were everywhere: a carburetor on the mantel, a tire rim on a love seat, pistons on the dining room table, half of an engine block on the floor.

She gestured toward the kitchen.

"Let's look in these drawers."

Elmer opened a drawer in the cabinet near the door and shuffled through a clump of butter knives and ice picks and spark plugs and hood ornaments and car door handles, the small metals clanging softly—everything but the tool they needed. Mrs. McNulty made a loud racket shaking a drawer near the washbasin.

"Hah. Got it," she said, holding up a screwdriver for him to see. She led him back to the porch. She crouched and began to loosen the screws within the claw feet. Elmer offered to help but she shook her head no.

He watched her for a few minutes until that eternal feeling of boredom came over him. He got tired of company right quick, couldn't stand to share a moment with anyone for too long. The five years he was married liked to have about killed him.

"Mrs. McNulty, I've got to get on back to work, I guess."

"What's that, Elmer?" She was still preoccupied with the feet. She had one foot loose and was working on the second.

He hustled his balls with his left hand.

"I said, I got to get on back to work."

"Why don't you have you a seat?" She turned and gestured to two rocking chairs on the other end of the porch.

"Naw, I gotta go."

"All right," she said, still not looking up. "Thank you for helping me hoist this old thing."

He inventoried her yard. She didn't have a car or truck and none of the vehicles in the junkyard had cranked in decades.

"Where you headed this evening?"

"What?"

"I said, where you headed this evening?"

She looked up at him directly like the idea of leaving the house had not even crossed her mind.

"You got to go somewhere," he said. "They shutting the floodgates tonight. The big water's coming."

He hustled his balls again. He was dying to get away from her and be by himself in the woods, having a smoke and listening to the birds chirping and the squirrels rooting around there one last time. He couldn't stand to be on the porch with her another minute.

She looked at him as though she had never seen him before.

"I guess one of your daughters is gonna come get you, ain't they?" He was nodding his head yes, answering his own question.

She nodded, though she looked like she didn't understand. The nod was good enough for Elmer. He *had* to go.

"All right, Mrs. McNulty. I'll see you in town sometime. Don't stay out here too late. The lake's a coming."

He turned on the porch and went down, the top step squeaking like a half-drowned bird.

"Bye . . . Elmer. You come back now, you heah?" she said weakly. But he was already down the steps and didn't hear.

ELMER GOT TO THE Magnolia Restaurant about the same time his uncle pulled up in his shiny police car, a big black Buick Century with white doors emblazoned with a star that announced *Sheriff Lloyd Finley* from three city blocks or a long bend in a country road away. Elmer didn't like to eat out in public with everyone in town stopping to speak to the sheriff and look down on their plates, but he had been summoned by his uncle and had no choice.

"Mornin', Elmer." His uncle extended his thick hand for a shake, his grip warm and strong.

Elmer clasped his hand and let go as quickly as he could. "Hey, Lloyd."

"Son, it's always good to see you."

Elmer didn't say anything but he held the door for his Uncle Lloyd, his girth in the taupe uniform beneath a white sheriff's hat filling the doorway. He was glad not to get another lecture about his need for a stronger handshake. He stood behind as his uncle surveyed the Magnolia, choosing a table in the back of the narrow greasy spoon, full with smells of fried sausage and cigarettes. He led Elmer down the aisle between the booths and the counter. Warm steam from pancake batter rose from the griddle and fogged the backsplash. Forks and knives on china and spoons tinkling in coffee cups slowed for a minute, as did the disorganized babble of voices, while everyone paused to see them pass. The sheriff nodded and spoke hello and mornin' to everyone, from the judge eating his waffle to the busboy with his dishrag. Elmer kept his eyes on the floor and spoke to no one, focusing instead on the black-and-white checkered pattern in the tile beneath his feet.

He slid into the seat facing the back wall while the sheriff stood for a moment studying the tables and the counter, his expression a mix of smile, smirk, and scowl, ready for whoever confronted him, child or criminal or college professor. Lloyd took off his hat and eased himself into the booth as the waitress whisked by and dropped off menus and cups of coffee. Elmer dumped a load of sugar in his cup and stirred it with a teaspoon. He stared at the black coffee and without looking up he knew his uncle was staring him down.

"Son, how you been?"

"I'm fine, Lloyd, fine. How 'bout you?"

"I tell you what. I ain't never been so busy with all these folks coming into town. Ain't no telling how many."

"Yeah. I been seeing it in the paper."

"It's the biggest thing ever happened 'round here."

Elmer said nothing. Lloyd took a sip of his coffee and set it down. They were quiet for a moment before Lloyd spoke.

"Did you see that new Ford out there? That pink and white one, the new Crown Vic Skyliner?"

"Naw," Elmer said.

"You oughta take a look at it. Sharp as a tack. It's the Guvnah's. First one like it I've seen."

"Pink and white? Sounds like a little girl's car to me."

"Nope. It's a cool ride. It has this green glass roof that lets the sun in."

"That old man's a fool. He's just showing his ass with that car."

"Aw, Elmer. It ain't like that. Aubrey just likes to have some fun, that's all."

Elmer took a long sip of coffee and turned around and looked at the front door before swiveling back to Lloyd's gaze.

"I hadn't seen you around in a while, son. You been working?"

"Every day. Out in the field."

"How's that going?"

"It's all right."

"Is today your last day?"

"Reckon so."

"What, uh . . . what you got planned?"

"Nothing, right now. Something'll come along."

"I hear Callaway is hiring."

"I ain't gonna be a linthead, Lloyd."

"It pays pretty good. Pretty damn good. You oughta think about it."

Elmer said nothing.

"If you don't want to do that, you know Otey always needs help at the sawmill."

"I sure as hell don't want no part of that."

Lloyd looked at Elmer and sighed.

"Well . . . Elmer, son . . . what you gonna do? Ain't nothing else 'round here. Lest you want to go back to school."

"Naw. Eleven years was enough."

Elmer checked his watch, avoided Lloyd's eyes.

"Son, you got to do something."

Elmer shrugged and moved his lips like he was going to speak but stayed quiet. He set the teaspoon down and looked at the menu. He knew what he wanted to order but studied the options anyway.

Lloyd sat up straight and leaned forward over the table.

"I warned you—did I not?—that that prison farm woman was trouble. You and she can say it was love, but the law says otherwise."

"I ain't the one said it was love."

"Well, son, I didn't think it was neither. I can't believe they didn't make me fire you the second time, much less the first. It ain't like the good old days when I was a boy. Them days is gone. A man can't get away with nothin' no more."

His uncle exhaled a long slow breath and sat back. "I know you've had a hard time of it, son."

Elmer looked straight into Lloyd's fixed stare.

"You all right?" Lloyd asked. "Is it bothering you?"

"I'm fine, Lloyd. I don't never think about it."

"You'd let me know, if things get to troubling you, wouldn't you?"

Elmer averted his eyes but nodded yes.

The waitress stopped by and they ordered. Elmer asked for biscuits and gravy, sausage, and grits, and the sheriff chose country ham, scrambled eggs, grits, and biscuits. She turned and the sheriff watched her go back down the aisle and behind the counter.

He winked at Elmer. "I think she's looking good, don't you? Putting on a little weight."

Elmer nodded and fingered the cigarettes in his pocket but

decided to wait to smoke until after he ate.

"You ever hear from Sherry?"

"Nope," Elmer said. "Not in a few years."

"Damn."

Elmer turned to look back to the counter and the griddle behind to see if their food might be coming out.

Lloyd asked, "You want me to try to fix you up with one of these young gals I know down in Macon? They'll be a lot of women in town today for the barbecue . . . and the party at Coach Hilliard's."

Elmer shook his head no. He finished off the last of his coffee and turned and looked down the aisle, gesturing to the waitress with his cup. She raised one finger to indicate she'd be there in a minute.

Elmer then saw State Senator Aubrey Terrell walk in the front door. Terrell was tall and had a high silver shock of hair parted on the side above his dark horn-rimmed glasses. He wore a dark blue suit with a bright red tie. He started shaking hands with everyone, working his way through the tables and down the counter. He walked stiffly like he wore a truss. His voice was smooth and slow as he complimented the women on how good they looked and asked the men how they were doing, telling them he was glad to see them and that they'd soon have a lake to go fishing and water skiing if they so desired, not to mention cheap electricity.

Elmer turned back around and stared into the sugary bottom of his cup. The sheriff was watching Terrell work his way down the aisle. Elmer could hear the senator having a discussion with the judge three booths away, something about valuable lakefront lots.

He lost track of his eavesdropping when the waitress set their plates and a cold butter dish on their table and refilled

their coffees. Elmer cut a chunk of butter and slathered it on
his grits, mashing it with his fork to melt it more quickly. The
sheriff, who had not taken his eyes off the state senator, slid
from the booth and stood.

"*Guvnah*, it's good to see you this mornin'."

The sharp scent of aftershave preceded the senator,
whom Elmer saw move into his peripheral vision and shake
hands with his uncle in a vigorous hold. Elmer took a bite
of grits.

"Lloyd, how in the heck are you, boy? You keeping everybody straight?"

"It ain't easy, but I'll die tryin'."

"Boy, I know that."

"That's a fine new car you got out there, Guvnah. Mighty
fine."

"Well, it's an old man's indulgence. But it rides mighty
sweet. I'll have to take you out for a ride in it sometime soon,
Lloyd."

"Anytime, Guvnah, anytime."

Elmer cut a large piece of the biscuit and sausage and ran
it through the thick gravy and put it in his mouth. His uncle
turned his way.

"Guvnah, you know my nephew here."

"Of course, of course. How are you doing, Elmer?"

Elmer put down his fork and turned in his seat and held
out his hand to shake with the senator.

"Yes sir," he said, speaking as best he could with his mouth
full. "I'm doing fine."

Lloyd said, "Elmer has been working for the power company.
If you hear of any jobs, you let us know."

Terrell tilted his head back and put his hand on his chin,
moving his fingers as though he had a beard he was pulling.

"Oh, that's right, I still think of Elmer as a deputy. Well, let me see . . . Come up front and see me this afternoon out at the dam. I'll introduce you around. There'll be a lot of folks down from Atlanta that could help you out."

Elmer didn't say anything. He was half-turned toward the senator but his eyes were watching his food cool off, the little wafts of steam reducing by the second.

Lloyd said, "Thank you, Guvnah. We'll do it. I'll be there. Elmer will get out there, too. Won't you, Elmer?"

"Yes, sir," Elmer said, taking another bite but not looking his way.

"Well, alrighty then,"Terrell said."I'm going to let y'all get back to your breakfast before it gets cold. Good seeing you Lloyd . . . Elmer."

Elmer half-waved his left hand as he took a sip of coffee. The sheriff gave the senator another vigorous handshake and got a healthy backslap in return.

"Thank you, Guvnah. We appreciate all you do for us."

"I do the best I can."

The state senator walked back to the front of the restaurant and sat in a booth with two lawyers who had been waiting for him. The sheriff sat down and attacked his food, but the ham and biscuit in his mouth didn't quell his angry whisper.

"Goddamn, Elmer, what's wrong with you, son? I can't do everything for you. You got to make an effort."

Elmer scowled and leaned toward his uncle.

"Why you call him 'Guvnah?' Ole Talmadge beat him like a stray dog."

"Son, you know everybody 'round here calls him Guvnah."

"Might as well call me sheriff." Elmer smiled a little at his own joke and would have scratched himself and spit had he not been sitting down and eating. "And I wonder who he stole from to buy that car?"

His uncle shook his head from side to side and let out another long sigh. He looked straight at Elmer, but Elmer spoke before Lloyd could, his eyes intense, his hand gripping his fork in the way he would hold a hammer.

"Goddammit Lloyd, that sumbitch took *our* land. Your parents' land, my mama's land. I don't see why I got to act like he didn't. He flat out stole it."

"That was a long time ago, Elmer. He did me and Billy and your mama a favor."

"A favor, shit. He favored a lot of dirt farmers right up the ass, didn't he? Then acted like he was our best friend. Most of the poor sumbitches believed him. I believed him for a long time, too."

"Elmer, it's not that way. It cost him something. He saved a lot of farmers 'round here from going to jail."

"Mama always said that giving up our land is what killed granddaddy and grandmama."

"They was old, Elmer, had lived hard lives. At least they died in the homeplace, not some old nigger shack. Aubrey's a good Christian. He did us a favor by not kicking us all out in the road."

"And doing us all favors made his ass rich. Helped him to take over the bank, helped him to get elected."

"He was already in the state house by then."

"That don't matter nohow. Goddammit, Lloyd, it's about our land. He took it, and now look what he's done with it. I'm supposed to be happy about that?"

Lloyd shifted in his seat and leaned forward over the table.

"Elmer, son, it was the big'un. I know that your mama and

Billy could've done worse, they could've lost everything. They never had to work in the factory. Your daddy could have gone to jail."

"My daddy might as well have ended up in the jailhouse."

"I ain't saying Billy wasn't sorry, Elmer. He was sorry—is sorry—and your mama would probably have been better off if she'd never seen him . . . but the Guvnah don't have nothing to do with his being sorry."

"I don't see what loyalty you got to the old sumbitch, Lloyd."

"The Guvnah has supported me all along. I was a young man, only thirty, when I got elected."

"Lloyd, everybody knows he ran you against old Rasmussen 'cause Rasmussen didn't let him get away with drinking liquor and gambling and screwing half the women in this county. Like you do, Lloyd."

"Elmer, don't you go there with me. Not today. I know you are in a bad place, but there ain't no cause to be mean. Brother Frank says every time somebody's being ugly, it's because they are hurting inside . . . and I know you are hurtin'. But I ain't gonna 'low it. I ain't. You hear me?"

"Don't quote no uppity preacher to me. You know what you oughta do, Lloyd? Go out and see your family's land one last time and say goodbye to Finley Shoals. You and your girls are the only Finleys left. You oughta take them out there and see what they lost. See the little crossroads that was once theirs, before it all goes down to the bottom of the lake. Maybe if you thought of it that way, you'd want to shoot that old sumbitch like I do, instead of giving him a goddamn gold medal."

"Elmer, keep your voice down, boy. You just talking again."

"I want to give the sumbitch some medals, all right, some *metal* from my gun, right in his ass."

"Elmer, hush now. You can't go around saying you are going to shoot somebody. I've heard you say it before. I know you just talking, you angry, but you ain't going to do anything of the sort . . . Go on home, cool off for a while. Think about things. He'll help you out if you just let him. He pulled some strings to help me keep you on as long as he could, until it got to where he couldn't do anything else."

"Shit. I don't believe 'at for a minute. He'll help me only if he can help himself."

"Well, it's the only help you gonna get, boy. The *only* help you gonna get. You better take it. Your mama would tell you the same thing if she was here. You family, son, I love you. I'm telling you that you better see things different. He's your best ticket to something new, a job, your future."

Elmer said nothing, avoiding eye contact with Lloyd.

"Son, I wish I knew what to say to you. You going to go out there this evening to this thing, ain't you? Wear your suit and a tie. You'll be there?"

Elmer cut another piece of gravy-soaked biscuit with his fork and put it in his mouth.

"Well, son, won't you? This is the best chance you gonna have."

Elmer chewed and swallowed. He looked up at his uncle's red face, then back down at his plate.

"C'mon, now, son. You look good in that blue dress suit of yours. Just for a little while, this afternoon."

Elmer set the fork tines down on the edge of his plate, listening to his uncle's labored breathing.

"I ain't going to promise you nothin'," he said, "but I'll think about it."

DOWNTOWN LYMANVILLE ON THURSDAY morning was slow, more than half the parking spaces empty. Silver aluminum stars with glittery tassels hung from the creosote-covered light posts above the street-side trees, bare gingkoes and crape myrtles dormant in the late fall as winter waited to begin. Elmer lit a cigarette and walked down Lyman Avenue and then turned right on Main Street toward the women's college, passing storefronts: the five and dime, the bank, the pool hall still dark, Woolworth's, the movie house, the Piggly Wiggly across from the courthouse. He finished the butt and tossed it on the ground.

He sulked along the street for a ways and then turned and went back up Main Street for a block and then left onto Lyman Avenue and crossed it and went up the high steps and into the Feed-and-Seed. He shut the screen door behind him and the smell of fertilizer and phosphorus rose up on him something powerful and phosphorous, the odorous promise of high corn and fat red tomatoes and world-record turnips. The store had dim lights and the smell in the air was like a relic of the last century; the old hardwood floors were clean but long worn and had not seen a coat of varnish in Elmer's lifetime. Exposed brick on the inside walls showed sloppy masonry from a bygone era. Four men, two gray and two bald, all in glasses and overalls, sat around a checkerboard on a wooden barrel near the front. They looked up at him and nodded. Mr. Worthington, the bald store owner who was the oldest and the only fat one, spoke.

"Mornin', Elmer."

"Mornin'."

"Something I can help you with today?"

"Naw sir. Just looking."

"Okay. Make yourself at home."

Elmer walked down the fertilizer aisle, stacked high with fifty-pound bags of phosphate dug up from deep in the ground in central Florida then crushed and burned before being bagged and shipped to farmers. The high strong chemical smell was oddly pleasing, the hard whiff Elmer could smell in his nose and eyes. His eyes watered slightly and he paused and rubbed his hands on his lids to clear his vision. He blinked a few times and moved slowly on down the aisle.

Hoes and shovels and pickaxes and posthole diggers and adzes hung on the rear wall. He turned and walked back down the middle aisle where red and white and blue bags of Jazz feeds for cows and chickens were stacked high on the sturdy blue metal shelves. He paused and studied on a bag of Red Heart dog food but moved on toward the front of the store where the men played checkers. He turned by them and walked down the last aisle where the seed was kept, its shelves empty except for some unsold bags of turnip seed from the previous growing season. In three months the shelves would fill up with seed for beans, peas, corn, tomatoes, okra, squash, potatoes and all other manner of vegetables, but now the aisle lay in wait for winter to do its cold business.

At the end of the aisle in the far back corner of the store he looked in a locked glass case with a selection of shotguns and pistols for sale, and next to that an open shelf of boxes of ammunition for everything from .410s to .45s. Mr. Worthington was a connoisseur of guns and known for his fine selection of weaponry. Elmer sorted through the boxes, mostly .22 bullets, and picked up a carton of 20-gauge shells, buckshot, and then one of the only two remaining boxes of bullets for a .38. He paused for a minute and set the shells down and looked into his wallet and then took inventory in his mind of what he had at home in the way of firepower. He put the shotgun shells back neatly into place and went up the feed aisle with the overpriced bullets. At the front of the store he walked to the cash register and held the box high so Mr. Worthington could see.

The store owner excused himself from checkers and went around behind the counter and rang up the sale, the bell clanging and the drawer popping open and the numbers 1-5-0 flashing white in the encased glass on the faded brass register. Elmer counted out the last two dollar bills from his wallet.

"I do thank you, Elmer." Mr. Worthington handed him two quarters. "You need a bag?"

Elmer shook his head no and took the dense box of bullets squarely in his right hand and cocked his fist into his side. He paused to look at the three old men waiting for Mr. Worthington's return to the checkerboard. He had known all of them his entire life, one-time farmers turned into go-getters. When the day ended and the mill whistle blew and their wives got off work, they would up and *go get her*.

He nodded a goodbye to them and walked out into the brightening sun, careful not to slam the screen door. He was going down the steps when behind him he heard a thin voice at the checkerboard make a wisecrack, something about a "deputy dawg," and then high laughter from their dry throats. He paused on the steps and glared down the street but did not turn around. He had half a mind to go back and ask them what was so goddamned funny, but he knew better than to fuss with the old plowboys. He went on down the steps and across the street.

ELMER CROSSED THE INTERSECTION of Lyman and Main at the top of the low hill downtown and looked south to where the courthouse stood, the enormous cedar on the lawn decorated with giant gold balls and four-foot candy canes and wide red ribbons. Friday would be the Christmas parade. He would be sure to steer clear of that.

He walked back to his pickup truck, a lightweight Chevrolet 3100 with a silver grille backed by the sloping blue fenders and hood. He'd bought it brand new five years ago, but the once shiny blue paint and chrome had lost its luster and the shifter wasn't always dependable. He kept an axe handle in the front stanchion hole for prying the linkage loose when it stuck and the three-speed transmission wouldn't budge. The wooden club was also handy if some farmer's cows got out in the road and needed a prod.

He got in and slammed the door and slid the bullets under the seat, next to his revolver. He turned the key in the ignition and pressed the starter button on the floorboard. The engine cranked and he sat for a second letting it idle. He looked in the glove compartment and found a fresh pack of Lucky Strikes. He smacked the pack on his palm and ripped it open and pulled a cigarette out and put it in his lips and lit it with the old Zippo that had been his daddy's, monogrammed W.E.B. He inhaled and laid the pack and the lighter on the gray dashboard.

He thought about running back into the Magnolia for another cup of coffee to go but he didn't want to have to speak to anyone again, especially Lymanville's beloved *Guvnah*. He decided to brew some at home.

He backed out of the parking space and drove toward his house but changed his mind about the coffee. He turned and looped around the main block of the courthouse and the women's college and headed out toward the dam north of town. He'd heard about all the manmade lakes up along the Tennessee River where women in swimsuits water-skied in packs, sometimes in two-high formations like cheerleaders at high school football games. He had seen pictures of the

Miss Guntersville Lake contestants in the newspaper that
he had not been able to believe. Sherry was off up that way
somewhere he had heard, and even though she had the body
for it, he doubted she wore one of those revealing swimsuits.
At least he hoped she didn't.

He pulled away from downtown on the hardtop two-lane
Aubrey Terrell had gotten the state to pave all the way to Atlanta. North Highway the new signs called it. Elmer passed
the lumberyard and the road off to the sawmill and the footings where the new school was going to go, but the outskirts
of town thinned out fast after that, nothing but shacks and
fields of dry brown cornstalks and new growths of shortleaf
pine from forests that had been clear-cut a few years before.
The black road ran sleek under his tires, making a whisking
sound on the clean asphalt. The freshly painted center stripe
shone a bright yellow.

Up ahead on his right in a long slow curve he saw the
Witcher boy at his family's boiled peanut stand under a pin-
ewood lean-to, the roof pitched with hay. Elmer pulled off
to the side of the road and parked on the shoulder about ten
yards shy of the boy. He turned off the engine and studied the
sootblack kettle hung over a fire of hickory and birch wood.
The boy, no more than eight or nine, wore dirty overalls and a
work shirt that was too big for him. He was alone, standing on
his tiptoes, dipping a big spoon into the boiling water.

Elmer slammed the truck door and walked around the hood
of his Chevy but the boy still didn't look up.

"Hey, son."

The boy didn't say anything but gave Elmer a sideways
glance, the way a cat turns its head when coming out of a
nap. He had a skinny neck and pointed ears and his towhead
was shaved down to a thin buzzcut. His eye slits were narrow,

almost Chinese-looking.

Elmer asked, "Your name's Walker, ain't it? Just like your daddy's?"

The boy nodded and stared at his feet and spoke a very faint, "Yessir."

"How's your daddy doing?"

Walker Witcher Jr. shrugged, his eyes still at his feet, the water boiling before him.

"He's all right."

Elmer looked into the kettle, the roiling water letting off steam and the rotation of the wet peanuts jostling like popcorn in a popper.

"How much you get for 'em?"

"Small bags is a quarter, big'uns fifty cent."

"Gimme a small one."

The boy got a paper sack and snapped it open with one jerk of his wrist. He dipped a ladle deep down into the kettle, his dark eyes peering into the bubbling surface of the water. He pulled out a full scoop and tilted it over the ground and the excess water poured out and then dribbled until he was satisfied and he dumped the peanuts into the sack. The brown paper soaked through and darkened with water. He held the bag out to Elmer.

"Thank you, son."

Elmer gave him a quarter and the boy examined it and put it in the bib pouch of his overalls. He looked back at Elmer as though he was going to say something but didn't.

"You going to be busy out here today, I bet," Elmer said. "All these people heading up to the dam this evening. Is your daddy out there doing the barbecue?"

"Yessir. They had some hogs on all night."

"Well, I guess that'll make for some good eatin'."

Elmer looked around and pawed his foot in the dirt. The little boy picked up a black metal lid that was next to the fire and stood and placed it over the kettle.

"Well, thank you for the goobers. I best be getting on."

The little boy didn't say anything.

Elmer opened his truck door and set the peanuts down in the seat next to him and cranked up the engine and pulled off. He drove slowly, watching in his rearview mirror as the little boy sat down on the shoulder of the road and stared blankly at the edge of the new highway.

HE DROVE FURTHER NORTH and the road pressed slightly west. He put a few peanuts in his mouth and worked them around, spitting the softened salty shells out of the window and swallowing the slimy delicious meat. He was reaching into the sack for another handful when he saw a red Buick Roadmaster convertible with the top down parked off to the side. A man in a suit and tie was out of the car and talking to the man in the driver's seat.

Elmer put more peanuts in his mouth and pressed the gas to pass but the man standing outside stepped to the edge of the highway and waved his arms at him to stop. Elmer slowed down and pulled over beyond them on the shoulder. He left the motor running and reached beneath his seat for his .38 and six bullets from the carton. He clicked open the cylinder and loaded the cartridges and snapped it shut. He placed the gun on the seat next to him behind the bag of the boiled peanuts.

"Hello," the man yelled.

Elmer, working the nuts between his molars, watched in the side mirror as the man in the car got out and slammed the shiny red door. The men were dressed identically in dark suits and red ties, and walked together up to his truck.

"Thank you, sir, for stopping," said the man who had waved and yelled. "We need some guidance."

Elmer spat the shells out the window that landed near their polished black dress shoes. The men took a step back and looked at each other. They were about his age and their ties had snow-white Coca-Cola logos on them. The first man took off his suit coat and revealed red suspenders, these also emblazoned with the Coca-Cola script.

"Hello, sir, this is Stan and I'm Howell," the first man said. He held his soft clean hand up as though to reach into the window to shake, but Elmer ignored it. His voice was like those Elmer had heard on newsreels. "We are down here today from Atlanta for the dam dedication."

"You workin' for the state?"

"Oh, no," Howell said, and he looked at Stan and they laughed, "not quite. *We* are employees of the Coca-Cola Corporation."

They glanced down at the logos on their ties as though Elmer had not seen. Elmer looked at the logos and then back at their faces.

"You must be doing it for the free clothing."

Howell looked down at his tie and then at Stan's. They laughed again.

"Well," he said, "that's a good one, I guess you could say that ... Really, though, we are guests of the governor and he said we could hang signs along the way to the dam. There's expected to be a big crowd out here this afternoon. Our maps, however—"

"Signs? What kind of signs?"

"Coca-Cola signs. Banners, really."

"You got them in the trunk of your car?"

"Oh, no," Howell laughed and again looked to Stan, whose smirk was heavy on his clean white chubby face. "A man in a truck hangs them. We just put up markers for the best placement."

"You got to get permission from the sheriff to post anything in Achena County."

"Well," Howell's voice took on a deeper tone and he raised his shoulders, "I do not believe that your sheriff would disagree with the *gov-er-nor* on this issue."

"I reckon you'd just have to ask him to know for sure. You can hang monkeys from the trees out here for all I care. I don't give a damn what you do. I got to get on down the road."

Elmer shifted into first and the truck began to roll. He reached for more peanuts.

"Wait, please. We need directions. Can you help us?"

Elmer revved the gas but pressed the clutch in as the men walked along to move with him and the truck rolled to a slow halt. Their faces held perpetual grins.

"Could you please tell us if we are on the right road to the dam, and how to get there?"

Elmer pulled his hand out of the peanut sack, lifted his finger to point, and was about to describe the directions when Stan stepped up beside Howell and cut him off.

"And also tell us"—Stan's voice was strong Yankee, guttural and fast—"if there's a half-decent golf course out this way."

Elmer grunted, a half-laugh. He spat out the window and started to reach for his gun, but instead put both hands on the wheel and popped the clutch. The tires growled and spewed pebbles back behind as he took off and left them there staring at his truck as he headed on up the road.

ELMER SPED UP THE two-lane, passing a pulpwood truck carrying a load of cut pines down to the sawmill. He ate several handfuls of peanuts and spat the shells out the window and watched the side mirror as they trailed and flickered in the headwind. He passed the turnoff for the new road to the dam without even slowing down, pressing ahead to the northwest. He drove by the turnoff for Finley Shoals Road where he had been out this morning to see Mrs. McNulty and kept on until he got to the first turn off down toward Ridleyville and Fish Creek. The dirt road was dry and rutted from the heavy rains back in August, but still no road scraper had run over it. He put it in second gear and rolled it slowly along the dirt road that declined all the way down to Fish Creek, a tributary to the Oogasula.

He came to the bottom of a long crest and saw the rickety wooden bridge over the creek. The Washingtons were out with cane poles hanging off the railings and along the banks beneath it. Their smooth ebony faces looked up to him in surprise. The youngest man, Maurice, picked up a small bottle from near his feet and hid it in his overalls pocket. The three men all scrunched to the bridge railing to let his truck get by. Instead Elmer stopped the truck just shy of the bridge in the road and turned the motor off. He moved the sack of peanuts and slid his revolver under the seat with the box of bullets.

He got out and surveyed the Washingtons' set up. The old man with the gray beard and two of his grown grandsons were on the bridge and down beneath it their sons—the old man's great-grandchildren—were in the buttonbush along the river's edge. All Elmer could see of the three boys were the tops of their dark heads and their hands holding onto the ten-foot poles protruding from the shrubby undergrowth along the creek's edge.

"Y'all catching anything?"

"Not yet," the senior Washington said. "But it's early and that sun will soon be shining on this water."

"That water's gonna warm 'em up, huh, make 'em hungry?"

"Yes, sir, deputy. That's what we're hopin'."

Elmer smiled at the old man but did not make eye contact with his two grandsons, Maurice and Lemon, nor did they look at him. Elmer figured they were still seeing him with that badge and gun on his belt, the scowl he put on whenever he had to go into the juke joint for a cutting or a shooting. Uncle Lloyd had put their daddy, the old man's son, in Reidsville for life for stabbing a man about ten years back, the week Elmer had gotten home from the war, a month after it ended in mushroom clouds over Hiroshima and Nagasaki. Maurice and Lemon stared down the end of the cane poles resting on the wooden railing and the lines disappearing into the creek. Elmer had no plans to disabuse them of their notion he was still with the sheriff's office.

Elmer took the pack of cigarettes from his breast pocket and shook one loose and put it between his lips. He lit up and studied the old man in overalls and a tattered hunting jacket and a homemade skullcap knitted together of maroon wool.

"Would y'all like one?" Elmer said, gesturing with the pack.

"I b'lieve I do," the old man said.

"Here you go, Mister Washington." Elmer popped open the Zippo and lit the old man's cigarette. The smoke paused in the air and then blew southward, the direction of the stream.

"Maurice, Lemon, what about you?"

Both men cut their eyes to him quick and then back to their cane poles. Maurice, the oldest and tallest of the two brothers, grunted an affirmative and moved toward Elmer and reached and took a cigarette from him. Elmer flicked the lighter and held the flame toward Maurice but he waved him away and pulled a pack of matches from his overalls pocket and lit it himself.

"Lemon?" Elmer said, but Lemon just shook his head and said, "Naw."

The old man said, "Thank you. We 'preciate it."

Elmer turned and looked back up the north side of the stream, the water running slowly along flat shoals out of the wild growth. A willow tree in the banks about one hundred feet up towered over the smaller hardwoods, its lithe branches catching a higher breeze and trembling for a second.

Elmer turned to the old man and asked, "Is y'all's place in the flood plain?"

"The what?" the old man said.

"The flood plain. Where the lake's gonna go. You ain't too far from the river back in there, are you?"

"What you mean? It s'posed to come a big rain?"

"No, sir, the state and power company is damming up the river—tonight. All the low spots around it are going to be under water, for good, 'cording to the government. Has anybody from the power company been out there to see you?"

"Well, no, we haven't heard from nobody."

"Have you seen that dam they built up there? It's the biggest piece of concrete in this part of Georgia."

"For electricity, right?"

"Yeah, but it's going to turn this half of the county into a lake. I guess you must be on a dry spot, or they'd moved you out by now. But I thought for sure Ridleyville'd be under water."

Down below the bridge there was a scurrying in the brush. One of the boys yelled, "Pull 'im out." The cane pole with the taut line shot straight up from the river and the biggest boy, about twelve, lifted it up and a foot-long bass, glistening green and silver and white, dangled at the end of the line. The second brother, about ten, grabbed the bass and pulled the hook out of its mouth and held it up for the men on the bridge to see.

"That's a good 'un, Tyrone," Maurice said. "About two pounds, I bet. String 'im up."

The old man chuckled, a rumbling laugh like a big cat's purr. Elmer and the men watched for a while as the boys ran a long piece of twine through the fish's gills and tied it to the low thick branch of a shrub and tossed the tethered bass in the water and then rebaited the hook with earthworms from an old shoebox. The sun was warming on the bridge and the blue water flowed serenely under the wooden trestle.

"I guess I best be getting on," Elmer said. "Y'all keep an eye on that river tonight. The power company says they know right where this lake will go and where it will flood and where it won't, but I don't see how somebody with a piece of paper and a little metal tool no bigger than a stapler can predict it."

"Yes, sir, deputy. And don't worry, we got these boys in school. We just giving them a day out 'fore it gets too cold to fish."

Elmer paused and looked over the bridge at the boys. The oldest one was easing the cane pole back out over the water, propping it on the low branch of a swamp dogwood.

"You do that, now, you hear." He nodded to each, speaking their names in the rhythm he'd say goodbye, but only the old man acknowledged his farewell.

Elmer got in his truck and turned the key in the ignition and pressed the starter button that cranked up the engine, but when he tried to put it into gear the column linkage stuck and he couldn't shift it out of neutral.

"Goddammit," he said under his breath, his face turning flush.

The men on the bridge had leaned tight against the railing to let him pass and were watching him curiously. The old man seemed to want to ask him a question but Elmer ignored him.

Elmer turned off the engine and got out and pulled the axe handle from the stanchion hole. He opened the hood and stood with his feet on the front bumper and leaned up over the engine and jammed the point of the handle into the linkage connectors and knocked them loose.

He stepped down and slammed the hood and dropped the axe handle back into its rightful slot. He got in and started the engine and popped it into first gear and sped over the wooden bridge, shifting into second as he passed the Washingtons, waving a curt goodbye without looking back.

HE WENT FARTHER UP Fish Creek Road, the dirt ruts widening out and rising after the creek. He drove into a stretch of older pines and tried to figure where the lake would go. Maybe the chainsaws hadn't gotten all the trees, but he knew the greedy bastards were too smart to drown their own forests. Where most men saw pine trees, some saw fat bank accounts, a fine car and a big-breasted woman waiting for them in the Imperial Hotel on Peachtree Street.

He looped around a back road to the north so he wouldn't have to pass back by the Washingtons. He got on the highway and then drove south for about ten miles until he started to get close to town. He came up on Dam Road, the new one they'd cut when construction started three years ago. It was freshly paved and marked with a big new sign announcing GEORGIA POWER COMPANY: LAKE TERRELL DAM on a white background. He turned off on the two-lane with red dirt shoulders a few yards wide, driving about a mile until he

saw two Cadillacs coming up fast behind him. Soon the first
one was riding his bumper. He immediately pulled off into a
short driveway leading to a fenced pasture. He stopped in front
of the locked iron gate and watched in his rearview mirror as
the Cadillacs passed by, all black and shiny and full of men
in suits. One of the men had on a military dress uniform of
some sort, Army perhaps, but Elmer couldn't get that good of
a look at it as they zoomed behind him, sleek and fast on the
smooth road.

He took his eyes off the mirror and looked at the pasture
ahead, busy with cows going about the business of eating grass
and drinking water from an old bathtub set out in the middle
of the field. Old bathtubs made good troughs for the cows once
the drains were plugged up to catch rain. Maybe he could give
Mrs. McNulty a dollar for that old tub of hers and sell it for
more to one of these farmers with the fields full of cows that
had been herded out of the low pastures that were soon to be
lake bottom. He smiled sideways and spat out the window. It
would be funny if some of the farmers had it wrong and their
cows ended up drowning and floating in the lake, all bloated
and stinky and their eyes glossed over and their waterlogged
hides ridden with maggots and worms. Especially if it was some
of Aubrey Terrell's cows. He shifted in his seat and scratched
his nuts, then tapped another cigarette out of the pack and lit
it. He inhaled deep and let the smoke glide out around him
like a cloud as he dropped the column into reverse.

He drove back to North Highway and turned right, passing three pulpwood trucks with cut sections of chained-down
logs. He turned onto Finley Shoals Road and drove on past
Drowning Creek Road about a mile until he turned left onto a
year-old logging road scraped out through a thicket of sapling
oaks and yellow poplars. He drove up a hill, the terrain changing

from flat clay to rocky, the small trees giving way to an open
field that had been clear-cut of pine trees and the road diverted
around a six-foot high wall of granite boulders. Trees grew
sideways and up from the low cliff. He remembered learning
in middle school that this had been the coastline millions of
years ago, back when dinosaurs and woolly mammoths had
roamed the Earth, pterodactyls flying overhead.

He followed the logging road around the boulders and
stopped and turned off the engine and left the blue Chevy
smack dab in the center of the one-lane road amidst a thicket.
No one would be able to get by his truck but no one was going to be back in here today, and if they were, they shouldn't
be. He got his revolver from under the seat and stuck it in the
back of his britches.

He walked along the ridge of rocks until he passed into a
swale and came up on the river where it broke over the shoals.
Boulders spanned the river, stopping anyone trying to get upstream in a rowboat or a raft. Hardwoods grew along the riverbanks, including a few grand willows whose long leaf-covered
branches drooped ceremoniously onto the grass below.

Elmer climbed up an incline to the top of a granite boulder
that stood almost six feet above the water's edge. He stood
there watching the river for a while and then lit a cigarette and
stepped onto the next boulder, following the narrow path across
the river on the top of exposed rocks, water flowing through
channels cut between the stones. He held his cigarette in his
lips and raised his hands out to his sides to keep his balance. A
few of the boulders were wet and slick where the river flowed
over them and he almost slipped at one point, the worn heels
of his old brogans not getting much traction on the wet stones.
Almost to the bank of the far side, two boulders were a good
three feet apart. He squatted on the rock at the gap and looked

downstream at the swirling water where it picked up speed as the land sloped downhill.

He finished the cigarette and turned north and flicked the butt upstream into the water and watched the white speck bob and sink and rise again, making a path between two boulders. It dropped down the mini-waterfall and disappeared but then bobbed up, like he'd seen those river jumpers from Niagara Falls do on the newsreels back when he went to the movies, back before the war when he didn't mind the company of others. His eyes followed the cigarette butt until it shrank, too small to see in the flattening water.

He noticed that the water smelled fresh, clearer here before it slipped down across the fall line and muddied with the loamier soil, and the temperature felt cooler in the midst of the wet boulders. He leaned down and cupped his hands and drank from the splashing current, swallowing several handfuls, splashing some on his face.

He stood and measured the space with his eyes and then stretched his legs and made the short jump across the gap in the boulders. He walked to the river's edge and headed up beneath a stand of oaks and poplars and red maples. From a dirt rise he could see through the thinning leaves of the hardwoods and could make out the shape of the dam, hulking and beige, the fresh concrete filling in the gap where the river ran between two sloping hills.

He went about half a mile in the low hardwoods, the leaves crunching under his feet, stopping only to push back the briars that hung across his path. His tooth that sometimes hurt began to bother him, an ache that came and went deep in his back right molar.

The hardwoods ended and he reached a narrow stand of small pines surviving on the edge of a field of stumps. He sat down beneath the few remaining trees that the pulpwooders had been too lazy to clear or hadn't had time to get to and leaned back on his elbows. He pulled the revolver out of his britches and laid it on the ground and reclined even more, tossing away a few pine cones. The loose brown needles made for a comfortable bed.

He turned his head and looked at the bark of a pine tree only a few feet from his face, the intricate patterns of the bark busy with ants, the trunk like a hazy map of roads and rivers and plateaus and valleys, little towns and big knotted cities, and vast lands of open pastures and virgin forests. The bark of the tree looked like what he remembered of his view of the country the time the Navy flew him on an airplane, the ants sorting themselves into highways just like people.

He lay there for a while and smoked, looking at the tree bark, until the sun moved to an angle where it shone down on him and it warmed his shirt and pants. He stubbed out the butt of his cigarette and licked his finger and then wet the remaining smolder to make sure it was out, just like they had taught him to do with matches in his three-week stint as a Cub Scout, something he quit because he had gotten tired of his daddy ridiculing his little blue suit and funny hat. He tossed the extinguished butt into the pine needles and put his hands behind his head and closed his eyes. He felt the sun on his eyelids and listened to the birds chirping and scraping the bark in the tree limbs above him, brown thrashers singing and blue jays anxiously calling. He heard the rustling of feathers and soft low clucking of quail and thought about flushing them out and shooting one or two, but a .38 revolver was no good for bird hunting. There was a time when he wouldn't have dreamed of coming into the woods without his shotgun and taking back a few of the plump birds, but it had been a year at least since he had messed with the old 20-gauge pump he kept in the back of his closet. The shotgun had been his daddy's. He had cleaned it and oiled it regularly but had not shot it in two hunting seasons.

He began to dream half-dreams of being a boy hunting in the woods alone with a .410 and then going home to his mama with a squirrel or a bird and her hugging him, his daddy being nowhere around and they liking it that way. Then the half-dreams became deep dreams, his fists uncoiled and his eyelids twitched and heavy sleep poured over and through him like a solid wall of water.

PERCY WAS OUT AGAIN, his morning visit with the old lady and his first nap of the day behind him. He trotted through a field to the narrow road and followed it until he saw the empty blue pickup truck. He stopped and sniffed the tires, the smell of oil and gasoline heavy from the warm motor, a globular spot expanding in the dirt under the engine block. He peed on the left front wheel.

He ran on down the road until he cut his path through the hardwoods where the boulders began and the cliff was red clay and sandy over and around the boulders. Trees here grew at strange angles, some with two trunks and others joined together at branch level and some split apart at the top, crazy like the old lady's hair got sometimes when no one had been to see her in the days and weeks when she stayed in the bed and didn't speak and forgot to feed him. He got by on bugs and grass and whatever varmints, maybe a squirrel or even a rabbit, he could catch in the woods. He missed the old man and the hambones and biscuits he used to throw him after supper. He saw three gray and brown mutts from a distance and barked angrily at them as they ran away over a hill. Many a stray dog

Percy had snarled at to keep away from the junkyard by the river, his home.

Percy went down from the road to his path through the brambles and leaves and fallen trees, trunks that had dropped sideways over time and sometimes were nudged by the hard winds of spring to lie horizontal and rot and become a home for snakes and lizards and even the occasional turtle if close enough to the water. He ran up on the boulders and looked downstream at the flow of the river and then tiptoed across. He had fallen off the boulders and into the water more than once in his younger days. The first time he had sucked water into his lungs and almost drowned. He had fought it with all his black chow fury and scrambled to the bank and coughed and gasped and rolled on the ground like a mad dog until he spewed up water and the pain stopped and he could breathe normally.

He didn't go back to the river rocks for a few months after that first splash, but then one warm day the water had smelled fresh and clear on the spring breezes blowing up to the house and he trotted down there and stood at the edge, studying the boulders with his black eyes, his tongue hanging and his wet nostrils taking in all the scents of the fish and the turtles and the blooming flowers along the wide stream of water that never stopped moving. A few days of that and he was back on the boulders again, standing there looking across the water at the other side where birds skittered in the trees and squirrels and rabbits played under a canopy of branches and leaves. He could see cows in the distance, their existence on the other side of the river taunting him until it became his daily ritual once more to cross the river on the boulders. One rainy day he lost his footing and fell off the boulder into the water, this time banging his head, and when he came to he was down river, washed onto a shoal with the water lapping softly around him.

So today he crossed the river carefully, keeping to the middle of the rocks and taking short, sure steps until he reached the gap where he had to jump, an easy leap when he was a younger dog and still not a hard leap for him now, although he was very sure to jump plenty far enough from the one boulder to the next. He moved on across and jumped down from the last high rock onto the riverbank and ran along the edge for a ways, beneath a series of willows hanging long and sad over the edge of the water, and then to a stretch where the river was blocked with deadfalls of poplar and oak trunks that had not survived a twister that sprang up back in the summer and knocked over the trees like matchsticks, uprooting some and breaking others off at the base. He stopped and sniffed the roots of an old oak, the earthen hole holding rain water, the hoof prints of deer fresh in the dry red clay around the suspended root system, intricate and wild and mysterious above ground.

A squirrel surprised him, skipping from one of the decaying trunks hanging into the river and onto the bank and scurrying up a dogwood tree that was supple and had survived the fierce tornado in August, unlike the stiff and unforgiving trunks of the big hardwoods that had stood majestically but tumbled down in the big winds to lie dead and proud in the river. The squirrel screeched and its claws scraped on the bark as it climbed to the top and looked down at him, its bushy tail flicking in the sunlight and its eyes bulging. It wasn't a flying squirrel so Percy let it be. He was getting too old to bark his lungs out at every varmint that crossed his path. Many a squirrel he had treed and waited out and crunched their fragile skulls and broken their pencil-thin necks between his teeth, but this one he let go. Squirrels were not meaty enough. Rabbits made for better eating.

He paused and let his eyes close for a minute and was tempted to trot back into the cut pines and curl there in the needles in the sunlight and nap when he heard yapping, a steady cry in the distance beyond the hill. He followed the yelps up a low rise to a narrow stretch of pines left standing near a clear-cut, the lonely stumps still oozing sap. He smelled the drift of cigarette smoke but ignored it and ran along the edge of the cleared forest to a new trail the pulpwooders had used to haul out the timber, a scratched-out path where longleaf pines had been dragged through clay and brown needles to the waiting trucks. The smell of young dogs rose in his nostrils and the sound of puppy cries got stronger. At the juncture of a dirt road plowed only a month ago, he followed his nose and ears to a side ditch. He stepped warily in their direction, eyes open for an angry mama dog to show up and protect her litter. But no dog appeared and he inched closer to the whines of the puppies. He looked down in a swirl of wiregrass and saw six skinny black and brown pups curled together, their eyes still closed and their attempts to walk on their feet shaky, their cries of thirst and hunger unanswered by their mama, who was nowhere near.

He put his nose into the squirming pile and they detected his warmth and yelped louder and suckled desperately at his nose, trampling on each other's heads. He pulled back and watched them and then sniffed at the pile again, this time rousing them even more as they cried and whined with all of their young might. A damp warmth rose from their young bodies. Most of the pups were all black or mostly black with white streaks on their bellies and legs and paws, but one yellowish one that was solid in color and fatter than the other scrawny ones managed to crawl across Percy's snout as he nuzzled them. It scratched his nose with a needle-like toenail. Percy shook his head and knocked the yellow dog to the ground beside the litter and barked loudly, the roar flattening the ears of the still-blind pups. He barked a few more times and then let out a low growl, a grumbling threat. They cowered and cried, holding their heads down between their front paws and their stumpy bodies squeezing together, helpless against his tirade. He stopped growling and turned and trotted off to explore in the direction of the cigarette smoke, fainter than it had been earlier. Maybe a man there had a hambone in his pocket. The whimpers of the pups faded as he ran away.

He crossed through the low valley, stopping to smell the fresh sap every now and then where the big trees had been felled and hauled off, leaving only two-foot high stumps and a mess of pine needles and cones and branches covering what had been the floor of the forest. The fresh pine oozings caused him to lose the odor of the cigarette smoke but he remembered where it came from and followed in the direction to the high edge of the valley.

He saw the man lying on his back beneath a small island of remaining trees. Percy took a wide arc and circled about fifty feet away, sniffing the man out. It was the same man who had been firing his gun at the squirrel this morning, the same man who had been to see the old lady and who had shuffled around on the porch with her and that tub, the same man who had smoked by the river and urinated into it and who spat regularly into the hydrangeas and who drove the big blue truck that was parked in the middle of the road across the river. Percy kept his distance from this man. His eyebrows worked in confusion over the man's behavior and he looked back in the direction of the truck, an uncustomary place for someone to park. It also was odd for a man to nap flat on the ground beneath the trees. Usually men would sit half in a daze with a gun and watch for dove or quail or deer, perhaps sipping from a small bottle, but never stretching out to sleep. Percy couldn't get his mind around the way people were acting, the changes in their routines. When he saw the man stir, moving his arm and beginning to raise his head, he hightailed it into the trees further up the hill and ran off and hid in the brush.

ELMER OPENED HIS EYES and raised his head and rubbed a stiff spot on the back of his neck. He detected movement and looked up the hill where small pines and briars and wayward shrubs grew thick. He reached for his revolver and aimed that direction, tensing his finger on the trigger, but he decided not to fire. He couldn't see what was causing the faint rustling through the thicket, a scuffling sound that faded off into the stillness of what remained of the pine forest. He didn't want to waste a bullet.

The forest here once had been the quietest place on earth in the daytime when the bugs and birds and squirrels were still, recumbent in their nests of straw and dirt, the longleaf pine trunks absorbing sound like a sponge takes up water, except the sound held in the trees forever. Now most of that pine was bound to be made into newspapers and paper plates and cardboard of all shapes, folding boxes and poster board, even the little tubes that toilet paper rolled around. How those trees went into those stinky factories and came out paper products he couldn't understand. He and Sherry once had been down to Savannah near the ocean where the paper mills sat on the mouth of a tidal river. They smelled that rotten-egg stench until they couldn't stand it anymore, rolling up the windows on a 98-degree day, his eyes burning, she holding her nose while he drove, cussing. All he knew about the tree business was that he wanted no part of it. Whatever he had learned was horrifying.

A man falling into a wood chipper and coming out mangled like a sausage. A man drowning in a vat of sulfuric acid. Other men getting rich and building golf courses on the north side of Atlanta along that pretty road where they wouldn't dare touch any of the majestic oak trees surrounding their homes that sat like palaces on the hills.

He stood up and tucked his pistol in the back of his britches and crossed straight through the valley of stumps, like low brown wooden gravestones in a cemetery blanketed with pine straw. He paused to watch small black beetles rushing around the globs of sap that were drying on the cut of the dead tree. He moved on through the chair-high remains of the longleaf pines until he came to an enormous stump, almost four feet across, a tree that had once been king of the forest with its green crown towering above the tree line. Perched atop the remaining stump sat a praying mantis, its long green front legs poised in sharp elbow bends and the bug's angular head cocked in an air of wisdom as though it was saying grace over the perished pine.

Elmer studied the stump, a cut less than two weeks old. The stump had the angled shape of a pine felled by an axe and not the smooth hewn surface that most of the nearby trees had, zipped through by the engine-powered teeth of the blade. This tall tree had fought like a sumbitch, forcing perhaps a second larger chainsaw with a bigger motor than the first to be called in and the blade sharpened and pressed at an angle and the engine gunned until they shouted timber and it fell downhill in the direction of the Oogasula.

Elmer raised his heel and kicked at the top side of the stump and the praying mantis fluttered its green wings and buzzed away. Elmer watched its flight and then looked back at the top of the stump and the rings there, too many to count, at least one hundred, maybe twice that many. He fired a cigarette and tilted his head back and blew the smoke up, a cloud drifting in the air, stiller after the early morning breeze. The sun had crossed the eastern sky and hung at the top of its arc, not yet having begun its downslide toward the evening, bound for an early quitting time as the days became shorter. He took a few more puffs and then started out through the pine stump field toward the river.

ELMER CROSSED THE BOULDERS on the river and returned to his pickup. He stuck his pistol under the seat and cranked it and drove slowly up the one-lane dirt road, the ruts getting rockier as he climbed the slight hill away from the river into a wild thicket. He had driven half of a mile when he saw a Ford F-100 coming from the other direction, the truck a shiny red, the biggest model Ford had on the market, the grille of the truck like an enormous goofy grin and its hood rising high in a pronounced arch concealing a V-8 engine. He stopped but the Ford continued coming forward and then got close enough for Elmer to see Warren Higginbotham Jr.'s broad face behind the windshield, his meaty hands on the steering wheel. There was a woman with him, dark-haired and small, sitting low in the passenger seat, not his wife. Warren smiled when he saw it was Elmer, pulling the truck up so close that the bumpers almost touched before shifting it into neutral and turning it off. The Ford towered over the squat blue Chevy.

Warren opened his door and got out. Elmer stayed put, lighting another cigarette.

"*Elll—merrr*! I figured that was your truck." Warren said everything loudly. "Boy, what in the hell you doing out here? You got me blocked in."

Elmer did not smile or take the cigarette from his lips. He

looked at the woman sitting low in Warren's passenger seat. She was barely visible, only her eyes and forehead and a big mass of dark hair poofed out.

Elmer stepped out of the truck and Warren approached, his thick hand out for a shake. Standing six inches taller and weighing at least one hundred pounds more than Elmer, he wore an untucked starched white shirt with a straight collar, the top three buttons unfastened, and navy dress pants and polished black cowboy boots.

"Hey, Warren."

"Good to see you, cousin."

Warren's grip was firm and he moved in with his left arm as though to scoop him up but Elmer escaped, extending the fire of his cigarette like a sharp sword and ducking behind the open truck door.

"S'that something the men in Atlanta do these days, Warren? Hug one another?"

"Damn, Elmer. It's been a while. We are blood."

"Blood?" He spat on the ground. "How is that again?"

"Aw, you know. Your grandma on your daddy's side was a Higginbotham, a great-aunt to my daddy. That makes us second—or is it third?—cousins."

"Next thing you gonna tell me is that I'm Aubrey Terrell's love child."

"He's got some Higginbotham in him. Some of the same blood you got."

"Yeah, and that's Pocahontas, my long-lost twin sister, over there." He pointed to Warren's truck.

The smile dropped from Warren's face. He turned and said, "You ain't changed much."

"What you expect? Grandpa Jones?"

"Naw, I shoulda figured. What are you doing out here?"

"Just scouting lake bottom for Georgia Power."

Elmer took a long glance around at the brush and hard-woods, a mess of dogwoods and red maples that crowded the road.

"What are you doing out here, Warren? I ain't seen you in five years or so, not since you left the sheriff's office to go to Atlanta. Where is it you work again? A bank, ain't it?"

"Yeah, I've been at the bank there five years now. It's a good place."

"A bank." Elmer shook his head and spat.

"I'm just out here checking on my cows," Warren said. Elmer looked back to the truck and the woman jerked her eyes away from his gaze. She had olive-colored skin and a sharp nose, was possibly Jewish, most likely from Atlanta or Columbus. He'd heard that the Jews had their own country clubs in the cities.

"You still got cows down in these parts?"

"Yeah, I been on up the hill there, checking on my old cow pasture, making sure there are none left, that they got 'em all moved."

"Ain't no pastures on this road. This is a logging road. Be-sides, I ain't seen no cows down this way since early summer. They moved 'em all up along the new Dam Road."

"S'that so? Well, just wanted to make sure one of mine doesn't drown here in this lake. It's something, ain't it? Just flooding the land like this."

"Some of this land used to be in my mama's family, long time ago, before my daddy got smart and tried to be a bidness man." Elmer hustled his balls and spat on the ground.

"That wasn't a good time to be in business for anybody. Didn't anybody make any money back then. 'Specially dirt farmers like your daddy."

"Certainly not him. But I guess it wouldn't pay to own the bottom of the lake these days, or maybe it would, shit, I don't know. I guess old Aubrey's doing all right with that farmland, selling it to the state for the lake. I reckon there's good money in selling what *used* to be my mama's land."

"Shoot, the Guvnah's done more good for this county than everybody else around here combined."

"Shit." Elmer said. "I wouldn't trust that sumbitch as far as I can throw him."

"You are wrong 'bout 'im, Elmer. I just stopped by and saw Uncle Lloyd and he said the Guvnah's trying to help you."

"We'll see about that."

"Yeah, Lloyd said he's probably going to help set you up with something if you'll let him. Lloyd's worried about you, Elmer. It don't pay to be so hardheaded all the time."

Elmer got into his truck. He put his hand on the open window to pull the door closed but Warren moved next to him and prevented his shutting it.

"Hold on, now, Elmer. I didn't mean to piss you off. Hold on."

Warren leaned toward Elmer and rested a big hand on his shoulder.

"After we are done out at the dam, you should come over to Coach Hilliard's house. He's having a party tonight and lots of folks will be in town. You can be my guest. Coach always has good liquor, and there's gonna be a lot of women around, from all over the state." Warren nodded his head back in the direction of his truck and raised his eyebrows. "Some fine young thangs."

"You ain't bringing your family down, I 'spect. Lloyd tells me you and Marilee got two young'uns."

"Yeah, that's right." Warren removed his hand from Elmer's

shoulder and stepped back, speaking lower. He looked at the truck and then back at Elmer. "Boys, three and six. They up in Atlanta with their mama. You'd be their cousin of some kind. You need to come up and see them. You're family."

Elmer spat on the ground near Warren's boots and slammed his door. He cranked up his truck and looked Warren in the eye. "I ain't shit," he said, and shifted into reverse.

ELMER BACKED DOWN THE narrow road using the side mirrors as his guide until he found a clear spot wide enough to turn around, and then sped off with Warren's Ford following. He watched the red truck in his rearview mirror and rode the gas hard, lashing out a batch of curses on Warren and his Jewess concubine, then Senator Aubrey Terrell and his Uncle Lloyd and their fondness for impure women and liquor and money and the love of their own images reflected in shiny glass. Elmer cut the wheel sharp as he turned left onto the pavement toward Finley Shoals, the place his great-grandfather had founded.

Elmer watched in his rearview as Warren stopped at the intersection with Finley Shoals Road and paused there before lurching slowly to the right and back toward Lymanville, dust trailing the tires of the F-100 as he exited the logging road. Elmer mashed the gas pedal even harder as the road flattened out, land where the longleaf pines had once grown high and pristine but were now clear-cut. Finley Shoals devoid of its trees was ugly and sad.

He slowed down as he got to the crossroads where the crumbling macadam of Finley Shoals Road met the red dirt of Sills Road. He sat there with the engine running, not a soul around the old general store that was catty-corner to where the church once stood. Across the street were a few clapboard houses with long porches running along the fronts and sides.

All of the doorknobs were gone from the homes, and some of the doors, many of the windows busted and a few knocked out altogether. Some gutter troughs were hanging down and others completely gone. The old weathervane atop the store was missing, as was the sign and the red Coke cooler that had sat out front.

His homeplace was to the south, but he avoided looking in that direction. He knew he didn't have the heart to go see it. He continued on toward the old gristmill at the very end of Finley Shoals Road on the banks of the Oogasula, only a quarter mile from the crossroads. He'd made this trip back as a boy when his daddy farmed and there was corn to be ground into grits. But his daddy had been gone a long time, twenty years, and the mill had been closed down almost ten. Finley Shoals' mill was like most of the gristmills and the cotton gins in Achena County these days, empty sagging buildings along the rivers and creeks, ghostlike structures of dried, rotten boards popping loose from their framing. Only the sawmills still thrived.

He parked by the gristmill at the end of the road, the mac-adam ending about fifty yards from the river where the route took to dirt, weeds growing high in the path that had seen very few travelers as of late. Only the oncoming cool of winter kept the wide path from vanishing altogether. Wild privet had sprung up around the loading dock where once corn had been loaded in and then shipped back out as bags of grits.

He got out of his truck and walked through the brush and surveyed the dock before stepping up onto the old wooden planks. The boards creaked underfoot. He carefully checked his steps and tried to judge where the joists below provided for more support. The boards were dusty and dry and brittle. The broad slanted tin awning over the dock blocked out any sun and made it seem dark despite the early afternoon sunshine.

The door to the mill was gone from its hinges but the room was very dim since the one window high above the floor had been boarded from the inside with a sheet of plywood. Only a slant of sunlight in the shape of the doorframe cut into the darkness.

He went through the doorway into the mill's large front warehouse room with the open ceiling reaching to the rafters and paused to let his eyes get adjusted. A strong smell he took to be a dead animal, or possibly shit from a dog or a coon or some other kind of varmint, rose up on him, odiferous like feces but also sharp and pungent, not unlike that of a skunk or stale urine in a neglected outhouse. Paper littered the floor, shreds of yellowed newspapers and magazines and feed sacks chewed by mice. Small round, dry turds dotted the floorboards. A hodgepodge of footwear was lined up neatly together in a corner. He paused a moment, studying on brogans with the soles gone, a pair of fisherman's hip waders and three black Army boots without laces, the tongues hanging awry.

He crossed the cavernous room toward a closed door. He remembered it as the office where the mill boss kept the cashbox. He put one hand on the doorknob and another over his nose and mouth and pushed it open, a cloud of dust drifting down from the doorframe and another puffing up from the floor when the rusty hinges creaked and the door opened, cracking the tomblike seal. A powerful stench and the glare of sunshine rushed at him simultaneously. The rectangular little room had a source of light, a small window on the end, and he covered his eyes at the brightness and then looked down waist high to see the bottom of a man's withered foot, toe bones protruding through black skin. He moved his hand down to cover his nose and mouth to keep from gagging at the smell and pushed the door wider and stood there and took in the decomposing body supine on an old metal table. He looked for only a second or two but the image etched in his head as though he'd gazed on it for an hour: the man had died in his overalls on top of a makeshift mattress of old sacks on the tabletop. His skin was molded black like a bad banana and was rotting away in patches revealing bones. What remained of his waist-length white beard was dry and yellowing and piled on his chest and fell down by his right side. One overall strap was loose but the other still fastened and he had one arm raised over his head but the other down by his side, the black deteriorating hand relaxed with long curling yellow fingernails. The man's eyeballs were missing, either decayed or plucked out by a coon or a king snake, and his teeth were bared in a ghoulish grin where the lips had sagged and the face rotted to reveal part of his jawbone and skull. Elmer darted his eyes to the other side of the room where a metal folding chair faced the window and a four-foot high stack of *Progressive Farmer* magazines and Sears, Roebuck and Co. catalogues stood piled neatly in the corner.

He turned and pulled the door shut. He walked swiftly across the dark main room and out, stepping lightly across the creaking floor of the dock and down through the wild privet to his truck parked in the low dry weeds at the dead end of Finley Shoals Road.

He squatted for a minute until his inhalations returned to normal, taking deep breaths of the fresh air. He stood and faced the river and leaned back against the right front fender of his truck and pulled a cigarette from his pocket and snapped open the Zippo and lit it and inhaled deep, holding the smoke and closing his eyes as he did.

It had been at least three, maybe even five years since he'd seen that old hermit, supposedly from Tennessee, who had taken up in the mill and lived there after it closed. If he had thought about him at all he had assumed he was long gone. Elmer remembered coming home after the war and seeing the man with the long beard walking into town with a goat on a leash to buy tobacco and newspapers. He heard stories from folks in Finley Shoals about the man swimming naked in the river and sunbathing in the rocks along the shoals, and that he never talked to anyone except his goat. While out in the patrol car Elmer had waved at him many times, and the man with his goat had waved begrudgingly back, but they had never spoken. The closest he'd ever been to him was today, finding his corpse.

Elmer smoked three cigarettes and turned as though to walk to the river's edge to look down at where the big water-powered wheel had been, the hydraulic force that had spun the gears of the mill's grist crusher, but he changed his mind. Finley Shoals' mill wheel had been sold to an antiques collector up north earlier in the year and there was nothing left to see except the steel axle jutting out over the edge of the river. He got in and cranked his truck, turning around in a long circle in the wide dead end of the road. Holding the cigarette in his lips, steering with both hands, he drove slowly back down the road a quarter mile to the Finley Shoals crossroads.

HE CROSSED OVER SILLS Road and pulled off in the dirt lot next to where the Finley Shoals Baptist Church had been. Its sign, a six-foot high portable billboard purchased by a preacher about seven years ago for posting Bible verses and messages of his own making, was blank, all of the letters gone, as were the small tires used for hauling it behind a truck. Somebody had unscrewed the wheels and carried them off, leaving the sign for lake bottom.

The sanctuary was gone except for the busted foundation.

About three months prior the county had tried to move the old A-frame structure on a wide flatbed, jamming supports of heavy beams underneath, lifting it with a giant crane from the sawmill and then tying it down with heavy ropes. It hadn't gone far when the gables began to crack and the trusses broke loose and the roof ultimately gave way and the white clapboard structure collapsed on its side, just sagging right off the flatbed into the ditch, its insides chewed up by termites, more little bugs in one church than there were people in the world. The county left the remnants of the church on the side of the road, and after darkness fell scavengers on mules came by and busted up the plank boards for firewood they piled in a wagon. They tied ropes to some of the old heart of pine joists that were still solid beneath the thin coating of bug-gnawed rot and dragged the beams away.

Elmer parked in what had been the preacher's spot. The foundation was cracked and littered with trash and broken wood from the process of ripping loose the sanctuary. A stand of pokeweed withered in the busted masonry beneath where the choir had sat.

He got out of the truck and slammed the door and walked around the church foundation into the violated burial ground. The coffins had been raised up and hauled away and the tombstones moved down to the dry ground near the dump, south and far from the impending lake. He saw a short-handled shovel in the weedy fringe that the chain gang must have left behind when they were digging up the graves. He picked it up, the metal flat head heavy and the wood handle starting to warp with weather. He pressed his heel on the blade and took a shallow stroke at the dry earth. The shovel was sturdy, worth keeping. He carried it over and set it down in the bed of his pickup.

He returned to the old graveyard, walking between the empty graves, about one hundred in all, past the Hawkins and Shepherds and McKibben plots, and, of course, the Finleys, his people. The dirt piles in the early afternoon sun were a rust-colored hue beside the rectangular holes in the red clay. Dents in the ground marked the earth where the oldest of the granite tombstones had sat for almost century and a half. Most of the grave markers had been moved, but at a small hole a short, cracked tombstone lay where it had fallen, grass growing up around the chiseled marble placard recording the life and death of a baby, dead in 1874, three months old. *George Finley Jr. May he walk with Jesus in the valley.* There had been a lot of dead babies in the old days. Elmer's mama had lost two before he came along.

He walked over to his mother's former grave. Elmer had not seen it since she had been dug up. He had visited the night before they exhumed her with the rest of all the Finley Shoals folks and carted them off down to the new cemetery built for those flooded out of their home burial grounds. He looked around for a flower to toss in the hole but it was December and nothing was blooming. The only colors in the landscape were the auburn leaves clinging to the red maples on the hill to the east and a touch of green in the patches of wiregrass. Everything within reach of the cemetery was barren or brown or weedy.

He heard a rumbling from across the cleared land and saw up Sills Road a pulpwood truck loaded with a stack of cut pine logs, its chains hanging and clanking, the engine groaning under the heavy weight. Dust kicked up at the sides of the truck as it motored toward the intersection of Finley Shoals and shifted into a lower gear and lurched as the clutch popped and the transmission caught hold and slowed it down, but strengthened the traction of the thick tires. A covey of quail near the side of the road in a grassy open spot took flight at the noise, scattering like brown specks over the blue-green horizon in the low southern sky. The truck driver slowed to watch the flapping fat birds. Elmer walked between the open graves to what had been the McKibben plot so he could get a look at the quail settling back down in the distance.

The truck came on and stopped near to the old graveyard, about fifty yards from where he was standing. The driver rolled down his window and waved at Elmer, gesturing for him.

"Hey, boy, come over here." The man's voice was gruff.

Elmer held his ground, just staring, while the man continued to summon him.

"Hey," the man yelled and waved again.

Elmer didn't answer.

The black-haired pulpwooder with leathery skin opened the truck door and climbed out and came around the front of the white cab, the engine idling rough. He was tall and had an enormous gut that hung down in a tucked white T-shirt like a sack over his belt, filling the shirt as tight as a water balloon that shook as he walked. His dark hair was slicked up high from his forehead in a pompadour and fiercely parted on one side.

Elmer stood and watched him come, his large fists clenched, his eyes set hard. The man walked to the edge of the graveyard and studied on it for a minute, as though surprised to see the ground pockmarked with holes. He walked as close as he could get to Elmer, about the distance of a baseball pitcher to home plate, without stepping onto the cemetery grounds. His rough skin had the look of a fresh-oiled baseball glove.

"Son, didn't you see me waving at you?"

"Yessir, I saw you."

"Well, why didn't you come over to me?"

"Just didn't."

"You dumb, boy? Or is you a haint?"

"I ain't nary of the two. I just don't got to take no orders from you."

"You what?"

"I ain't being bossed by no pulpwooder in my own home."

"You in the graveyard, you dumbass."

Elmer extended his right arm rigid in front of him and let his middle finger point to the sky.

"Fuck you," he said.

The man walked into the cemetery and came for Elmer, winding a fast path around the open graves. Elmer instantly regretted leaving his gun in his truck and considered rushing to it, but instead held his ground. He had never run from anyone. He clenched his fists and dug in his heels and the big man was soon on him, throwing a punch that glanced off Elmer's forehead. The man was too tall for Elmer to punch squarely in the face so he slugged the man's huge gut. It was like hitting a sack of feed and the man didn't flinch but kept coming and punching and the weight of his body came behind it and pushed Elmer down onto the ground and the pulpwooder landed hard on top of him. The man smelled of sweat and coffee and pine trees and gasoline. Elmer scrabbled in the dirt to stay out of the two graves they were between but the big man was hitting him, alternating between gut blows and head blows that hurt like hell with the big slow lumps of the man's fist, his girth pinning Elmer to the ground.

Elmer pushed at the man and surged as hard as he could to get loose, sliding to the side, but the man clung to him. The earth began to fall away and he and the man tumbled like an entwined couple six feet down into the hole, landing with a thud in the clumps of mud at the bottom of the empty grave where Waddie McKibben had rested for fifteen years. The blow of landing under the man in the empty grave knocked Elmer's breath from him. His chest felt like it was being crushed and he desperately tried to breathe. The big man quit throwing punches and cussed a string of "goddamns" and "sumbitches" and stood and tried to climb out, a boot heel stepping hard on Elmer's left elbow. On his first try the man stretched one leg up on the top edge of the grave and tried to leap out on his other leg but he fell back on top of Elmer, his ass landing on Elmer's thighs, painful as hell, but somehow the hurt in his legs shocked his breath back into him. The man kept cussing and this time got better footing and hoisted one leg up on the rim of the grave and then groaned and yelled "shit" and pushed against the side with his other leg. He struggled until he cleared the edge and was out.

Elmer lay at the bottom of the grave, his head and stomach and legs hurting, the ground damp despite the recent dry spell, furious he didn't have his gun. Elmer heard the man let loose another string of profanities in between groaning and wheezing to try and catch his breath. The man cussed for a while and breathed heavy and then fell into a coughing fit.

After a few minutes the pulpwooder stopped coughing and appeared, looking down on Elmer from graveside. His white T-shirt was filthy with mud and he moved where he stood over Elmer's head. He seemed to be a little shaky on his feet, still wheezing. His face was a dark crimson beneath his greasy black hair that was mashed sideways on his large head. He hawked his throat and pursed his lips and spat into the grave, hitting Elmer in the cheek. Elmer wiped the glob away with his forearm.

"You dumb sumbitch," the man said, his voice a groan,

raspier than before. "All I wanted is you to tell me . . . to tell me . . . the way back to town."

Elmer didn't say anything and kept his eyes averted away from the man over the hole, his face hard to make out against the backdrop of the bright blue midday sky.

"Well, which way is it, you sorry sumbitch?" The man weaved a little as though he was losing his balance. "You . . . you want me to get in there and kick your ass some more? I get in there again . . . I'll leave you so you ain't ever getting out. I'll give you a real ass whuppin'."

Elmer pointed the direction of town and looked at the man.

"Turn right at the road. That'll take you in."

The man let forth a short laugh, almost a grunt and said, "Lemmee thank you."

The pulpwooder pulled off his filthy T-shirt and his gut sagged ponderous and white in the sunlight. He slowly undid his fly and reached shakily into his pants. Elmer put his hands over his face. A moment or two passed before he heard a stream and immediately felt a warm rain of acrid urine come splashing down on him.

The flow was steady but wavering as though the man's balance was not good. It trickled off, and then Elmer heard the pulpwooder's fly zipping up, heard him coughing again and mutter "Crazy sumbitch" and other curses and then the sound of his bootsteps walking away. He could barely hear the pulpwood truck engine idling and he waited until he heard the door creak open. It had taken longer than he thought it would for the man to get back to his truck. He listened for the door to slam shut and the truck to drive off but he did not hear it. The big engine continued to rumble.

Elmer uncovered his face and looked straight up into the

blue. His hair and his shirt had gotten wet and there was a puddle near his left shoulder that he scooted away from. The movement caused him to hurt, especially his gut and his knee and his left elbow. He sat up and most of his body ached and his bad tooth was throbbing again. A chill from the ground ran through him, the cold dampness of the grave he had not noticed before when he was hot from the struggle.

He stood up gingerly, the rim of the grave about six inches above his head. He moved to the end where there was no piss and reached his arms up to climb out, gripping the ledge as best he could. Despite the pain, he pushed his legs behind him and walked his feet backwards up the earthen wall until his head was above ground.

From that position he could see the man by his pulpwood truck with the door open. The big man appeared to be slouching against the running board, holding onto the steering wheel with one hand, his feet on the ground, still shirtless with his bare gut hanging. Elmer kept pushing, trying to ignore the sharp pains in his left elbow and his knees, until his feet reached the top edge of the grave and he rolled over toward the end and out of the hole in the earth. He shielded his eyes from the sunlight as he stood.

He headed straight for his pickup truck, keeping an eye on the pulpwooder. He took a hurried stride despite the aches shooting through his legs and gut and arms. The big man didn't move, still hanging onto the steering wheel with his right hand, leaning up into his high-riding truck through the open door.

Elmer grabbed his revolver from beneath his seat, positioned himself behind his truck door and got a drop on the man, but the pulpwooder didn't react. Elmer studied the man to make sure he was unarmed. He lowered the revolver but kept his finger on the trigger. He retrieved the shovel from the bed of his pickup and, with his gun in his right hand and the shovel in his left, began walking toward the pulpwooder.

Elmer stepped closer, moving in slowly. The man's face was twisted, a dark red with hints of blue, and his eyes were crazy, one bulging and the other barely open. He was gasping for breath, his mouth gaped wide and his tongue swollen and purple. He held his right hand on the steering wheel as though he was hanging onto a cliff. The man's left hand clutched at his bare chest. When Elmer approached, the man reached out in a gesture for help.

Elmer tucked the pistol into the back of his britches and then gripped the shovel like a baseball bat. He raised it over his head and stepped forward and swung the flat side of the blade down squarely into the man's forehead, knocking him loose from the steering wheel. The pulpwood man slid from the open truck door and collapsed onto the ground like several bags of fertilizer bound together, desperately grabbing at the seat and the gearshift as he fell, unable to catch his hands on any surfaces and hold himself up. He slid down onto his ass and tried to sit but couldn't. He ended up supine on the ground next to the truck, the engine still rumbling, his arms twitching at his sides. The man's ponderous belly rose and fell with his labored breathing. He groaned and seemed to say something about Jesus but all else that came from his mouth was unintelligible garble.

Elmer looked down at the man's face, blood beginning to flow into his eyes from the wound square in his brow.

"Who's getting the ass whuppin' now?" he said, and in one long loop of motion he raised the shovel and swung it down hard and flat across the top of the pulpwooder's face. The rusty metal gave off a solid low ding, pressing the back of the man's head into the red earth.

The blow flattened the man's nose and knocked out his two front teeth. Blood ran from the corners of his mouth and his eyes went blank and gazed out to nowhere through the pools of blood forming in his deep sockets. The man's arms lurched up and he seemed to try to sit but only let out a loud groan and exhaled a deep breath before rolling back motionless. His breathing stopped for good.

Elmer watched him for a few minutes, his own breathing fast from swinging the shovel that he held by his side, the blade in the dirt and the handle leaning against his thigh. Blood on the man's face began to thicken and some had run down onto his bare chest. The pulpwood truck engine continued its low, smooth rumble. Elmer turned and looked back down Finley Shoals Road and then north up Sills Road, the direction the truck had come from.

He stared down at the dead man.

"Goddamn you, you sumbitch. Goddamn you to hell."

Elmer set the shovel down on the ground and grabbed the man by the top of his low work boots, curling his fingers into the lining to get a good grip. He began pulling the man feet first across the dry red dirt. The man's arms naturally fell to his sides and then over his head as they trailed behind.

The pulpwooder weighed a ton. Elmer rested after getting him only about ten feet, still holding onto the man's smelly boots. He resumed pulling and got some momentum going, dragging the man as he walked backwards toward the closest grave at the corner of the cemetery, one that had belonged to Eula Mae Swanson.

Elmer pulled the corpse alongside the opening in the earth. He stood for a moment and then repositioned himself with his right foot wedged under the man's large midsection and turned him over with a kick so he fell face first into the hole. The man landed in the damp bottom with a heavy wet thump.

Elmer walked back and got the shovel and tossed in a few scoopfuls of dirt on the corpse, just enough to cover him up. He paused and leaned on the shovel for a minute and caught his breath, studying the lump that the man made under the thin coat of red clay. Elmer spat on the ground and threw the shovel in the hole and turned and walked off. He went to his pickup and put his gun back under the seat.

He then headed for the pulpwood truck sitting there, still idling, and he contemplated what to do with it. Most likely nobody would be back in here today, but if the truck didn't show up at the sawmill, someone would come looking for him. A man they could spare, but a missing load would not go unnoticed.

He climbed up in the cab of the pulpwood truck and left the door ajar. He gnashed the gears a bit getting it into first but he got it moving, the truck lurching forward with a keening groan. He turned it on Finley Shoals Road toward the river by the gristmill.

Once pointed toward the river he shifted it into second and then third and pressed the gas and built up speed, gunning it up to thirty miles an hour by the time he neared the end of the road at the river's edge. About ten yards from the river he shoved the door open wide and dived out onto the ground, hitting hard on his left shoulder and rolling in the weeds.

When he stopped tumbling, he rested on his side to watch the tail end of the truck descend and turn sideways as it plunged down the riverbank. The sections of pine wood broke loose from the chains and spilled on the embankment as the twisting truck nose-dived into the edge of the river. It rested on the driver's side with the front down in the water but the back tires sticking out and the cut pines logs scattered in a giant messy woodpile. The passenger side wheels kept spinning.

He sat up and checked his watch. It read fifteen until one, the second hand still moving despite cracks in the glass face. His hands were stained from the mud of the graveyard and he touched his nose and big drops of red came off on his fingers. He wiped the mud and the blood on his pants and got up and slowly limped back the quarter of a mile to his truck, assessing all of his injuries as he went. He walked slow, taking short steps. He couldn't think about anything except how much he hurt.

Back at the church grounds he got into his truck. He found an unused handkerchief in his glove compartment, a dressy one with a bright red argyle pattern that his mother had ordered for him from Sears, Roebuck and Co. years ago. He wiped his face with it, staining it with a trickle of blood from his nose. He shifted in his seat, and his arms and legs and stomach hurt. He studied how the blood stains and the red of the handkerchief merged. He wished he had not ruined this gift his mama had given him.

He cranked up his pickup truck and the engine roared to life, seeming small after the pulpwood engine. He put it in reverse and backed out onto Finley Shoals Road. He shifted gears, relieved that the linkage didn't stick, and lurched forward away from the crossroads where he had lived from birth until marriage. Sherry had insisted they buy the little house in Lymanville where he still lived. He wished aloud that he had never moved from Finley Shoals. He cursed the fact that he could never go back.

He drove west and watched Finley Shoals fade out in his rearview mirror, merging with the land of stumps that the woods around it had become. He turned up Drowning Creek Road and then veered onto Junkyard Road and saw Mrs. McNulty sitting out on the porch with her black dog and that bathtub.

He waved but did not look to see if she waved back. He sped up, driving the truck hard through the long curve that mimicked the slow bend of the river until it looped back to Drowning Creek Road at its northernmost reach. He turned south and rode it back two miles to the worn macadam of Finley Shoals Road and then he turned in the direction of the main highway. From there he followed the smooth paved road back into Lymanville, dreading all that awaited him in town.

Afternoon into Evening

A ubrey Terrell looked out the window and saw Mr. Henry's black Cadillac waiting at the corner, his driver Alfred in a chauffeur's hat. He crumpled up the speech he had been trying to write, tossed it into the wastebasket, and took the last sip from a glass of Old Grand-Dad. He put down his pen and took up the thick folder with the deeds and the map. He put on his suit jacket, patted his pocket to make sure he had his cigarette case, checked his silver hair in a wall mirror, and made his way down the stairs.

Alfred held open the car door for him and he got in back with Mr. Henry, the pudgy Coca-Cola president in a dark suit with a red tie, his bald head white above horn-rims.

"How're you, Mr. Henry?" He shook his hand vigorously. "I appreciate the ride this afternoon."

"You are welcome. Alfred and I have never been down here before, so we appreciate your giving us directions."

Aubrey leaned forward and told Alfred to turn around and head toward the courthouse, then to take a left at the light and follow that road north for about ten miles.

"Yes, sir, Senator," Alfred said. "You just let me know when we start to get close."

Aubrey had always been very fond of Alfred, the charming Negro with the big smile and bright eyes, as pleasant and friendly as he could be. Alfred was neat, too, always in a crisp white shirt and pressed black jacket, and he always laughed heartily at Aubrey's jokes. Aubrey wished he could sit up front with him instead of in the back with the ponderous Mr. Henry.

"This town doesn't seem so bad, Senator," Mr. Henry said to him when he leaned back.

"Well, I'm glad you could get out of that big city and come see us. It's a big night for Achena County. We appreciate your support."

"How many people are you anticipating this evening?"

"Up to three thousand folks for the music and the speaking and the barbecue, but that won't get started until later. It'll be just five of us for the poker game, the regulars from our game and the colonel from the Army Corps."

"Those are the five main investors?"

"That's right."

As the Cadillac rolled out the narrow road into the countryside, they talked more of the size of the lake, when it would be filled and stocked with fish, and where the first lakeside golf course might go. Aubrey directed Alfred to turn off at the sign for the dam, and then down the hill toward the river. A few cars were already beginning to line the road down to the water's edge where the concrete wall was built across it. At the bottom of the low hill, where they could see the chairs and the stage set up beneath the shadow of the dam, he directed Alfred to pull around to a parking area near the door to the office building, next to several large black sedans in the paved lot. Beyond the dais and chairs, green Sanders and Sons Funeral Home tents were in place along the riverbank. The smell of barbecued pork wafted up from the tents in thin, sweet smoke.

Aubrey and Mr. Henry greeted the other three poker players, already at the dam and waiting on the couches in the reception area of the office: Georgia Power President Frank Kines, retired Colonel Blake Johnson of the Army Corps of Engineers, and attorney Johnny King, owner of so much real estate and so many companies that some called him King John.

Aubrey led them through the office of the dam and to the boardroom, tucked away at the end of a far hallway. Alfred hung their coats on wood hangers in a spacious closet in Aubrey's office, adjacent to the boardroom, and carefully arranged each man's hat—fine felt fedoras all except for the colonel's military dress cap—on the rack made of the same mahogany wood as Aubrey's wide desk.

"Get comfortable, everybody," Aubrey said, his voice lush and slow, gesturing to chairs around the boardroom table, covered in a green cloth. "Smoke 'em if you got 'em. I've got each of you something to remember this day."

From a box on the table he handed each man his own commemorative ashtray, a square, white ceramic piece that had a message painted around the edges in a glazed burgundy script: *Terrell Dam—Built for the People of Georgia and the United States—1953–1955*, and below that, *Courtesy of the Honorable Senator Aubrey Terrell.* A small image of a dam, that actually looked more like an Egyptian pyramid, was in the bowl where cigarettes were to be stubbed out.

Aubrey gestured and said, "Have a seat, y'all."

The men took seats around the boardroom table, settling in the dark wood chairs with padded leather seats and armrests. Aubrey sat at the head of the table and produced a pack of cards from his pocket and shuffled. Everything in the windowless office space was new—the furniture, the light green paint on the cinderblock walls, the terrazzo floors that were slick and shiny, the oil paintings of bird dogs in the office and the boardroom. He'd had the dam manager set up a side table on which Alfred lined up liquor bottles next to the silver ice bucket with matching tongs and an ice pick. Aubrey sent Alfred to the kitchen for ice.

Alfred knew what each man wanted to drink without having to ask. He fixed the highballs in thick tall glasses and brought them out, all bourbons, except for Johnny King, who had a gin and tonic. He set the drinks on silver metal coasters before each man, next to their stacks of chips: blacks, blues, reds, and whites.

Aubrey lit a Camel and rested it in his ashtray and then held the deck of cards toward Mr. Henry. He split the deck in the middle and stacked the bottom on the top, and then Aubrey dealt out five cards to each man, one card at a time, all face down on the green tablecloth.

"You know the rules," Aubrey said, "so ante up. One lake lot to play."

"All the lots the same size, *Guvnah?*" Johnny King said. "Who is going to be choosing the surveyors? You going to get one of your boys to size it up in your favor?"

"Now Johnny," Aubrey said, smiling and showing all of his teeth. "You know you should expect nothing less. But when you got a lake as big as this one going in, there are too many lots for me to keep it all for myself." He'd already had three glasses of Old Grand-Dad that afternoon and his voice was relaxed, smooth and slow and deep, even more so than usual.

"So all these lots are the same size—ten acres?" Mr. Henry asked, trying to speak Southern although he had a Yankee sharpness to his voice when he was nervous. He was only fifty, fifteen years junior to the Guvnah. He wore red suspenders that matched his tie, both emblazoned with the Coca-Cola logo. His mama was a New Yorker, as was his wife, and Aubrey could hear those sharp tongues in his speech as much as he tried to suppress it. He kept asking questions before anyone could answer them. "About two acres wide along the lakeshore and five acres deep, correct? All these chips equal one thousand acres?"

"That's right, Mr. Henry. You got one thousand acres of prime lakefront sitting there in front of you. Coca-Cola's law firm even drew up the paperwork." He winked at Johnny King. " But if you want, we can hold up the game while you get a second opinion."

Johnny King laughed loudly, and Aubrey joined in, and they all chuckled, a low rumble of smoky laughter.

"All right," Aubrey said, "get your antes in. We'll start up with one lake lot to play."

Five white poker chips clicked together as they met in the middle of the table.

"The bet's to you, Frank."

The Georgia Power president was the tallest of the men, and he wore horn-rimmed glasses and had bad teeth and a pockmarked complexion. He tapped his big fist on the table twice.

"Colonel, Frank is checking," Aubrey said.

The retired Army lifer slid one white chip out in front of him. The slim and usually conservative colonel surprised Aubrey by placing a bet. Aubrey figured he must have drawn at least three-of-a-kind.

"Your highness," Aubrey said to Johnny King, "the colonel's raising ten acres."

"I see that Aubrey," Johnny King said, the handsome old lawyer's voice as soft and smooth as that of golfer Bobby Jones, a friend and neighbor of King's.

"I'll call," Johnny King said, sliding a chip into the pot. This was the first time Aubrey had ever seen Johnny King not raise on the first bet. The smooth lawyer almost always came out swinging and played his poker fast and loose.

"All right, Mr. Henry, it's one chip to you, but you can go all in if you want."

Aubrey laughed at his own joke and the others chuckled, shaking their heads, all except Mr. Henry. Mr. Henry studied his cards, his eyes darting all around. A few more drops of sweat beaded on his furrowed brow, his bald head starting to glisten in the fluorescent lights of the room. Mr. Henry had joined the games only two years back and had proved himself to be the worst poker player Aubrey had ever seen. Aubrey figured selling sugar water must be an easy job.

Mr. Henry's voice was sharp and fast. "I'll raise five," he said, pushing a white chip and a red chip across the table into the pot.

"Whewwwww, Mis-ter Hen-ry," Aubrey said, "you trying to take this lakeshore over? I give up my family farm of seventeen hundred acres and you drive down from Atlanta intent on putting it in your name, ain't you?"

Aubrey took a quick glance at his cards—nothing: ten high, no pairs, every suit but spades represented. Good sense told him to fold and fast, but he didn't want this fat Coca-Cola salesman to bully him out of the first hand. Not from the lake he was building in his home county.

"I'll call you," Aubrey said. "Sixty acres ain't even enough space for the front nine."

Aubrey flipped a red chip and a white chip into the air that landed on the pot with a clack.

"I'm out," Kines said, dumping his cards toward Aubrey.

"Me too," the colonel said, flicking his hand into the fold stack.

"Take it, boys," Johnny King said, also tossing his cards past

Mr. Henry toward Aubrey. Aubrey collected the surrendered cards and pushed them to the side.

"All right, Mr. Henry, how many you want?"

Mr. Henry didn't hesitate. "One," he said, flipping a card onto the out pile.

Aubrey dealt him one card, watched him read it, his eyes opening wide for a quick second.

"And the dealer takes three." He put three cards in the reject stack and took three fresh ones from the deck, dealing them to himself face down. He didn't look at his new cards.

"All right, Mr. Henry, it's your bet." Mr. Henry looked at his cards, at the pot, and at his cards again. Aubrey could tell he was bewildered as to why Aubrey had not even looked at his own hand. It was something he might normally comment about, make a smartass crack, but this game was bigger than the normal cash games they played a few times a year, either in Aubrey's room in the Imperial Hotel in Atlanta during the legislative sessions, Johnny King's cabin at Augusta National, or in the Hotel Denechaud in New Orleans during Sugar Bowl week.

Aubrey watched Mr. Henry move his head like he was about to speak and then stop himself. He studied his cards, protecting them carefully until he set them down, unwittingly flashing the hand open enough so that Aubrey could see he had at least three face cards.

"I'll raise you ten," Mr. Henry said, his plump fingers steering a blue chip across the green cloth into the pot.

"Whew, Mis-tah Henry, you trying to claim land from the lake I got built? I believe your New York manners are coming through."

"You were the one suggested we divide up the lots in a poker game," Mr. Henry said, his voice cold. "We can quit if you want to, or just play for money. I'm happy with one thousand acres."

Aubrey still hadn't looked at his cards.

"Aw, Mr. Henry, you know I'm just funning. I'll call your bet and raise you twenty-five." He smiled, tossing three blue chips and one red one into the pot. "That will be enough land for your very own front nine."

Johnny King shook his head and smiled. "Take it easy now boys, this is only the first hand."

"It's all right, your kingship," Aubrey said. "We might as well start fast—we ain't got but about two hours until old Vinson and Eisenhower's boys get here and try to take all the credit for building this dam. Then we got to act all proper, you know, so old Mr. Squeaky Clean and the feds will approve."

He noticed the colonel shifted uneasily in his chair. Aubrey winked at him, shaking his head like there was nothing to worry about.

"Marvin's coming too, isn't he?" Johnny King said.

"Yeah, he'll be here," Aubrey said. "At least that crazy damn Little Talmadge ain't coming. Thank God we got him out of office. Let's hope his Senate campaign doesn't take."

"Here's to that," Johnny King said. "And thank God his daddy's dead. This whole state'd still be stuck in the mud if he were still around." He raised his glass in a mock toast. "Here's to the dead old demagogue, rolling in his grave, cussing about these lakes and this federal money, riling up the ghosts of the dirt farmers."

"Amen, brother," Aubrey said, reaching over the table, in front of Mr. Henry, to Johnny King. They clinked glasses and took long pulls on their highballs.

Mr. Henry, oblivious to the chatter, broke into what seemed to be a full sweat. He wiped his soft hand across his brow, and then dried it on the stomach of his shirt. His eyes darted from Aubrey's hand and back to his cards. He nervously caressed his suspenders, fingering the white Coca-Cola logo. Aubrey watched him alternate from studying his cards to counting his chips. He parsed out twenty-five and began to push them forward.

"I'll ... I'll *ca*—no, you take it," he said, pulling the chips back. He tossed his cards down into the fold pile and released a deep breath.

"Aw, c'mon now, Mister Henry. You should play a little bit. I'll let you take these cards back if you want. You sure you want to cave in on the first hand? That's 160 acres you got sitting in there already."

Mr. Henry just shook his head from side to side, the glare spot on his bald dome flickering as he did.

"*Well*, all right," Aubrey said, raking the pot into his stack. "I do thank you for the donation." He took a peek at his refreshed cards—nothing again, only a pair of fours. "How 'bout that?" he said, and then mixed his hand with the cards from the fold pile and the deck. He shuffled, the crisp cards riffling together like a paper zipper.

"Hey, Guvnah, what did you have?" Johnny King asked, amused.

"I had five cards, your highness. Now I have another 220 acres of lakefront living. What about you?"

"I was sitting on nothing," Johnny King said. "Henry, what kind of hand did you have there? You must have had something pretty strong."

"C'mon now Mr. Henry, you can tell King John," Aubrey said, giving him a playful jab in his fat arm. "He will honor lawyer confidentiality and all."

Mr. Henry didn't look up from his chips, still counting them as though he could see the lake lots he had lost.

"Full house," he said sadly. He drained the rest of the drink in his glass.

"You might have just had you more lake lots full of houses if you'd stayed in," Aubrey said, still shuffling the deck. "But we'll never know." He handed the deck to Kines on his left.

"Hey, before Frank deals up a hand, let's freshen up these libations. I want to get you boys properly lubricated." Aubrey craned his neck around and said loudly toward the door, "How 'bout it, Alfred?"

They heard Alfred's footsteps coming down the hall from where Aubrey had told him to him wait in the straight-backed chair outside the office.

"Yes sir, Senator Terrell," Alfred said. He took Mr. Henry's glass to the side table. He took the silver tongs and dug into the ice bucket and dropped two big ice cubes in and then filled it with Glenmore. He set the glass down to Mr. Henry's right, the Coca-Cola man's head still down.

"How is that Glenmore?" Aubrey asked Mr. Henry. "You mind if I take a little splash of it? You can have all of the Old Grand-Dad you want to drink."

Mr. Henry turned to Alfred. "Fix the senator from my bottle. Pour him a big one."

"Yes, sir. I'll get him a fresh glass, too."

"You a fine fellow, Alfred."

"Mr. Henry, you ain't too bad yourself."

Alfred fixed Aubrey's drink, and then took Johnny King's glass to the table.

"Thank you, Alfred," Johnny King said. "So, Guvnah, what are you going to tell all these fine folks coming down here tonight?"

"Son," he said, despite the fact that Johnny King at age sixty-four was only one year younger than he was, "there's a woman I know in New Orleans, down there on Bourbon Street, who'd tell you the same thing I'm going to tell you—don't never give away your secrets before show time. Isn't that what she'd say, Mr. Henry? You know who I'm talking about. 'Member that Sugar Bowl trip two years ago?"

Mr. Henry gave way to a slight smile. "Yeah, Guvnah," he said, trying to drawl, "you got that right. She has secrets worth keeping, too."

"Okay, Guvnah," Johnny King said, "but what do people around here think is happening with the land? Surely some folks out here want some lakefront."

Kines cut in, his voice gravelly and deep.

"Johnny, we told them we are building a big park, courtesy of Georgia Power, where they can fish and put in their boats. We'll tell them that again. And Aubrey will talk about giving up his homeplace for the umpteenth time. And the jobs and the cheap power that dam will bring. It's the best day in the history of Achena County. You have been a part of this from the very beginning, have heard it all a dozen times, so I don't see why you are even asking." His sandpaper face was all seriousness, and he stared hard at the lawyer.

Johnny King only smiled.

"Frankie, I'm just having a little fun with the Guvnah— ain't that right Aubrey? Don't get your big ole panties tied up in a wad. Legal counsel has a right to ask a few questions if he wants to."

Kines bristled, shifting as though he was going to get up.

"All right, fellas," Aubrey said, putting his hand on Kines's forearm. "You know this state has too many lawyers and not enough fistfights." He winked at Johnny King, and Kines laughed a short, hard laugh.

"Frank, deal us up. What game you got in mind?"

"Seven-card stud. Deuces wild." He set the deck in front of Aubrey. "Cut these up for me, Guvnah."

Aubrey just tapped the deck. He trusted Kines, a fellow country boy native to Lizella, down east of Macon. And as president of Georgia Power, Kines had all the lake lots he could ever want on Lake Lanier, the new lake north of Atlanta. Aubrey didn't expect he would see him down here in Achena County very often.

While Kines dealt out the cards, Aubrey noticed that Mr. Henry had already knocked down all of his glass of Glenmore. Aubrey picked up his glass and stood, and took Mr. Henry's as well. He went to the side table and dropped in two ice cubes. When the cubes clinked, Alfred appeared. "You want me to get that for you, Mr. Henry?"

"No, son, I got it," he said, and winked at Alfred. Aubrey filled both glasses to the brim from his bottle and went back to the table and set a glass down in front of Mr. Henry.

"Hank, I got you a glass of my Old Grand-Dad. See how you like that. It's smooth as a baby's ass."

Mr. Henry nodded his appreciation. He seemed to be over his loss of the first hand—Aubrey figured he must have reminded himself of his fortune of Coca-Cola stock in the Trust Company Bank in Atlanta. Probably in the same vault where they kept the secret formula.

Aubrey was glad to see Kines chose seven-card stud, a game that created big pots with five rounds of betting. That would be what he'd choose when it was his deal. He figured they'd get in only ten or eleven hands at most before it was time for the public festivities.

Johnny King won the second hand, and then Kines won a hand, then Mr. Henry, then Aubrey again, all the bets conservative so no one person lost more than five lots in a given hand, although the pots of twenty lots or more—more than two hundred acres—were a good take for the winner. Aubrey could see that no one was willing to take risks but instead they were content to break even.

Alfred kept coming and refilling drinks, and Johnny King, Mr. Henry, and Aubrey were knocking them back fast, firing up cigarettes one after the other. Kines and the colonel slow-sipped, particularly the colonel, whose second drink was still more than half full, the cubes long melted.

After the seventh hand, everyone had won a pot except the colonel. He was down about twenty-five lake lots when he said, "Aubrey, I've enjoyed playing, but I'm going to hang on to what I got left."

"Now, Colonel," Aubrey said, the military title that had become the man's name long and slow on his tongue. "You don't want to get out before you win a hand. You could leave here with more than you started—you're due. All it would take is one hand. We are going to play only five more. We've got an hour before folks start showing up."

"No, Aubrey, I'm going to cash out. Johnny, put me down for seventy-five lots."

Johnny King pulled out a tiny notepad with a brown leather cover from his back pocket and made a quick note with a silver pen, monogrammed with his initials, JJK.

"I got you covered, Colonel."

"Thank you, Johnny."

The colonel stood and placed his almost full glass on the side table. "I'll see you all at the party," he said.

Aubrey and Johnny King stood and shook hands with the colonel. Kines and Mr. Henry kept their seats and nodded farewell.

The next four hands were smaller pots, and Aubrey and Mr. Henry each won two.

Aubrey looked at his watch. "Last hand," he said when it was his turn to deal. "Our esteemed guests will start rolling in any minute. How about we up the ante? Ten lots to get in."

Johnny King said, "I don't know about that, Aubrey." He was more subdued after losing all but one hand. "That's a big chunk of land just for the ante."

Kines spoke before Aubrey could. "Sit out then," he said. "It's Aubrey's game. Ten lots to play." He reached out and slammed a blue chip into the center of the table. "Deal 'em up, Guvnah."

"C'mon, Johnny," Aubrey said. "Just one more hand. You ain't gonna starve if you lose."

Aubrey flicked a blue chip into the middle of the table and it skidded into the chip Kines had put there. Mr. Henry followed, adding his ante. Johnny King took his time, his face downcast, talking a little to himself as he pushed his chip into the pot.

"All right, King John, that's the man I know. Okay, seven-card stud, suicide kings and one-eyed jacks are wild."

"Aubrey, let's play a standard game," Johnny King said, his voice higher than usual.

"Quit your griping," Kines said. "It's Aubrey's game. It's his game to call. It takes a goddamn lawyer to complain about the rules."

Aubrey didn't respond to Kines's anger, but inwardly he was tickled by it. He shuffled the cards one more time and slid the deck in front of Mr. Henry.

"Cut these up for me, Hank."

Mr. Henry, his attitude happily adjusted after about six drinks and a couple of wins, stubbed out a Chesterfield and exhaled a stream of smoke. He then drained his glass and took the deck, cutting it only about eight cards from the bottom, before handing it back.

"There you go, Guvnah."

Aubrey was feeling loose too, the Old Grand-Dad and Glenmore buzz at its peak, warm and gentle in his veins, the old nerves numb and quiet. He took the deck and dealt the four hands, two cards down and one up to each man. Aubrey showed a seven, Kines an ace.

"Your bet, Frank."

Kines, who had about the same number of chips he had started with, glanced hard at Johnny King, whose up card was a five, and said, "Raise twenty," his voice almost a hiss.

"That's it for me," Johnny King said, "I'm out."

He stood and dropped his cards near Aubrey's hand. Kines laughed, a harsh bark.

"Chickenshit," he said to Johnny King. "Make sure you count up your chips honest, counselor. How many you got?"

Johnny King gave him a quick look but he turned his eyes away when Kines's glare was unwavering. Aubrey figured Kines wasn't above grabbing the Atlanta lawyer and choking the stuffing out of him.

Johnny King stacked the chips, clicking them on the green tablecloth, letting them fall through his fingers into the stack. He pulled his notebook out of his pants pocket and looked at Aubrey.

"I'm cashing out at fifty." He made a short note and put the pad back in his pocket.

"All right, Johnny. Stay and watch the rest of this hand. Let's see what old Mr. Henry is going to do."

Mr. Henry had a nine showing but a confident look on his face. He thumped another cigarette out of his pack and fired his gold-plated lighter, the tip glowing with his deep inhalation. Aubrey had watched this routine practically every time he had a good hand. He figured Mr. Henry must have a wild card and something else high in his hold cards.

"I'll call the twenty, and raise five."

"All right, Mr. Henry," Aubrey said. "The pot's getting big here now." He took a quick peek at his hand, an ace and a one-eyed jack to go with the seven, but gave his best mock look of disappointment. "My daddy would have told me to fold, but then again he never would have supported the lake either. He'd have called us all damn fools for messing with the river and drowning all that fine farmland . . . I'm *in*." He slid twenty-five lots worth of chips into the pot.

"Frank, you going to call Mr. Henry's raise?"

Kines had lit a cigar and was smoking it, gazing at the floor to his right.

Aubrey addressed him again, "Frank, what's your move?"

"Oh yeah, I'm in," he said, but he seemed to have lost interest in the game after Johnny King dropped out. King watched from the side table, sipping a gin and tonic and smoking a Benson & Hedges.

Aubrey dealt another round of cards, one face up to each man. Kines still had the highest visible hand, an ace and a queen showing. Aubrey noted that he had never bothered to look at his down cards. Mr. Henry was showing king and nine, while Aubrey had a seven and a ten showing.

"Some mighty fine hands out here," Aubrey said. "But the bet is still to you, Frankie." Kines glanced at Aubrey, an angry but short look. Aubrey remembered that Kines had never liked the nickname, one that Johnny King often called him.

"I'll tell you what," Kines said, "I don't give a shit about these lots and poker don't mean nothing if something ain't at risk. I'm going to fold, but I'm going to put all these in so you two can fight for them. I got all the lakefront I'll ever need already." He used both hands to push all of his chips into the pot. "One of you boys can have this."

Johnny King sighed deeply and hung his head. He picked up the gin bottle and refilled his glass.

Aubrey was speechless for a moment, something that almost never happened to him, as he watched Kines slide all 750 acres worth of poker chips into the pot.

"That's mighty generous of you, Frank," he said, speaking without his usual bravado.

Mr. Henry's eyes widened behind his dark horn-rimmed glasses and he smiled broadly until he saw Aubrey watching. Mr. Henry tried to shift into a docile expression, but Aubrey winked at him.

"Okay, Mister Henry, no reason in dragging the suspense out. What's your bet?"

Mr. Henry took a sip of his Glenmore. Then he peeked at his cards so quick that Aubrey knew it was a ploy. He knew damn well what his cards were. He was just stalling, trying to bluff. Mr. Henry then began counting and recounting his chips. Aubrey pretended to neaten up the folded stack and snuck a peek at the hand Kines had thrown away—his down cards had been an ace and a three. He did it so fast and casually that none of the players saw him.

"C'mon, Hank," Aubrey said. "These federal boys are going to be rolling in soon. Drop a bet on me."

"Twenty," he said, plunking two blue chips into the big stack.

"Damn, Mr. Henry, you trying to take over all of Middle Georgia's lakefront, ain't you?"

But Aubrey's feigned indignation was brief.

"I'll call you," Aubrey said, changing his tone to matter-of-fact, flicking two chips into the big pot with his right hand, and at the same time palming Kines's two folded down cards in his left hand. He slipped the two cards on top of the deck. He then dealt out the fifth round of cards, the three to Mr. Henry and the ace to himself.

"Well, I'll be. How 'bout that? We better finish this hand up. Maybe we should check and see if anyone's here yet. It won't look too good if WSB pops in here with a microphone and hears how the lakefront is being divided up." Aubrey turned his head toward the door. "Alfred!"

They heard Alfred's footsteps and saw his face appear in the door.

"Alfred, Mr. Henry wants you to go see if anyone is here yet, especially the federal boys. If they are here, let them know we'll be out in about ten minutes. Tell them we've been fishing and we are changing clothes. Offer them something to drink."

"Yes, sir, Senator." Alfred moved away quick down the hall.

"Okay, Mr. Henry, where were we? An ace showing, I guess it's my bet. I'll raise ten."

"I'll call that," Mr. Henry said.

"Okay, the pot's right. One more face up?" he asked as though he'd never dealt a hand of seven-card stud in his life.

He waited on Mr. Henry to nod, and he dealt out the last up card: a king for Mr. Henry and a six for himself.

"A pair of kings, Hank. That's a good-looking hand. Now you are sitting in the catbird seat."

Mr. Henry kept a straight face, but he wasn't sweating and his brow was relaxed. Aubrey noted that Mr. Henry's glass was dry yet again, as was his own.

"You think about your bet, Hank," Aubrey said, standing up. "I'll fix us up one more round."

The side table with the liquor was behind Mr. Henry and Aubrey watched him from there, the back of his broad puffy shoulders, his thick white bald head, trimmed in patches of graying brown hair above each ear. He was counting his chips intently, rearranging the stacks, letting them fall onto the table from his palm to the tips of his fingers, keeping the piles in line, the *clack-clack-clack-clack* of the chips against each other as he dropped them onto the green tablecloth.

Aubrey stood at the end of the side table, pouring the drinks, straight liquor now that the ice was gone, but keeping an eye on Mr. Henry, waiting for him to peek at his cards—but he wasn't peeking. That meant he was certain to have a pair of kings underneath, or the equivalent with a wild card. When Mr. Henry had doubts, he would check his cards repeatedly as though he was hoping they would change into a better hand since the last time he looked. This time he hadn't peeked once, and Aubrey knew that a smart poker player in his position would fold, not risk another dime, much less several hundred acres of land stretched along the lakeshore, prime property in the New South renaissance. But folding meant turning over as much as two hundred lake lots—two thousand acres!—to this pudgy half-Yankee from Atlanta. He was not about to let that much of his county, *his* land, fall into the hands of Mr. Henry Bickford of the Coca-Cola Company.

He placed the full glass of Glenmore by Mr. Henry, still counting his chips. He took a sip of his drink and lit another cigarette, the smoke swirling about his head before lazily rising to join the cloud that hugged the ceiling. The white ceramic trays had long since filled up, obscuring the image of the Terrell Dam in gray ash.

"What's your bet, Hank?"

"Twenty," he said, sliding two blue chips into the sprawling pot that covered the entire middle of the table, stacks of chips tilting every which way.

"I'll call you, Mr. Henry." He dropped another two blue chips into the pot. Aubrey was now down to about fifty lake lots, slightly more than Mr. Henry had in front of him. Most of the lakefront real estate sat in the middle of the table, a sloppy pile of chips waiting to be claimed.

"Final card coming out. This one's down."

He dealt a card down to Mr. Henry, but paused before dealing his last card. As Mr. Henry checked his card, he dealt himself one and then dropped the remaining deck messily onto the fold pile that was next to his hand.

"All right, Mr. Henry. The bet is still to you."

"Guvnah," Mr. Henry said, trying to affect a drawl. "I'm going to go *all* in."

He used both hands to push the stack to the middle.

"Hold on, podnuh," Aubrey said. "How much is that? You got to count it up before you just push it in there."

"Forty-six—I counted it three times."

"Well, I want to count it up myself."

Aubrey leaned toward Mr. Henry and with his right hand stacked and restacked the chips, rearranging the stacks of five Mr. Henry had into stacks of ten, mixing chips of different colors in the same piles. While he did that he ran his left hand through the unused deck, his index finger searching for a needle hole. He felt the tiny pin prick he was looking for and surreptitiously slid the ace with his left hand into his cards, all the while counting Mr. Henry's chips. A magician would have been proud.

"Okay, Hank, I guess you can count. That's forty-six. I'll see your bet, and raise you six lots—I've got fifty-two here, and I'm putting it all in."

Mr. Henry's face went pale and he moved his head like he was startled by a loud noise. He poised like he was going to ask a question, but then said nothing.

"Goddamn, boys," Johnny King said, still standing near the side table with the liquor. "Y'all sure you want to do this? Why don't y'all just split it all even? That's about 375 lots sitting out there, almost *four thousand* acres."

"Hell, man," Aubrey said. "We are going to play this like men. We ain't in the big-city country club, we are out here in the country. Where we do things *big*. Ain't that right, Hank?"

Mr. Henry didn't say anything, but Kines spoke up. "That's goddamned right. Y'all take it down. What you boys got? Let's see all them cards."

"Hold on now, Frank," Aubrey said. "Mr. Henry has to count me up, and then offer something to cover the bet." He turned his head toward Mr. Henry. "Okay, Hank, count 'em—I think it's fifty-two."

Big drops of sweat had popped up on Mr. Henry's forehead and were sliding down into his brow. He pulled off his glasses and wiped his eyes with a handkerchief from his front pocket. Aubrey took the opportunity to neaten up his hand, moving the pilfered ace into place and the unwanted card into the fold pile.

Mr. Henry counted three times, rearranging the stacks much like Aubrey had done to his chips.

"What's your count there, Hank?"

"Fifty-two," he said, his voice Yankee cool.

"All right, what you gonna put in to cover the bet? You know our rule, if you can't match it, you got to fold out and lose it all."

"I only have about one thousand cash with me. Can I write you a check to cover the difference? What would you estimate each lot is worth?"

"It's two thousand a lot for tax purposes," Johnny King said, "but you could probably sell them tomorrow for five to six thousand each."

"Mr. Henry," Aubrey said, his voice starting high and then low as though he was talking to a child. "You know our long-standing rule. No checks. We never have wanted anything on paper about these games."

"I don't know what else to do. Why don't you just keep six lots and we'll be even? Nobody anywhere else plays poker like this, forcing someone to fold if they can't match a bet."

"Hank, I got news for you—we ain't anywhere else—we are right here. And we've always done it this way. You've never had a problem with our rules before."

"We've never played for real estate before, either," Mr. Henry said.

"I tell you what," Aubrey said. "You probably don't believe me, but I feel sorry for you." He leaned over close to Mr. Henry but kept speaking as loud as he had been before. "You throw in Alfred, to work for me, for five years. You keep paying him what you are now. I'll call that fair."

"Jesus," Mr. Henry said, all New Yorker now. "You can't be serious." Mr. Henry shook his head, his brow furrowed violently, his eyes narrowed behind his horn-rims.

"I'm as serious as I'm sitting here. I'm as serious as the flood gates that are going to knock that river shut tonight."

Mr. Henry kept shaking his large head. He looked back over his right shoulder to Johnny King. "Johnny, what do you think?"

"Who gives a shit what he thinks?" Kines shouted, slamming his fist on the table so hard the chips moved. "This ain't no fucking courtroom. You got to work it out with the Senator. Man-to-man."

"Settle down now, Frank," Aubrey said. "It's all right. Mr. Henry and I can take care of our business."

Mr. Henry sat staring at the enormous pot of chips in front of them.

"You can have Alfred for two years."

"Three," Aubrey said. "And I'm being kind. I'm sure you don't pay him more than two or three thousand a year."

Mr. Henry sighed, heavily. "Yes, but you've got to give him somewhere to live if you bring him down here."

"That won't be a problem. I'll give him one hundred acres of his own if I win this hand. What do you say?"

Mr. Henry nodded, "All right."

"Okay, Mr. Henry, what have you got?"

"Four kings," Mr. Henry said, a dejected tone, flipping the three down cards. "Three kings and a one-eyed jack."

Aubrey tried not to gloat but the bourbon in his blood and the knowledge that his four aces had just made him the biggest landowner in Achena County got the best of him. He sat up straight and leaned back and smiled his biggest shit-eating grin.

"Well, Hank," he said, reaching his right hand over and gripping Mr. Henry's soft left shoulder. "How about that? I've got a one-eyed jack myself," he flipped the jack over, "and three single friends to go with him." He lined up the ace that was face up, and then slowly flipped the other two aces. "Four aces. A helluva hand."

Mr. Henry bolted up, his face as red as his Coca-Cola suspenders, and stormed through the door and down the hallway.

"Don't forget your hat and jacket in my office, Henry," Aubrey shouted, stifling a laugh. "You can help yourself. I'm giving Alfred the rest of the afternoon off."

Johnny King shook his head and half-smiled on his way out, jotting in his notebook.

"Aubrey, you got the deeds, right? Just send me the ones that aren't yours and I'll record them in the courthouse and distribute."

"You got it, King John. See y'all later."

Kines rose and thumped Aubrey on the back with his meaty hand, giving him a knowing wink.

"Fine job there, Aubrey. A damned fine job, sticking it to these Atlanta pussy boys. I'll see you out at the speaking."

"You got it, Frank. Come on down and see me out at the lake sometime."

Aubrey lit a Camel and inhaled, holding the cigarette in his mouth while he counted up the pot. He arranged the chips in the stacks of colors and neatened the piles. He retrieved the stray cards scattered on the table and put them back in the pack.

Alfred appeared in the door.

"Can I help you, Senator?" he said. He began lining up the bottles on the side table neatly, and when he finished that, he began emptying the full ashtrays from the boardroom table into a trash bag.

"No, Alfred, have a seat. I want to talk with you for a bit."

Alfred's eyes darted to Aubrey, wide and frightened.

"No, don't you fret. I've got some good news for you. Have a seat and wait right here."

Aubrey stood and went into his office and retrieved the file with the deeds and the map. Alfred sat down slowly, looking at the leather padded chair as though it was concrete.

Aubrey returned with the thick file under his arm. He spoke over his shoulder while pouring himself another drink, this time Glenmore from Mr. Henry's almost empty bottle.

"Son, I'm going to make you one of the richest Negroes in all of Georgia, certainly the richest in Achena County."

"But, sir . . . I, uh . . . I live in Atlanta."

"Well, Alfred, most of the time you will, 'cause I stay up there more than half the year now, too. But Mr. Henry and I made a deal where you are going to work for me for the next three years. I don't require much, just rides here and there and a little help with odd jobs."

Alfred's face was expressionless, his usual smile gone.

"And I'm going to set you up on the lake. See this map here . . ." Aubrey paused as he unfolded the blueprint. He smoothed it out and rotated it so both he and Alfred could see.

"This," he gestured over it, "is Lake Terrell. It's going to start filling in tonight and in a few weeks, will be all the way up to these shorelines. Right over here," he ran his finger along a section on the map near the mouth of the dam, "is where I'm going to set up the Alfred . . . what's your last name, son?"

"Jenkins."

"The Alfred Jenkins Negro Recreational Center. It will have half a mile of lakefront for fishing, swimming, recreation for all your people. I'll even build you a house on it. What do you think of that, Alfred?"

"Yes, sir," Alfred said. "That's good," but he sounded doubtful. He paused before speaking. "What about my family? My wife works up in Atlanta, a schoolteacher. Our children are up there, too. All my family."

"Well, son, maybe you can bring them down here in the summer. And, like I said, I'm in Atlanta more than half the year anyway."

"But will we be able to stay in Mr. Henry's carriage house? We've gotten mighty comfortable in there. I've been there fifteen years."

"How old are you now, Alfred?"

"Thirty-nine, sir."

"Well, son, you don't want to live in a carriage house all your life, now do you? I'll help you sell some acreage, and you can buy you a house of your own in Atlanta. You don't want to live at Mr. Henry's if you're not working for him. He'll probably put a new boy in there."

"Yes, sir," he said quietly.

"That's more like it, Alfred. Now stand up. Let's shake on it."

They both stood, and Alfred shook Aubrey's hand. Aubrey was disappointed he didn't get a big smile or a strong grip or even a hug from Alfred, instead only a limp-fish handshake and a sullen downward gaze at the floor. He'd always cherished seeing Alfred's smiling face, his cheerful demeanor. Aubrey had always imagined that they were the same type of person beneath the obvious difference in their skin and their last names.

"All right, Alfred. If you want, take you a break and get out of here for a while. Or just rest in my office. Make yourself at home. We'll get you something to eat after the speaking. Later on tonight, I'll need you to give me a ride. I got me a hot date." He winked and patted Alfred on the back.

"Yes, sir," Alfred said, his voice low. He turned slowly and walked out.

Aubrey watched him go, trying to figure out why he wasn't acting like it was the best day of his life. "Niggers and women," he said, "I can't never figure 'em out."

Percy curled himself into a ball near the steps of the house and rested his head on his right haunch. He faced the river, the sunlight dancing on the slow-moving water and the wind rustling easy through the last few leaves on the mostly bare oak tree. The heavy sounds of the huge trucks and the road scrapers and the yellow metal bulldozers that rearranged the earth where they had built the concrete wall across the river had ceased a few weeks back. The blasting and grinding and the shouts of the men from the construction only a mile away had gone on for more than three years, starting back in the hot weather a long time ago. Percy had been scared off by the explosions, louder than any deer rifle he had ever heard, and had hid under the house when he heard the blasts, followed then by the scared cries of all the animals of the forest and riverside, the skittering screams of squirrels and groundhogs and raccoons and the high throaty shrieks of birds flying from the trees in all directions, away from the loud boom. Even under the house it was loud, and he could feel the earth below him vibrate with the echo of the concussive noise.

The scraping and the clearing and the explosions had been when the old lady began to change, muttering to herself, taking to the bed for days and forgetting to feed him, cutting out the weekly trips to town, generally just letting herself and the house go. She had been into town only twice since the previous winter, and saw no visitors except for the man who had dropped in on her that morning. A few cars or trucks each day would speed past the dirt road by the junkyard and the house, but they never stopped. The only vehicle back in here today had been the blue pickup truck of the man Percy did not trust, the spitting-scratching man who flaunted his gun.

Although the loud noises from the high concrete wall across the river had ceased, Percy's ears picked up what sounded like heavy traffic. Last night he smelled a big charcoal fire and then this morning the scent of a hog slow-roasting over ashy coals. And even though Percy was scared of the big wall straddling the river, he was drawn to it by the warm sweet promise of barbecued meat.

He lay there not sleeping and his mouth watered thinking about the taste of pork when it was cooked over a fire, the tangy sauce the men put on it, the bones they would toss to him after the meal was done, gnawing the white crunchy calcifications until they dissolved in his mouth and the marrow inside was soft and delicious. He got up and trotted to the river's edge and looked south down to where they had built the concrete wall over the water, a hulking construct unlike anything he had ever seen. They had even moved the river temporarily, rerouting it while they built the wall across the riverbed.

From this distance, all he could see was the top of the concrete wall between the hills in the mid-afternoon sun. He set off in that direction, following the route of the river, ducking beneath a fence to the pastures where the cows had roamed until a few weeks ago, and then down beneath another fence to the edge of the water where a farmer had occasionally moved the cows to drink and cool off in the sweltering days of summer. He wondered where all the cows had gone, where was the farmer with his shotgun, the big yellow labs that barked clumsily at Percy and chased him until he turned and snarled and scared them, even though they had him outnumbered.

He passed through the open fields along the edge of the river and ducked under a fence until he got near the town of Finley Shoals where the crossroads had once been busy. He cut more inland and trotted to the west of the old mill where men once labored and traded. The smell of ground corn had given way years ago to the solitary man with the long beard and the mean goat, and then the idleness and the stench that had arisen in the past few years.

He moved on south toward the concrete and he could hear the traffic of cars on the new blacktop road they had built leading to the structure. He had been down that far a few months ago when they were paving it and saw the big trucks full of the hot tar and the road graders spreading it flat and the steamroller mashing it into a smooth dark surface. In prior years he had come down to spy on the work but had been scared off by the explosions and the mysterious men in red hardhats, their voices loud and the dynamiting of hills ferocious.

He normally wouldn't come down here, but today the smell of the barbecuing hog signaled a special occasion. And it wasn't just the hog, a marker of ceremonies and celebrations. He sensed that today was different, a turning point of some kind for him, the old lady and the river. He was an old dog and while scared of the unknown, he also was without fear of the future, an innate knowledge that the end was perhaps near, that the time designated for him was running out, like it had for the old man.

He trotted within about two hundred yards of the dam, watching the cars running up and down the new road, sunlight glinting on windshields and chrome, parking back behind the dam from where the smell of cooking was coming. The concrete wall sat against bases of earth on both sides of the river that they had built up almost as high as the hills on each side, contoured mounds that mimicked the terrain with the man-made berms. He studied the top of the white wall. Two men in red hardhats were walking across and pointing down to the river, gesturing this way and then back downstream. They were small in comparison to the mighty monument, like bugs on a dinner plate. Percy ran away from the river and beneath the fence leaving the pasture and went into the edge of a stand of brush. He considered moving closer, to get nearer the roasting hog, but the men on the top of the wall across the river scared him, the sun intense on their plastic hats. He held his ground and watched, his eyebrows going up and down as he tried to make sense of all the change in the landscape.

The warmth of the day still hung on, unseasonable this close to the tree-in-the-house time, the time when he remembered the man and woman singing a whole new set of songs, songs he only heard once a year. He liked the happy rhythms of the holiday and the ritual of the tree in the house, the extra food that came with it, but he didn't count on it this year. The world was nothing like when he was a pup. The old man was long dead and the old lady was gone in the head. Armies of men and machines had built a giant wall across the river. The land had changed. People had changed. His life had changed. He couldn't understand it. But he knew that he smelled the sweet juices of a slow-roasting hog. And he knew that he was hungry. He watched the dam from the cusp of the remaining tree line, hiding in the brush, sniffing, looking, waiting.

ELMER WAS GETTING OUT of his tub where he had soaked his sore body for about fifteen minutes when the phone rang. He let it ring and reached for a towel on the rack of the small bathroom. The modern tub, a rectangular block the shape of a bar of soap carved out to hold water, took up more than half the floor space and, the door opening against it, bumped the side at full swing, not going all the way to the wall like it would with a smaller tub. The two-bedroom house with one bathroom on the edge of the mill village was not much square footage but it was plenty enough space for him. The fancy tub had been Sherry's idea. It was Art Deco, she had said.

The phone kept ringing, its loud *tring . . . tring . . . tring . . .* accentuated by pauses between each bell. A phone in the house was a curse, he had told Sherry, but she had insisted that they get it. "How can I talk to my mama down in Macon?" He'd told her, "Go see your mama." But like most of their disputes she had won out and they had gotten the black telephone with its shrill ringing interrupting them all hours of the day and night. Nobody in Finley Shoals had ever had a telephone in their home and that was the way it ought to be. The community line they all shared at the general store had served them all just fine. A telephone in the home made communication too easy, too trivial, allowing anybody who could remember three numbers in a row to call you up any time they felt like it. Elmer hated the telephone and rued the day he agreed to get one. He didn't know why he had not turned it off after she left. He listened to it continue . . . *tring . . . tring . . . tring* . . . and cursed.

He dried himself and looked at his face in the mirror, flush red from the bath and puffy along the left jaw where the pulpwooder had landed several thick punches, but otherwise not bad injuries considering the pummeling he had taken. The bruises on his body were another matter. His left knee and right elbow ached with stiffness and his stomach and thighs were bluing rapidly into dark, sprawling shapes. The bruise on his right thigh overlapped the long jagged scar where Jap shrapnel had cut into his leg during the war.

The phone continued. Elmer knew it was his Uncle Lloyd, the only person who knew him well enough to know that getting him to answer required letting it ring incessantly. The few other people who called him gave up after about ten rings. He could envision Lloyd sitting on the other end, persistent and stubborn enough to let it ring until kingdom come if he had to do it to get Elmer on the line. He also knew Lloyd well enough to know that he would come by in person for very bad news, such as suspecting Elmer of killing a pulpwooder.

The phone rang a few more times. Elmer wrapped a towel around his waist and walked slowly into the den and picked up the receiver and answered. It was Lloyd.

"Elmer, son, why don't you answer the phone? I knew you were there."

"What you want, Lloyd?"

"I need you to do me a favor. Po' Baby is down at the courthouse and the Guvnah wants to make sure we get him out to the dam for the ceremony this afternoon. I want you to go down there and take him out to the dam with you."

Elmer paused before speaking. "Why I got to haul his niggers around?"

"Son, c'mon, now. You knowed Po' Baby all your life. He thinks the world of you. He knowed you since you was a baby. Still asks me about you whenever I'm down at the courthouse. Tells me to tell you he misses seeing you around down there. The Guvnah's been quite generous with his time, making sure Po' Baby gets a ride out there, that he doesn't miss it."

"Shit. It's something he oughta want to miss. It's the worst damn thing this county's ever seen."

There was a long pause on the line and then Elmer could hear the sheriff sighing, a long exhalation finished with an almost crylike *ahhhh*.

"Son, I don't know what I'm going to do about you. We have talked about this 'til I'm blue in the face. You got to think about your future. I know you don't like how things have turned out, but son, things don't always turn out to our likin'."

Elmer grunted.

"And son, I ain't got time to fool with a lecture for you now,"

Lloyd said. "The question I need to know is this: Will you or won't you go get Po' Baby and take him out there? Don't do it for Aubrey—do it for Po' Baby, do it for me, do it for yourself. If I can't rely on you, son, if you won't let me help you, I'm going to have to wash my hands of you at some point. It don't make a lick of sense, the way you acting."

Elmer closed his eyes and rubbed his hand gently along his swollen jawline.

"I'll go get him, Lloyd. Be down there in a little while."

"All right, Elmer. Be sure to have him out there by two. The Guvnah wants everyone there early. There'll be a nigra section in the back. Po' Baby'll know where to go. It's already after one, so you better get moving."

Elmer hung up the phone. If he'd been a drinking man, he would have taken a whole bottle and chugged it, but liquor and his stomach had never agreed. All he would do was puke after a few sips. Lots of men had called him pussy for refusing to drink, his daddy among them, but he had never acted so smart after he got into the bottle.

Elmer pulled his dark blue dress suit out of the closet and laid it over a chair. Before they married, Sherry had ordered it from the Sears, Roebuck and Co. catalogue despite his objections to the $14 price. He'd worn it very little, the first time at the wedding, and probably only four times in five years since, almost $3 per wearing. He had known he was right when he objected to buying it but went along to make her happy, just so she would quit talking about it.

The last time he had put on the suit had been about six months ago for his meeting with his uncle and the warden from the women's prison and a man from Atlanta who worked for the state. Lloyd and the man from the state had done most of the talking, agreeing that Elmer would no longer be a deputy but that he wouldn't face criminal charges. Elmer had spent most of the time staring at the warden's rug until Lloyd cued him to apologize.

He opened his drawer and took out boxers, a T-shirt and a wrinkled dress shirt and pulled them on, then the suit from the chair. He had a lone red tie that had been on the hanger under the suit. He had to knot the tie twice to get it right, looking at himself in the mirror on the dresser. He cinched the outfit with his everyday brown belt with the big silver buckle.

He sat on the edge of the bed and put on a pair of gray hunting socks that came up almost to his knees. Then he pulled on his brown cowboy boots. He'd gotten the boots at a store near the port in Los Angeles after the war was over, before they flew him home. He saved the boots for special occasions, infrequent though they were.

Dressed, he lifted his .38 from the nightstand. He got a piece of cheesecloth from a drawer and wiped it down and blew a cool breath on the muzzle. He put the revolver into the inner coat pocket over his left breast and looked at himself in the mirror over the dresser, hands by his sides. He stood taller in the boots and liked the extra height. The suit coat was loose, bought five years ago when he was carrying a little more weight, and the lump where the gun rested showed only slightly.

He lit a cigarette and studied his reflection. He didn't think anyone could tell his jaw had been punched. His elbow and knee hurt like hell, but he walked slow as it was—folks would not be suspicious of him taking his time. He would not permit a limp or a grimace. The nosebleed had stopped and it seemed that cigarette smoke helped stem the flow.

He took a deep suck on the Lucky Strike. He debated getting his shotgun for the ride but thought better of it. His trusty .38 could do what he needed.

"ELMER, GOOD TO SEE you," Po' Baby said, his voice warm and smooth. He rose from his chair and gestured with a towel for Elmer to have a seat in the shoeshine stand. "What happened to your jaw? Somebody try to knock your lights out?"

"Naw, just bumped it working on my truck," Elmer said, keeping his voice quiet, surveying the basement hallway of the courthouse. No one was around. The coffee room was dark and the clerk's office empty, even though Elmer suspected Gail Troutwick was back in there with her door shut where she couldn't hear them. She always kept to herself that way.

Po' Baby flicked the towel again, the white cloth whisking the seat in the elevated chair with the cast-iron footrests.

"Lemme give them boots a shine 'fore we head out to the meeting."

Elmer hesitated and looked at his watch.

"C'mon, Elmer. We got time. I'll make it quick."

"All right."

Elmer stepped up into the chair and his knee ached but he held his face stern, hiding the pain. He'd always been good at concealing hurt, had done so with his leg wound in the Navy, so he wouldn't let a little soreness show. He eased his boots onto the black metal rests with the inverse shoe sole to hold his heels in place. Sitting there with his feet up soothed the tenderness in his knee.

Po' Baby rolled the cuffs of Elmer's slacks above his shin. He then rummaged through his black leather shoe-shine kit and pulled out a metal canister and began rubbing up a rag stained with the brown polish and then slathered it on the leather boots, his hands vigorous and fast on the cowhide.

"It sure is good to see you down here again, Elmer, my man. I hadn't seen you in several months, I guess it is."

"I been laying low, I guess you could say."

"That's the only way to lay," Po' Baby said. He laughed, a deep rumbling chuckle, a gold crown flashing deep in his otherwise white smile. Elmer watched the top of his head while he worked, his dome black and shiny with silver hair around the temples manicured into neat sideburns. Up above the ears the gray bristles were trimmed in a flush line.

"This old lake here is something, ain't it? We going to be the first county in Middle Georgia with a manmade lake. And the Guvnah says everybody in the county's going to have 'lectricity, and it's going to be cheap, too. We going to be catching up, putting Lymanville on the map."

Po' Baby paused to give Elmer an entry but he said nothing, staring at a spot on the far wall. Po' Baby worked polish into Elmer's boots with a flourish, rubbing hard with the rag. He then reached for a cleaner cloth and began to remove the brown cream from the leather.

"I don't guess I've seen these boots in a couple of years, have I, Elmer?"

"Naw, two at least. I never wear 'em that much."

"They's a nice pair of boots. I've missed having you come down here for a shine."

"Yep," Elmer said, and begrudged a smile. He had liked sitting up here in this chair with that taupe uniform and his gun on his belt holster, the raised chair giving him a long view down the hallway, just slightly above everyone else, the happy black man polishing his footwear.

The heavy froth of polish removed, Po' Baby grabbed another towel, this one almost pure white. He stretched it tight between his hands and buffed Elmer's boots, fast snaps of the taut towel back and forth, raising a sheen on the brown leather with the swirled stitching.

"Yes, sir, this is a fine pair of boots," Po' Baby said.

The rubbing was hypnotic and Elmer leaned back in the chair and closed his eyes. He dozed for a moment, and the past rushed up on him like a dream.

HIS MAMA'S FUNERAL HAD been the middle of August 1949. They held it in the Finley Shoals Baptist Church in the morning with the doors and windows open and everyone there fanning themselves, ninety-two in the shade by nine-thirty. The sanctuary was crowded with her fellow lunchroom ladies and teachers and all of the church's members, practically everyone from Finley Shoals. Elmer sat on the end of the row next to Sherry. On her other side was Lloyd and his wife and Elmer's Aunt Matilda, his mama's oldest sister, an old maid from down in Macon. Aubrey Terrell sat in the row behind them.

Elmer's daddy had been gone fourteen years by the time she died and hadn't bothered to return from Alabama for the funeral. Elmer was damn glad he hadn't. He had been tempted to shoot his father if he showed, carrying his pistol beneath his suit coat in one of Lloyd's shoulder holsters.

The preacher preached and the congregation sang, but the service was a blur to Elmer. Afterward they all filed by the open casket. Elmer peered down at his mama's corpse: it didn't look like her, her face shiny and hair coiffed, wearing a dress he had never seen. He could not understand why everyone was always so determined to stare at someone's body one last time after they died.

Lloyd had met with the undertaker to make the arrangements, refusing Elmer's suggestions that his mama would have wanted something more simple. "Nothing to be ashamed about a pine box," he'd said, but Lloyd and Sherry had fought him and, as usual, won.

At the grave Aubrey Terrell stood right behind them and

put his hand on Lloyd's and Elmer's shoulders. Three times he said, "That Mrs. Blizzard was a good woman, the salt of the earth."

Elmer wanted to say to Lloyd, "He only liked her cause she gave him our land," but he said nothing at all that day except to grunt "Thank you" to people who told him they were sorry about her passing.

They lowered her into the ground and the preacher said a final prayer for his mama. Most everyone went on their way, but Elmer insisted on staying. He and Sherry watched quietly while two high school boys who worked for the funeral home filled in the hole with the red clay and tamped it down with spades.

Two TAPS ON THE soles of Elmer's boots, beneath the balls of his feet, woke him. Elmer opened his eyes and saw Po' Baby there, closing up his shine bag, clicking the clasps shut.

Po' Baby said he'd be right back. He took the shine bag and went into a closet at the end of the hall and left the door cracked open. Elmer could see him change out of his short-sleeve work shirt, which he put on a hanger, and into a pressed white dress shirt he adorned with red suspenders and a matching bow tie.

Elmer stepped down from the chair. He reached for his wallet, looked inside, and then put it back in his pocket. Po' Baby locked the closet door and came back down the hallway with a red newsboy style cap in his hand.

"What I owe you for the shine?" Elmer asked. "I'm going to have to bring it to you next week."

"Not a cent, Elmer, not a cent."

"Naw, Leonard, I'm going to pay you, just a little short today. I'll get it to you Monday when I get paid. I apologize."

Po' Baby just nodded. Elmer looked around uncomfortably.

"How's your business been?"

"It's been mighty good. Lots of folks getting shined up for the big doings out there this evening. I made almost fifteen dollars in the past two days." Po' Baby snapped the red cap in his hand and put it on his head. "Best I done in a while."

"I'll bring you a dollar next week."

"You ain't gonna to do it. We'll trade a shine for a ride."

Po' Baby walked in front of the coffee room door with the big window and checked out his reflection. Elmer watched him in the glass, the natural pout his face had when he relaxed, the protruding bottom lip that inspired his nickname. Po' Baby straightened the hat and bow tie and lightly licked his fingers and brushed them over his short silvery sideburns.

He turned and faced Elmer.

"I'm ready whenever you are, Deputy Blizzard."

"I'm not a deputy. Don't call me that anymore."

"Sorry, Elmer, just habit."

"That's all right. But you know I'm not with the sheriff's office anymore. This way. I'm parked out on the street."

"I'm right with you."

Elmer looked Po' Baby up and down, dapper in the red bow tie, suspenders, and newsboy cap. He was at least seventy years old, maybe older.

"Why you still go by 'Po' Baby,' Leonard? You don't like that name, do you?"

"That's what the Guvnah called me a long time ago, back when he was first on the county commission. He was only twenty-one years old. And that's who I've been ever since. It's my name as much as Leonard ever was. I like it just as well."

Elmer's truck was one of the only vehicles parked downtown. The Christmas decorations strung on the street lamps swayed lonesome and sad in a soft breeze. Elmer got in and waited on Po' Baby, moving slowly, to climb into the passenger side. As he stepped in, Elmer remembered the bloody handkerchief on the floorboard and reached to flick it under the seat. He saw that Po' Baby noticed it but said nothing.

Elmer turned the key and hit the starter button and the engine roared to life, but the truck would not move when he tried to shift gears. His face reddened and he grunted a half-curse and bit his lip to keep himself from going into a tirade. He could feel the black man watching him inquisitively.

Elmer shut off the truck and got out and grabbed the axe handle and opened the hood. He climbed up on the fender and slammed the column linkage joint with the point of the axe handle and knocked it loose. He slammed the hood and slid the handle into the front stanchion hole.

He got back in his seat and slammed the door and started the engine and revved it, barking the tires a little as the truck pulled off.

"Sorry about that," he said. "This ain't no Cadillac. But it beats walking."

He drove toward North Highway for the run out to Dam Road. He turned on the radio and the local announcers were talking about the impending lake as if it was the greatest event ever in Achena County. Po' Baby listened earnestly, smiling. "Is that so?" he said. "How about that?" and "Is that right?" Elmer thought he sounded like a trained parrot.

At the edge of town where Lymanville began to fade away to fields, the traffic on the two-lane road picked up. North Highway was busy, people coming in from both north and south, and all were turning onto Dam Road, a jam-up like he had never seen in this part of the county. Cars and pickup trucks were parked along the shoulders of the fresh blacktop and people were walking, a mix of families, couples, businessmen in suits, farmers in overalls and hats. Everybody was leaning forward eagerly, looking toward the dam, and then turning back to see the crowd behind them. Only kind of crowd like this the county ever had was west of town when high school football season was going on and everybody tried to get their car into the parking lot with only the one narrow entrance and exit, waiting in the long slow line before giving up and parking along the roadway.

"Lawd have mercy, look at all these folks," Po' Baby said.

Lloyd's new deputy, that Coggins boy, and a state patrolman were out directing traffic, the hatless Coggins boy in a brand new sheriff's uniform, the light taupe in sharp contrast to the trooper's crisp blues and World War I campaign-style hat. The sun was still bright and the sky clear but the hint of the evening was coming on with a slant toward the western sky.

"If you think this traffic is bad now, wait till everybody tries to get out of here tonight after dark," Elmer said. "It's going to be a sure enough goat fuck."

Po' Baby didn't say anything but turned his head and stared out the side window.

Elmer and Po' Baby inched along listening to the radio until Elmer switched it off. They covered only one hundred yards in ten minutes, and were about a dozen cars from turning when the Coggins boy saw Elmer and waved him to the front of the line. Elmer cut out into the empty oncoming lane and slowly pulled up to the intersection. The former all-state offensive lineman walked around to the driver's side.

"Hey there, Elmer," Ricky Coggins said, his fat white face smiling as he bent his big frame down to talk through the truck window. "Lloyd told us to look out for you. If you want to park out here on the road, I'll put you and Po' Baby in the patrol car and run you down there right now."

Po' Baby reached for the door handle.

"You take him on in," Elmer said. "I've got an errand to run, but I'll be back."

The Coggins boy's thick brows wrinkled and his top teeth showed.

"You sure? Lloyd said he wants to see you."

Elmer gestured to Po' Baby, still holding the door handle, to go on, flicking his hand in a shooing wave at him. Po' Baby got out and gently shut the door. He walked toward the corner where the patrol car was parked.

Elmer turned a scowl on the Coggins boy.

"Don't never ask me if I'm sure. Just tell Lloyd I got on my suit and I'll be back in time."

"Okay, Elmer, okay. I didn't mean nothin'," Ricky Coggins said, and started to walk off.

Elmer nodded and turned his truck around and drove straight back to town, moving fast against the line of traffic.

Lymanville was empty as if it had been abandoned, like in one of those newsreels about towns about to be hit by a hurricane or atomic bomb or some other such apocalypse. Elmer parked down the street from the sheriff's office and sat in his truck watching the traffic light change colors. He wondered if Marla was there, listening to the radio, doing her nails or smoking, waiting on the phone to ring, a bead of sweat on her brow even on cool days, her beehive hairdo lacquered to her head as hard as pottery. He guessed she was out at the dam, that Lloyd wouldn't make her miss it.

Six years his senior, Marla had been friendly to him in

the beginning, when he was back from the war, in fact, much too friendly. One late afternoon when Lloyd was in Atlanta on business she followed him down the back hallway to the jail cell and pinned him there and kissed him on the mouth before he could wriggle away. He was engaged to Sherry at the time and Marla was married with three kids. They'd never talked about it, and she'd been cordial but noticeably cooler after that. He'd kept his distance, especially when Lloyd was out of the office. Almost seven years later, when they were both divorced, she made another pass at him, this time in the back parking lot, after they had ridden together to a meeting over in Macon, reaching down to his crotch and rubbing him through his pants. He didn't resist, but he didn't respond either, no erection, no anything, he just stared out the windshield at the brick back wall of the sheriff's office and smoked while she worked her hand up and down. She was really cool to him after that, and when his trouble first happened at the women's prison farm she got downright malicious, refusing to acknowledge his existence and referring to him only as "deputy" if required to speak to him. She didn't even tell him goodbye on the day he got fired.

He got out of his truck and walked down the sidewalk past the front of the office, the thick glass door with the steel trim giving a view into the fluorescent-lit lobby and the Formica counter where Marla usually sat with her small green reading lamp, attendant to the big black telephone. She was not there. He walked on down the sidewalk and then around the corner to the alley that led to the small parking lot and rear entrance. He still had his keys to the back door and Lloyd's gun locker. Lloyd had let him keep the keys in case it all hit the fan, an ambush or hostage-taking or a gun battle, and his help was needed.

Elmer's key took some jiggling in the solid red wooden back door to the jail before it opened. He went straight into Lloyd's office and took the small key on his chain and unlocked the heavy padlock on the long trunk in the far corner. He dug beneath three 12-gauge shotguns to find two of Lloyd's prized Smith & Wesson .38-.44 Heavy Duty models. He picked up one of the big revolvers and studied the frame, much more powerful than the .38 Model 10 that he carried. Lloyd was proud of his handguns, the famed Smith & Wesson produced for lawmen as an answer to the high-caliber weapons used by gangsters in the twenties. The revolver was rare around these parts, and Lloyd was the only sheriff in Middle Georgia who carried it.

Elmer turned the .38-.44 in his hands. It was sleek black, cool metal, a big solid chunk of steel. It was a gun you wanted in your hands if you were dead-set on killing. If you didn't hit someone in the head or the heart with the standard-issue .38, you might have to shoot all six bullets into their hide to put them down. But the .38-.44 was a stopper. He pulled his smaller revolver out of his pocket and wiped it clean on his slacks. He stacked it in the bottom of the trunk. He slid the big piece into his coat pocket, the gun too big to fit all the way in, the wood-handled butt of the revolver riding out against his dress shirt.

Elmer reached into the trunk and found a box of high-velocity rounds for the .38-.44. He took a box of twenty cartridges that was only three inches wide and long but heavy as a brick with the dense weight. He flipped open the box and made sure these had been hollowed out, rubbing his finger in the concave bullets. He had spent many an afternoon with a drill and a vise hollowing out the tops of the magnum rounds for Lloyd. Elmer recalled the autopsy of an escapee from the state prison Lloyd shot with a hollow point in the chest at close range—the hole going in his breastbone was small, but out his back the exit wound was as big around as a plump garden tomato.

Elmer stood from his crouch and closed the top of the long trunk and set the box of bullets on the corner of Lloyd's desk. The bigger pistol tugged on his breast pocket, dragging down the side of his suit coat with its denseness, twice as heavy as his revolver had been.

He went to the hallway closet and pulled the door open. His uniform was still there, cleaned and pressed with heavy starch. He pulled it off the hanging rod and held it up in front of himself and admired the way he looked in the long mirror hung on the back of the door. He pictured how he had worn the taupe uniform, the crisp outfit that bespoke authority on his thin frame. That gal down at the prison farm had loved it, couldn't take her eyes off him every time he went down there, and he let her go with it. She wasn't that bad to look at either, a little older than he was, and not able to gussy herself up in a prison farm, but she had held him tight and would not stop kissing him and it had been nice. Afterwards, it was much better than being married. She would sneak back across the prison yard so he could go home and get a good night's sleep and not have to be woken up in the night to investigate strange noises or to stomp spiders or the next morning be summoned to open jars or to hear her complain about the smallness of their closets or the incessant ringing of the loud black telephone when her mother called.

He didn't know what happened to her after they got busted the third time, his uniform mostly off, his britches all the way down and his shirt unbuttoned, her naked as a jaybird in the backseat of his car, right in the front of the prison farm, just after dark, like a damned idiot, the assistant warden with his flashlight in the tower up above getting a good look at his skinny ass pumping like a piston in a two-cycle lawnmower. Her name was Wanda and she was from way down in Thomasville, almost into Florida. He still thought about her from time to time.

He was tempted to keep the uniform, to put it on, wear it out to the dam—who else would wear his uniform? It was much too small for Lloyd or the Coggins boy. But the uniform was only a cloth symbol. The .38-.44 was tangible, heavy, cold steel—a gun so goddamn mean it had two numbers.

He hung his uniform back in the closet. He rummaged around in shoe boxes and bags on the shelf above the hanging rod and found a shoulder holster, another one of Lloyd's many prized possessions. It was worn brown leather, made by the George Lawrence Co. in Portland, Oregon, the famed provider of holsters and saddles to the U.S. Army during World War I. He took off his suit coat and put the holster on over his shirt and then put the gun in and buttoned the clasp over the revolver's big grip. It hung comfortably under his arm, beneath his bicep where the jacket was loose.

He stood there before the mirror and rubbed along his jawline, tender to the touch but the slight bruises and swelling were not obvious. His legs and arms and even his stomach hurt much more, stiffening and weary. But if he stood up straight, no one would know his ailments. He made sure the closet was the way he had found it, then slammed the door tight.

He double-checked that the gun locker was fastened securely. He looked around the sheriff's office one last time. He had spent many a day in here, the quiet hum of the lights and the loud ringing of the telephone and Lloyd's voice heavy like syrup. Aside from his mama, this office and the Navy were the only family he had known. Sherry had talked about family, starting one, but that had never seemed to work and he had refused to go to the doctor when she had pleaded with him to get his testicles checked out. No country club sawbones was going to touch his balls and pecker. He figured it was meant to be and now it turned out that it was just as well, considering how things had worked out between him and Sherry. He had never liked little kids much anyhow.

He went back into Lloyd's office, the cowboy boots making a soft click on the hardwood floor. He removed six bullets from the box he'd left on the desk. He unholstered the revolver and loaded the hollow points into the cylinder and spun it and then clicked it into place. He put the gun back in the holster under his suit coat and buttoned it tight before going out, taking the rest of the bullets in the box with him. He closed the door and locked it, his key again giving him trouble before he finally wrestled the deadbolt shut.

ELMER DROVE BACK NORTH with the truck windows down. The traffic from earlier had cleared and the road was wide open. As soon as he was within two miles of the dam he began to see cars and pickup trucks parked all along the sides of North Highway.

He sped on up the road, past the haphazardly arranged parked cars, until he turned onto Dam Road where the Coggins boy sat in his patrol car, that goofy half-grin on his face. Elmer waved but didn't stop. He drove down the fresh asphalt road that descended a mile, gradually declining to the river, to where the lake would begin at the base of the enormous concrete wall spanning the Oogasula. At first he could only see the towering concrete and some of the colors of the bunting and banners strewn across it and the red and silver patch that was the Lymanville Rebels marching band, but as he came closer, passing cars parallel-parked along the shoulders and ditches, he could make out the crowd, bigger even than the crowd for the football game against Sills County, gathered before an enormous dais on the riverbank that had four rows of chairs and a lectern for a speaker, with several microphones bunched together. *Welcome to the Lake Terrell Dam* said a huge banner above the stage, flanked by Coca-Cola signage. The smell of barbecuing pork drifted up toward him, emanating from the line of dark green funeral home tents set up along the river's edge.

He slowed down as he got within a few hundred yards of the crowd at the bottom of the hill. All of the parking spaces along the sides of Dam Road were taken so Elmer pulled up tight to a dark blue Cadillac that belonged to Reverend Frank Fincher, pastor of the First Baptist Church, and double-parked. He killed the engine and opened the door and got out and closed it softly.

The festivities had not yet begun, although he heard random honks of the brass horns and short drum rolls from the two ensembles, the high school band and the Fourteenth Air Force Band. An enormous sign along the road indicated both were scheduled to play beginning at three o'clock, only a few minutes away. An occasional cymbal crashed, then stilled. The crowd buzzed with hundreds of melded conversations. He began to walk slowly down the hill. His knee hurt like hell in the boots on the hardtop and he steeled himself to make sure he didn't limp.

The crowd came into focus as he descended the new asphalt road. The men in front were all dressed in suits and hats and ties, the women in colorful dresses. Workers from the dam wore their red hardhats like they were medals earned in a war.

Farmers in overalls stood in the back. Practically all of Achena County's white folks were there, and in the back on the right side near the river was a section made up of about one hundred of Achena County's oldest colored folks. None of the young blacks had showed up.

He could see many in the crowd looking up at him, watching him descend. Everybody in this town was always up in your business. He imagined what those in the crowd looking up his way might be thinking of him, about him and that woman at the prison, about his mama who died, *bless her heart*, about what he was going to do with his life now that there were no more scout jobs for the power company. The eyes of the crowd were like matches burning his skin and his cheeks got hot and his neck itched. He suspected they all thought he was sorry, a disgrace. Elmer balled his fists and kept going slowly down the hill, scanning for Lloyd, whom he knew would be up in the front of the crowd and would wave him up there and make him talk to people. He fought the urge to turn and hightail it out of there, heading for anywhere but the dam. He paused to light a cigarette and inhaled deep. It calmed his nerves a bit and then he kept on down the road.

The smooth asphalt leveled out the last hundred yards and ended in the parking lot by the office. Elmer walked up to the back of the crowd as the high school band began to play that patriotic tune, the one they had played for him when he came home from the war and rode in the parade, the heavy brass sounds echoing up the hill and carrying far into the woods, driven by the steady percussion and periodic crash of the cymbals that marked the divide between the distinct sections of the song. The band was situated to the front left side of the crowd, beneath the end of the stage but higher than the rest of the audience. Sunlight gleamed on the tubas and trombones, gold and brassy. Three majorettes out in front of the band began dancing, twirling the silver batons into the air and catching them and then doing synchronized cartwheels in the hard-packed dirt. Elmer had been attached to that tune for a few years after he got home, imagining it his own, written and played just for him, until he went to one of Aubrey Terrell's campaign speeches in '48 and heard the same song, played ad nauseam while the old hustler stood up there and waved and smiled. Between playings of the song, Terrell had promised a life lived high on the hog if they elected him governor.

Elmer stood and listened to the music for a while, before walking into the back fringe of the crowd. Farmers were gathered there in overalls with jackets and hats, older men who once had been hard workers but now lived off their wives who worked in the mills or their young'uns, most of whom likely worked in factories or offices or the military, down in Macon or up in Augusta or even Atlanta, some as far away as South Carolina, laboring somewhere inside big brick walls where the New Deal meant they were shackled to either a machine or a desk with a telephone for handcuffs, their lives no different from a hamster on a wheel. Some of the old men in overalls wore their Sunday navy blue jackets over their denim, and they topped off the costumes with tattered hats, a poor man's mimicry of the finely dressed men on the dais.

Elmer veered through the back of the crowd and saw the three old farmers who had been playing checkers with Mr. Worthington at the Feed-and-Seed in the morning. They stood watching the band, not speaking to one another, tired expressions on their wrinkled faces beneath weather-beaten hats. Mr. Worthington had money and most likely had a seat up front or on the stage, but his checker-playing partners were resigned to standing in the back.

Elmer studied the aging plowboys. His right eye twitched a little with anger. He walked right up to them.

"What was it y'all called me this morning?" he asked, speaking loudly so they could hear him over the band. "After I left, what the hell was it you called me?"

Two of the men looked away, but the oldest, Reese Whisner, stared him down.

"What's that, boy?"

Whisner stepped forward, his eyes angry, glassy and thin, the skin around them paper-like, crinkled like a croker sack that had been opened and closed a hundred times. His nose was red and his ears crooked. Elmer moved up closer to him and shouted.

"Didn't you call me a deputy dawg this morning?" he said loudly, his fists clenched at his side as though ready to throw a punch.

The tall, weathered man had spittle on his lips and his breath smelled of moonshine and his body of piss. He took off his hat and held it in his hand. Some of the skin on his head was flaking off around a dark scab the size of a silver dollar. The other two men walked away as though they were glad to be shed of him. He poked a knobby finger into Elmer's chest and looked down at him.

"You're damn right, you goddamned smart aleck," he said, his voice wispy and audible only to Elmer over the music because he was so close. "I remember you when you was no bigger than a goober pea. Farming this damn land before you was born, I was. You turned out to be nothing but sorry, just like your daddy. Your mama was the only good thing about you."

He got a faraway look in his eye and the anger in his voice faded but he continued in a raspy speech.

"I used to farm here and do pretty good at it until everything went to hell. Goddamn boll weevils. Your daddy wasn't a bad farmer except he drank too much, got lazy. After the boll weevil, then the big'un hit us, and it all went bad. He didn't have a chance. None of us did."

Whisner moved forward as he talked, and he bumped Elmer and inadvertently pressed the .38-.44 into Elmer's side. The ranting old farmer didn't notice the concealed gun but it reminded Elmer that he had six heavy shots hanging next to his ribs. Elmer held his ground and raised his hand and was about to curse him when Lloyd intervened, stepping his big body in between them

"Elmer! Reese! What in the world is y'all doing? Dancing?" His voice was loud and deep, and he put his arms around both men. "Y'all look like you aren't enjoying yourselves like you should be."

Reese Whisner moved his mouth as if to talk, but no words came out although the dewlap on his thin neck quivered. His gray eyes were lost and crazy. He turned slowly from Lloyd's clutches and walked away from the crowd, moving off toward the road where the cars were parked.

Lloyd and Elmer watched him go, then Lloyd turned to Elmer.

"Your suit looks good, son, sharp."

Lloyd brushed off one of Elmer's shoulders and then put both hands on his tie and straightened it, tightening the knot.

"I'm glad you're here. C'mon up front with me. Let me show you around."

Lloyd put his arm around Elmer's shoulder and guided him along the side of the crowd toward the front as the band continued to play, brassy and thunderous. Elmer kept his left arm pressed against the gun to keep it tight against his side so

Lloyd wouldn't feel it. Lloyd talked loudly into his ear about who all was there, the governor and various executives and politicians down from Atlanta, and four men from Washington with Congressman Vinson, but Elmer paid only slight attention. Lloyd was too busy scanning the crowd for people he knew to notice the slight bruises on Elmer's face.

"C'mon, son, before we go up on the stage, I want to show you the inside of this plant, how this thing will make electricity. It's sumpin' else. There's a man here from Georgia Power giving tours to the VIPs."

"The who?"

"You know, very ... important ... persons ... V-I-Ps. Elected officials and other big dawgs, like me. Let's go. We ain't got a lotta time."

Lloyd let go of Elmer's arm and walked ahead, leading him up the hill from the crowd gathered on the bottomland next to the river. They went up a newly laid sidewalk toward the office, the one-story cinderblock structure painted a light green with dark green trim and official letters on the heavy glass door. They passed around the building and went up to the base of the dam that began on the west bank of the river and crossed the Oogasula.

The dam had two levels, and they went up a short flight of metal stairs that started where the walkway ended in the raised earth, earth that had been combed and sculpted by bulldozers and men from the chain gang with shovels and hoes. Elmer had come up and watched them work back three years ago when they were using dynamite to blast the hills into the shapes they wanted. He was there when they built another channel for the river and rerouted it west so they could lay concrete across the riverbed to make the dam. The rerouting of the river had taken a few months and brought with it prime fishing. He had brought his rod and reel and a long net and caught catfish and bass by the armfuls when they drained a whole hundred yards of streambed. Once the dam was done, they filled in the temporary channel and returned the river to its original route but let the water flow under the dam, all the gates open so the river would keep flowing until they shut it off tonight.

Elmer and Lloyd stood on the lower deck and looked up at the high wall that rose another seventy-five feet above them. They were on the downriver side of the dam, the upriver side prepared to hold back an entire lake's worth of water. The concrete wall seemed endless above their heads, looming like one of the cliffs Elmer had seen in Hawaii when he had passed through there in the war. He had seen the dam many times before, but he had never stood up under it, so close to it, and something about climbing partway up to it stunned him, making him feel small and bug-like before the hydroelectricity machine. Never had he seen so much concrete in one place, and he had been to Atlanta. He also noticed something that he had not seen before from a distance. Along the side there was a ladder that led up to the very top of the dam.

Lloyd tapped him on the back and pointed ahead of them toward two huge, round metal covers, about three feet high and fifty feet in diameter, that jutted above the level where they walked.

"Them's the caps on the generators," Lloyd said. "Them big engines is down below."

He led Elmer to a thick glass door where they could see into a hallway brightly lit with fluorescent ceiling fixtures. Before Lloyd could knock on the door, a man in a blue suit with a Georgia Power hardhat appeared and welcomed them inside. He was all smiles and handshakes. Lloyd introduced him as Billy Bramlett, the plant manager, and he shook hands with

Elmer. Beneath the hardhat, Bramlett had neat black hair that was beginning to be tinged with gray in the temples, framing his sharp profile. His skin was tanned and ruddy.

"Y'all c'mon in here," he said, and led them to a room with a big metal console that faced a curved wall paneled with gauges of all kinds. "This here is the control room." He explained how the man who was on duty sat here and monitored the dam and the flow of water under it into the river downstream.

"It comes a big rain, we can open it up and keep the lake from flooding," Bramlett said. "It's dry, like it has been lately, we can shut the river down and keep the lake nice and full. You might say we are giving Mother Nature a helping hand."

Bramlett, who said he was from Savannah and had gone to Georgia Tech, continued with details about water flow, megawatts, and the lake. Elmer tuned him out, shutting down his expression. Lloyd nodded agreement to everything Bramlett said and checked out Elmer with an occasional glance.

Bramlett ended his spiel about the control room and led them down a hallway to a stairwell behind a gray metal door. They climbed down two flights and went out a door that opened into a cavernous room, the walls angled in and the ceiling supported on enormous concrete pillars. It was high and narrow, maybe only ten yards wide, but one hundred yards long. The ceiling was at least fifty yards high. Their steps echoed in the stillness of the huge room, particularly the click of Elmer's cowboy boots. The only thing Elmer could compare it to was the inside of the aircraft carriers he had seen on the Pacific or the giant hangars in Hawaii where the B-25s had waited. He thought he heard Bramlett say something about how many airplanes could fit inside the dam, but he wasn't sure. He couldn't concentrate on anything the man said and he didn't try, but he just gazed at the high ceilings. He heard

a machine crank up and then caught what Bramlett was saying as he gestured to a wall that jutted out with enormous
round curves.

"Behind here is where the electricity will be made. We've
got two generators. When the water is in the lake and we
open up the gates, it will fall down through the channel and
spin these and that's where the juice will come from. It will
put out enough to power everything from here to Columbus,
including all of Macon."

He turned and gestured to the other wall. "Over here is
twelve solid feet of concrete that will hold up the south end
of Lake Terrell."

"Twelve solid feet of concrete," Lloyd said. "Ain't that
something, Elmer?"

Elmer didn't respond, but stared at the wall as though he
were trying to see through it.

Billy Bramlett paused as though he were waiting for questions and then said, "C'mon around here, I'll show you the very
bottom of the dam."

He led them back to the stairwell and down four flights to
where the steps ended. They went through a door that opened
up into a narrow hallway with a low concrete ceiling, only about
seven feet high. The lights in the four-foot-wide space were
much dimmer. Elmer could hear Lloyd taking short breaths,
trying to keep up with the Georgia Power man.

They came to another long hallway that ran perpendicular
to the one they had come from. It was also narrow, but had
a high ceiling of about twenty feet. The floor consisted of a
three-foot wide walkway with six-inch wide gutters on either
side, each of which had a sheen of water. It occurred to Elmer
that he could kill them both and leave them down here and no
one would find them for hours, if not a day or more. Bramlett

walked ahead a few steps before turning around to face Elmer and Lloyd.

"This is the absolute bottom of the dam," Bramlett said. He stomped his right foot on the concrete. "This is as deep as you can go."

Lloyd moved forward and put his arm around Elmer's shoulder.

"Billy, tell him how deep we are down in the ground right now. What is it, six stories?"

"That's right, Sheriff, six stories down. You ever seen the Georgia Power headquarters in Atlanta? It's five stories high. That whole building would fit down in here, and we'd still have room to cover it up."

Despite being only a few feet from Bramlett, Elmer avoided making eye contact with him by staring down at the small little streams flowing on either side of the walkway.

"These here," Bramlett said, pointing down to the gutters, "are the water monitoring stations for the lake. We let a little bit of water seep in and we test it to make sure it is not contaminated."

"Contaminated?" Elmer said.

"There can be cases of pollution when rivers are dammed, or cases of changes in the hydrosphere, that can affect the water's drinkability."

"Hydrosphere?" Elmer said.

"Yes, that's the term for natural waters."

Elmer looked him in the eyes.

"That you want to make sure that you don't poison?"

"Yes. Georgia Power has always been committed to being a good citizen, wherever we serve."

Elmer scratched his nuts and spat right into the gutter stream. Then the urge hit him to get out of this huge mass of concrete deep in the earth before he took the gun out of his shoulder holster and shot them both. He turned around and was facing Lloyd. Lloyd swallowed and was about to say something, but Elmer stepped down into the narrow, shallow stream with his cowboy boots and brushed against the cool concrete wall as he moved around Lloyd and back onto the walkway. He cut a path toward the stairs they had come from. Behind him he heard Lloyd talking to Bramlett.

"I appreciate you taking us down here, Billy. It's impressive, and I've seen it three times. I bet you Elmer got claustrophobic down in here. I know that's what it is, he just doesn't want to say nothing."

Elmer kept walking but their voices carried in the hallways, and he heard Bramlett's response. "That's fine, Sheriff, just fine. I should have warned y'all about the tight space down here. To some folks it's like being in a grave, and they panic. We had a lady faint earlier today, and a few children who came down here started to cry."

Elmer reached the end of the narrow hallway and opened the stairwell door and began to climb. He ascended the stairs fast, the stiffness of the suit and his sore knee slowing him down but he still made good time, getting well ahead of Lloyd and Bramlett, glad to be alone and not touched or breathed on or spoken to.

He kept climbing until he reached the door marked Control Room and opened it and stepped into the well-lit concourse where he could see the glass exit door leading onto the lower level of the dam. He went out and breathed in the fresh air, cooling as the afternoon wore down, and he heard the music of the band, more pronounced and stronger and tighter somehow, like music he might hear on the radio.

He was relieved to be outside, and the low-hanging sun

in his face caused him to squint. He walked to the railing and looked down at the gathering and saw that the high school band had finished playing. The Fourteenth Air Force Band now was performing, blowing their horns and beating their drums, sounding much more professional than the high school musicians. The high school majorettes continued to dance and twirl.

He paused there, watching the scene on the riverbank, people milling about and getting barbecue and talking despite the loud brass of the band. There were several clumps of men in suits on the stage, including a large crowd around Aubrey Terrell. The sun was falling in the sky, with only about two hours of daylight left. It was cool but warmer than usual for an early December afternoon. He pulled his cigarettes out of his right front pocket and then rebuttoned the jacket to ensure the gun in the shoulder holster remained hidden. He clicked fire out of the Zippo lighter and inhaled deep on the first drag.

He heard the door open across the deck behind him. Lloyd came out with Bramlett and they walked over to Elmer.

"Elmer, I was thanking Billy for our tour. That thing's something, ain't it?"

Elmer nodded and reached forward and shook Bramlett's hand.

"Thank you," he said, and turned to the railing looking over the river.

"You are welcome," Bramlett said. "In a few weeks, you won't even recognize this part of the world, or at least the other side of the dam. The lake will start filling in tonight, and much of the land along the riverbank will flood in the next few days. Then it will keep going. If we get any rain, it will hurry it up even more. By Christmas there will be about seventeen thousand acres of water here in Achena County. The more it rains, the faster it will fill up."

Elmer turned and gave him a mean stare.

"How about Finley Shoals? How fast will it fill up?"

"You mean the little crossroads town just north of here? Where that old mill sits?"

"Yeah, that's it. That's where Lloyd and I grew up."

"Oh, excuse me. As I said, I'm not from around here . . . Savannah, I think I told you. As close as that land is to the river, the water will rise up on it by this time tomorrow. Certainly the mill will be underwater, and probably the crossroads, too."

Elmer turned his back to Bramlett and looked over the railing at the gathering on the riverbank. The Georgia Power man continued to talk to him, loud enough to be heard over the music of the band below.

"I know you must have mixed emotions about the flooding of your homeplace, your farmland. But I'm proud of how much Georgia Power pays when we put in a lake. We normally pay 15 to 20 percent more than the Army Corps, and as much as 25 percent more than TVA did. I know you were well-rewarded for your land."

Lloyd stepped up so close to Elmer that he bumped against him, gesturing as he spoke to Bramlett.

"That's right, Billy, we did all right. We ain't made any money farming since I was a child. You can't make no money selling cotton or corn or sweet potatoes, and we are a little too far north here to grow them good sweet onions. Life's changing around here, and we are changing with it." He put his arm around Elmer and squeezed his shoulder. "Idn't 'at right, Elmer?"

Elmer moved out of Lloyd's grasp, spat over the railing, hustled his balls, and stormed off, the gun in the shoulder holster itching under his arm. He heard Lloyd thank Bramlett as he walked away. He soon heard Lloyd following, his ponderous weight clanging on the metal stairs.

Elmer got to the bottom of the steps and was heading around the office toward his truck when Lloyd caught up to him along the concrete walkway.

"Elmer," he said, breathing hard in his pursuit, "I don't know what's wrong with you. But you better snap out of it quick. Let me take you up on the stage, have you speak to the Guvnah. Maybe it'll lead to something. Nobody here has got anything against you, son."

Elmer hesitated, but Lloyd took him by the arm and pulled him toward the crowd like a child being led by his father. They paused for a moment while Lloyd caught his breath, then he led Elmer through standing workers in their red hardhats and then rows of chairs where families sat. The bands sat to the left side of the stage on a rise where the earth had been contoured into a plateau as the ground led up to the dam. The Air Force Band began a Christmas medley and a county commissioner dressed as Santa Claus started to work his way down from the stage and into the audience, handing out candy from a big red bag to children, patting them on the head and repeatedly doing his best *ho-ho-ho*.

Lloyd paused and gestured for Elmer to stop. They stood behind a row of chairs, listening to the music and watching the children run to Santa Claus, their hands outstretched for candy from his bag. The band segued into "Jingle Bells" and everyone began to sing and clap their hands, including Lloyd whose deep voice was out-of-tune, but it didn't hold him back. The song went on for what seemed like an hour to Elmer before they finished to a loud roar and enthusiastic round of clapping. The bandleader took the stage and spoke briefly, thanking everyone for their applause and saying that there would be a twenty-minute break before the ceremony began, at which time the high school and Air Force bands would play together the "Star Spangled Banner" and "God Bless America."

When the Air Force bandleader finished, Lloyd led Elmer to the front of the stage where a short set of stairs went up onto the dais. Four rows of chairs were decked up there, facing the crowd on the ground as though there was a choir behind a preacher.

"C'mon up here," Lloyd said.

Lloyd grabbed the lead-pipe railing and pulled himself up, the staircase shifting under his weight. Elmer waited until Lloyd was up before he climbed the creaky stairs to the temporary stage. He squinted as he reached the top, the reflection of the sun on the white dam wall an orange glow.

"Let's go, boy, let me introduce you around."

On the stage behind the chairs, Elmer saw groups of men in suits milling around, talking and drinking from paper cups. Lloyd reached his arm around Elmer's shoulders and pushed him toward a circle of well-dressed Atlantans.

"How y'all doin?" Lloyd said to the group that included the two men from the Coca-Cola Company whom Elmer had seen on the road in the morning. "Good to see y'all."

The Coca-Cola men acted like they did not recognize Elmer. They were crowded around a scowling older man, baldheaded and heavy, whose picture Elmer had seen in the paper, but he could not name. They all raised their cups in acknowledgment and smiled as Lloyd and Elmer moved past.

"Hello, again, Sheriff," the big man said without a smile.

"Thank you, Mr. Henry. Let me know if y'all need anything."

"I will."

Lloyd and Elmer moved on by them, and Lloyd whispered without looking back, "You know who that is, don't you?"

Elmer shrugged. Lloyd took a quick glance to see if they were being watched.

"That's Henry Bickford, president of the Co-Cola Company. Maybe the richest man in Georgia. First time he's ever been to Lymanville."

"And probably the last," Elmer said.

"I doubt it, son. He and all these folks will be coming down to the lake. Fishing, and bringing their daughters water skiing. One day there will be lake houses all along here, docks and boats to beat the band."

Elmer grunted and Lloyd paused, and they stopped walking as Lloyd gave him a sharp glare.

"Behave yourself, now, boy, you hear me?" His voice was a threatening whisper. He tightened his grip around Elmer's shoulders, squeezing him. "You hear me now, don't ya?"

Lloyd's expression changed. Elmer thought that he was going to say something about his bruise until Lloyd shifted his forearm and pressed on his shoulder so that it rubbed over the leather band of the holster beneath his suit coat. He knitted his brow into a questioning look and looped his elbow up around Elmer's neck.

"You got a shoulder holster on, don't you? Where'd you get that? And why you got a gun out here? You got your .38 under there?"

Elmer nodded.

"We got time to talk about this later," Lloyd said. "You keep that coat buttoned up, Elmer. You hear me? I don't want nobody out here seeing that gun today. No-body. You know you ain't got no use for it."

Elmer stood up straight and looked at Lloyd, but said

nothing. Ahead of them was another circle of men, four Army Corps of Engineers officers decked out in blue dress uniforms and brass medals, and three men in suits and crew cuts whom Lloyd said were Georgia Power executives. Lloyd greeted them, and the men nodded and replied in turn, but he led Elmer past them toward the far end of the stage where Terrell was holding court.

Terrell was standing in the far corner, sipping from a paper cup and telling stories to a dozen men in suits, all local lawyers and politicians except for Reverend Fincher and the newspaper publisher. It looked like he was preaching, the men gathered around him in some kind of religious awe. They were all laughing and smiling as Terrell gestured one way and mugged another. The men hooted and guffawed far beyond what was necessary.

"C'mon, son, let's move in there. You should speak to the Guvnah." Lloyd steered Elmer into the back of the circle.

They got close enough to hear the joke Terrell was telling, something about a coon dog and a monkey. He was pouring it on thick, his voice reaching a rhythmic fever pitch.

"And that monkey took the gun and pointed it at that old dog's head and *ka-blowie*—shot him dead." Terrell took steps back, staggered, and put his hand over his heart before resuming the joke. "The man was upset and asked the monkey, 'What in the hell did you do that for?' And the monkey said, 'if there's one thing I can't stand, it's a lying coon dog.'"

The men in the circle all exploded in laughter. Lloyd seemed to be trying to hee-haw loudest.

"Hooooo boy, that's a good one, Guvnah," Lloyd said, "that's a good one."

They were all catching their breath, letting the last laughs trickle out, when Terrell said, "Hey there, Lloyd," reaching his long arm for a handshake, "good to see you up here on the big stage." Lloyd lunged through the wall of suits and shook hands with him, patting him on the arm with his left hand.

Bobby Wilson, a young attorney, turned to Elmer and said, "You shoulda been here to hear the Guvnah tell the one about jerking off an elephant." The blond-headed, chubby-faced lawyer laughed again, smiling so hard it looked like his jowls would hurt. Elmer got a strong whiff of bourbon from the paper cup he was holding.

"You wanna snort, Elmer?" The young lawyer gestured with his libation. "The Guvnah's got a few bottles back up under the stage. I'll get you a drink."

Elmer shook his head in a definitive "no" and stepped away from him.

Lloyd and Terrell finished their vigorous handshaking and backslapping. Terrell turned to see Elmer, and reached his hand out to shake but didn't advance toward him.

"And good to see you too, cousin Elmer." Elmer paused and didn't raise his hand until Lloyd looked over with his eyes wide and twitched his head the direction of the tall politician.

Elmer's shoulders sagged, but he moved over and shook hands with Terrell.

"Yes, sir, good to see you—but I'm his nephew, not his cousin."

Lloyd moved up close next to Elmer and pushed an elbow against him.

"What's that, son?" Terrell asked. The change in his tone of voice brought the peanut gallery's chuckling to an end. The blond-haired Wilson boy's fat face dropped like he heard someone had just died.

"I'm his nephew," Elmer said, not loud, but it seemed that way in the new quiet of the group, "not his cousin."

"Aw, son, I know that," Terrell said, his voice warm again and giving it his best aw-shucks gesture, returning the smiles to the faces of his entourage.

"Yeah, that's right, Elmer," Lloyd said, "he was only using it as a figure of speech."

Elmer scowled at Lloyd and then turned to look back at Terrell.

"I figure you would know our family tree pretty well, all the Finley farmland you've owned."

The seemingly permanent grin faded from Terrell's face and the group fell cold again.

"Son, I did my best to help your daddy and your mama out, to keep that farm. But there wasn't nothing else I could do. I'm sorry things had to happen like that, like they did. I did my best to be fair, to help 'em out."

Elmer smirked, made a *ppfft* sound with his lips. He hustled his balls and spat off the stage in the direction of the dam bathed with the late afternoon sunlight.

"Mama always wanted to buy some of the farm back from you."

"Son, I know she did. She was a fine woman, and we all miss her. I'm sorry she took sick. But there just wasn't any thing I could do to help her. There was no money to be made in farming. For any of us."

Lloyd wanted to say something, but Terrell held up his hand to him and continued. "Farming is just a doomed business, son. There wasn't any other way I could help your mama out. That's the hand we were all dealt."

Elmer's voice was an angry hiss. "None of it matters one damn bit now—does it?—with this lake coming? All my family's farmland will be lake bottom. So ain't no reason to care about it now."

Terrell, who had been leaning forward to hear what Elmer had to say, bunched up his mouth in a knowing smile and shook his head slowly side-to-side.

"You're right, Elmer, you are right." Sounding like he was trying to comfort a child. "Ain't no point in farming anymore, it's gotten so hard to make a living at it. Tree-farming is 'bout the only money to come from our land these days. And you can't harvest 'em but once every two decades. Things is changing, and this lake is going to help us out. We ain't never going to amount to nothing if we keep on trying to be sharecroppers. I've been saying that all along. That's why I was willing to give up all my land for this lake. I'm gonna talk about it in my speech here later on. I think you are going to like my speech. We all got to sacrifice for the future."

The tall old man reached to pat Elmer on the shoulder, but Elmer was seething, unable to speak. *Your land?* was the only thought he could muster. *Your land?* he asked in his mind again, but he couldn't get his mouth around the words. Elmer didn't move, but Lloyd next to him put his arm around him and pushed him forward.

"It's all right, son, it's all right," Terrell said, and laid a hand on Elmer's shoulder.

Elmer had the urge to curse Terrell and spit on him and tell him all the things he had done wrong, but he never had been the talking kind and knew he could never speak the words he wanted to say. He gritted his teeth. He was no verbal match for this smooth-talking legislator.

He turned and walked briskly through the groups of men and to the other end of the stage. He ignored Lloyd's calls to him to come back, descending the stairs into the babble of the crowd.

ELMER KEPT HIS HEAD down, avoiding eye contact with anyone who might be looking at him, and cut through the audience. He freed himself from the mob and walked a loop around the band and up the incline toward the dam wall, the fresh concrete bright in the flat sunlight of the late afternoon. He got off behind the office building far enough where no one would bother him, and he smoked a cigarette and studied on the scene, muttering.

Near the side of the dam wall he looked at the bottom rung of the metal ladder he had noticed earlier. The ladder led up the side of the dam, up to the very top, two hundred feet above the river and the low ground where Achena County's residents were gathered to bid the river farewell. He stubbed out his cigarette with his boot heel and headed toward the bottom rungs.

He began climbing the ladder and felt foolish ascending in a suit, the handgun dangling heavily in the holster beneath his jacket. He passed by the first level of the dam where he and Lloyd had met Billy Bramlett and he kept climbing, the earth below receding with each step. He was getting winded but kept moving up, his knee and elbow sore under the strain. He willed himself not to pause or look down as he neared the highest rungs. He reached the top of the ladder and climbed onto the eight-foot wide walkway with railings on each side atop the dam wall. At the far ends where the concrete sloped to meet the hills that had been shaped with bulldozers, a twelve-foot high chain-link fence kept men and animals alike from clambering up the sides.

He stood upon the dam and took in the view. He could see more of Achena County from here than he ever had before, the softly undulating shape of the rolling terrain south all the way to Lymanville. He saw the metal trestle of the river bridge in town and he thought he could make out the spire on top of the courthouse, blurry and tiny from this distance, but standing tall above the rest of the indistinguishable group of buildings that was the county seat. Further south, the land was as flat as a table-top in the far-off horizon, Georgia's Coastal Plain that ran level all the way to the Atlantic Ocean.

He turned and looked north of the dam where it was cleared and brown and barren until it gave way to green further up. He could see the boulders along the fall line that cut across the river, and he followed with his eyes the blue route of water as it wound and crooked down from the north to the dam and then passed under it and straightened out and got a little muddier as it flowed south in a straight shot down the west side of Lymanville.

He turned back to the north and crossed to the other side of the walkway atop the dam and directed his gaze down, where he saw the abandoned town of Finley Shoals, his once hometown, the aging general store standing rickety at the corner crossroads. Across the macadam, the barren spot where the church and the empty graves had been was heavy in shadow. He ran his eyes along the tail-end of Finley Shoals Road to the old gristmill, just a waterfront building now that the water-wheel was gone. He could not see his family homeplace amongst the old oak trees south of the crossroads. He shook his head and spat over the side and watched his glob of spit fall, wavering in the air and following the easy wind until it disappeared from sight.

The music started again, and the sound of the drums and the horns traveled up to him as though they could be heard a hundred miles away, yet still distant up on top of the dam. He crossed back over the walkway and looked down at the crowd gathered there. The high school and Air Force bands played together, that patriotic song again, and the lead majorette, Raynelle Watson, a curvy young redhead with her hair in a tight bun, performed on the end of the dais where chairs had been cleared for her. The men from Atlanta and Terrell all stood nearby in a clump, smiling and nodding their heads, smug about who they were and what they were doing and that they could get this sexy high school girl to dance and spin and do handstands right in front of them for everyone in Achena County to see. Elmer watched her dance for a while. She was easily the best-looking woman in Lymanville.

Elmer turned and scanned the land to the north again. All he viewed from here—the blue winding river and the farms and the cleared timberland—none of that meant anything to the Atlantans, to Aubrey Terrell, to most of the folks here in fact. It was only dirt and water and wood. A blight on the map. Exchanging fertile soil and a river and forests for cheap electricity seemed like the best deal in the world to them. So what if a few graves had to be moved, a few churches had to find new homes, a cluster of houses succumbed to water? They would all have somewhere to water ski. Some of these folks, Terrell foremost among them, were even idiotic enough to thank God for the boll weevil for killing off their cotton and forcing them to pursue a more sophisticated way of life through concrete, lakes, and hydroelectricity.

Elmer leaned his hand on the railing and watched Raynelle strutting her stuff, the baton flying higher and higher with each toss. The silver stick rose up toward him fighting gravity until it lost its momentum, wavering there seemingly in limbo for a moment or two, before dropping back down to earth to be snatched up by her hands and then passed around her back and twirled and slid quickly through her legs with a smile on her face and a sly, lightning-fast wink to the men on the stage.

Elmer glared down at Terrell, standing there, nodding,

drinking bourbon from his paper cup, smiling, proud of himself as he could be. He wasn't even dead yet and the dam and the lake were being named for him. He ought to be dead to have something like the biggest lake in Middle Georgia named for him.

Elmer pulled the .38-.44 Heavy Duty Smith & Wesson revolver from the leather holster and turned away from the crowd below so no one could see him with it. He leaned back against the rail and held the gun close to his body and opened the cylinder and spun it and listened to its synchronous clicks as it rotated. It was loaded, magnum bullets he had hollowed out himself on their tops, waiting to fire. He sighted down the target at a dirty speck on the walkway, the long barrel a different sight line than the shorter gun he was accustomed to but better for aiming.

The bands brought the music to a rousing finish of cymbal-crashing and horn-blowing and baton-spinning. The crowd cheered and applauded yet again. There was a pause, and he heard Terrell's voice over the loudspeaker, strong but smooth even up to where Elmer was, high above the ceremony.

"Wasn't that something?" Terrell said, drawling it out. "Let's give these young folks a big hand. The Fourteenth Air Force Band, ladies and gentlemen, and our very own Lymanville High School Marching Rebels."

Elmer turned to watch and put the gun under his coat and kept his finger tense on the trigger as Terrell spoke. The tall, proud old man stepped back from the microphone for a minute and applauded, holding his hands up high before bowing in the direction of the band. Elmer's angle was such that to shoot to kill he would have to hit him square in the back or the base of the skull. He gauged the distance to be about three hundred feet, most of the path of the bullet straight down, a long way for a pistol shot. He'd have to be accurate to avoid accidentally hitting someone else.

Terrell stepped back up to the microphone. "I'm only going to speak with you a moment now, but I'll be back later. Right now I want to recognize some of the dignitaries we have visiting us today, many of whom will be coming up here to talk to you, but many others who we don't have time to hear from but should be so honored."

Elmer watched as the old man pulled his glasses out of his suit coat and put them on. He unfolded a piece of paper and held it, adjusting the distance from his eyes, moving it farther, so he could read. "From Atlanta, Dr. Arsey Lorcasterman, personal physician to four of Georgia's governors. A fine gentleman. Please stand, Arsey . . ." An old man in the first row of chairs behind the lectern stood up. The crowd applauded and Terrell went on down his list of people. "Eugene Loftis, an extraordinary attorney, partner in Atlanta's leading law firm . . ."

Elmer's hands sweated and he held the pistol tighter under his coat, his finger bent around the trigger. He scanned the crowd to see if anyone was looking up at him, but it didn't appear they were. He could see the fat Coca-Cola man sitting in the front row next to the congressman and the governor. Everyone was focused on the dignitaries on the stage.

Elmer's finger twitched, flinching as though he was going to draw. It was a single motion to pull back the trigger and the hammer would go up and fall and the gun would fire. He paused listening to Terrell's reading of the names, looking for another place to get down, to make a quick getaway. Even if he shot Aubrey Terrell, he'd have to shoot himself or be shot, because he'd never escape. They had him surrounded. It seemed like he'd been blocked in his whole life by these people. Shooting his way out wouldn't stop the dam and he would end up

dead, or worse, down in Reidsville with all the hoodlums and
lunatics that would beat the shit out of him and even fuck him
because he had been a deputy once. He knew about prisons
and what happened to ex-lawmen inside there.

He relaxed his hand and put the big Smith & Wesson back
in the shoulder holster, fastening the catch. He took hold of the
railing and stepped on the top rung and began climbing down
the ladder. He favored his injured arm and knee, grimacing in
pain when he had to put weight on the aching limbs. Going
down was slow, and he stopped to rest a few times and made
the mistake of looking down. The red earth below seemed to
almost glower at him, taunting him to let loose and fall.

But he hung on. He reached the bottom of the ladder and
walked around the crowd as quickly as he could, his eyes down
on the ground. He cut a straight path up the hill to his truck.
He heard Aubrey Terrell finish thanking the bigwigs on stage
and the band start to play again.

Elmer slammed his truck door and cranked the engine
and turned around and drove off, relieved that the linkage did
not stick and he was able to get away quick, the good people
of Achena County bunched together like ants in his rearview
mirror.

PERCY EDGED ALONG WHAT remained of the tree line toward
the Oogasula, a mile from the shack where he lived with the
old lady, a half-mile beyond the abandoned crossroads and
gristmill, his eyes darting around, studying the dam as he got
closer, his nose following the scent of barbecue. He trotted
with his wet black tongue hanging slack. He heard noises like
he had never heard before, music that honked and clashed of
brass and a heavy beat, a determined loud clanging that carried
across the landscape like a harmonious machine of some kind,

but pretty in a way too, except for an occasional high-pitched squeak of some of the instruments that dinged his ear drums. The voices were thick and boisterous, a rising and swirling mix of chattering men and women and children. At regular intervals they would smack their hands together like they were mimicking a heavy summer rain shower. He was near starving or he would have never persisted in following the sweet smell of cooking meat to this crazy ruckus.

The men who had been on top of the dam in red hardhats were gone, so Percy left the cover of the tree line and trotted up the side of the manmade hill on the west side of the river that had been built to run up to the top of the dam, a perfectly angled slope that rose up to the ledge of the concrete wall and connected it with the natural hills. A high chain-link fence kept him from going onto the top of the concrete wall—not that he wanted to do so. From the top of the artificial hill he could look down on the mass of people situated in a flat spot on the other side of the dam. Years ago, the shoals here had been a regular hunting ground for him and he had chased the cows that used to be in the riverside pastures. He had not been down this far south along the Oogasula since the blasting and building began three years ago. Much had changed. A new building was there with a shiny glass door, a new black road with brightly colored lines and a large patch of hardtop where cars parked. Beyond that were more people than he had ever seen, more than he knew existed, all gathered there beneath some kind of riser where more men sat, higher than the rest. His brows worked, moving and wrinkling above his busy eyes as he took it all in, letting out a low half-growl, barking a time or two at the large crowd that did not notice the half-chow dog on the hill overlooking their festivities. He saw the spitting-scratching man on up the road where cars were parked, his steps fast in a tense stride. The man got into his truck and cranked it up and turned around and drove over the hill and away.

Percy turned his head back toward the crowd. He sniffed the smell of the meat, the distinct waft of pork so tender they could pull it right from the rib cage of the slow-cooked hog, the bones left over moist and malleable. Nothing was better than gnawing on a warm bone. He saw the clouds of smoke coming from under big green tents along the edge of the river where they were serving up plates of pork and vegetables and cornbread. There was no way for Percy to get to the food without cutting through the mass of people except for perhaps swimming across the river and running down and then swimming back across. But the water was too cold for swimming, despite the warmth of the sun.

He was an old dog now, and sometimes he moved slow like the old man had. If the old man were here at this event, he would have gone down first thing and gotten Percy a bone with a mess of meat on it and brought it back to him and scratched his head and fed it to him, talking to him in those warm, slow tones, the only word of which Percy understood was his name, but not caring, knowing that the man's voice was affectionate, just like the old man had known that his barks and pants were his only audible expression of his love for his master, the hand that had fed him well. But the old man was dead, long gone.

So Percy stood up above the crowd and measured with his dark eyes how to best get to the food. He was a shy country dog and would have avoided any such noise, hightailing it to the safety of the deep woods, but everything had changed. Even the cows in the fields near where he lived had vanished. He was hungry and his lupine instinct to eat drove him down the hill toward the people. The first group he would come to were decked out in red and silver uniforms, many of them holding noisy brass-colored instruments and honking on them. In front of the resplendent colors of the band there were three young-looking women in strange half-costumes with bare legs and shoulders spinning short silvery sticks with little white balls on each end high above their heads and dancing crazy while they were in the air, sometimes going head over heels, before getting in a position to catch them when they came to the ground. He eyed the twirling silver as the sticks spun high in the sky and then waggled and dropped back to earth into the hands of the girls.

On the other side of the costumed music-makers were rows of chairs where white people in their Sunday best sat, many old folks and children, in folding chairs like he had seen at the graveyard in years past when they buried a pine box in the ground and some of the women wailed and the men had stood around sad-eyed. But no one looked sad today. Behind the chairs were more white folks standing, including a clump of men wearing shiny, red hardhats. There also were many farmers in overalls and tattered straw hats like the old man had worn, and for a minute Percy watched the group of farmers in overalls but none of them were the old man, his old man. None moved like he had, those slow, shuffling steps and forward-hanging head with the long, pointed chin and missing top teeth, the jaws seeming to always be chewing on something. Beyond the farmers were loose groups of white children, running and playing in the dirt, boys tossing a football and girls sitting in circles handing something back and forth, pieces of string trailing from their fingers. He watched as one of the boys snatched something from a very small girl and then one of the older girls chased the boy and tackled him on the ground and his crying echoed loud above the other noises of the valley filled with people. Other children moved about the little boy in a flurry, and they swarmed back and forth. He didn't see another dog anywhere.

Percy eyeballed a path between the red and silver of the uniforms of the band and the people in their Sunday clothes, men mostly, and through that route to behind the last row of chairs and then through some of the standing farmers to the food. The only part of the crowd through which he would not have to pass was the small section of black faces, most of them trimmed with gray hair, standing in the very back behind the farmers and away from the white children who seemed to know to keep their distance, and the blacks seeming to know to keep to themselves a safe distance away from the food and the farmers and the white children. There were no black children that Percy could see, and he was glad he didn't have to go near the blacks as the old man had taught him as a pup to hate and fear anyone with a black face. Even being this near to them caused him to bristle.

Everything went back to the old man. He had taken Percy in when he was a pup and his first memories were of sitting in the old man's denim lap, the rough hands scratching him and the smell of sweat and car parts and warm, greasy meats. It was natural to bark at anyone who was not the old man. He had barked at everyone who did not feed him, but the old man had called him off the white faces, the old man's voice calm and gentle, "down, boy, down" a pat on the head and a strong rub of his rough hand along Percy's back, maybe even a snack as a reward.

But black faces, which were much less frequent along the road between the junkyard and the river, had scared Percy with their strangeness and brought out venom in the old man, something that caused him to point his finger, wagging it angrily, "sic 'em, boy, sic 'em," his voice razor sharp and bitter. Percy learned that any non-white faces should be scared off and run away, they were neither to be customers or thieves at the junkyard, and they could not stop to fish with their long cane poles from the river there. If they didn't run when he barked, his fangs came out. Percy knew to bite, be it man, woman or child, as long as they had dark skin, until they ran away and left the old man and Percy and the old lady in peace.

So Percy ran down the hill toward the bank, trotting slow but steady, his black eyes intent on his line through the crowd of people, on getting to the tent with the barbecued hog. He paused along the way and circled back a few times to observe. The people in the crowd were acting strange, oblivious to the earth and sky and water around them, seeming to worship only the concrete monument across the river.

The only time Percy had ever seen people behave this way was when the old lady had gone to church. He had sometimes walked down through the woods to the crossroads and watched from the edge of the tree line while she had gone into the old building that was no longer there. He had listened to the singing and hollering and puzzled over their actions. Once a year they had set up a tent in the field next to the church and then he watched with amazement how they sang and hollered and cried and carried on every night for a week, led by one emotional man at a podium who paced and cajoled and screamed. Sometimes it went on for hours, well into the darkness of the night. The old man never went down to the church, and Percy could understand why the old man didn't want any part of it. The old man had been all Percy had understood. All the rest of it was just human strangeness.

Percy stood watching the hubbub while the music played and the crowd moved to and fro and more people walked down the road and joined the celebration. There were cars as far as he could see parked along the new road leading down to the river. The band stopped playing and he trotted toward the mob. He reached the bottom of the hill and went around the far side of the new building where many cars and trucks were parked out front. He jogged around the parking lot and alongside the crowd until he was about halfway down, past the bright red and silver costumes of the musicians.

He cut through a walkway behind the band, slipping by a group of chubby high school boys in the back row, some with sticks and big silver barrels and others with enormous gold horns that wrapped around their bodies, almost as big as they were. He heard them laughing and pestering one another but they did not see him behind them. To his right were the farmers in overalls, standing and watching him but not showing any mind to a black chow-mutt mix trotting through the crowd. He made note of the fact that none of them were eating, even though they had lean, slack-jawed, hungry looks on their old white faces.

He was sneaking through the aisle past the farmers when he heard a loud voice from the stage, a voice that carried and echoed throughout the valley. Most everyone smacked their hands together and some hooted and hollered as the voice reached a higher pitch. Then another man's voice was on the loudspeaker, this one smooth and warm and lilting in its gratefulness. Percy came upon a short, stout farmer with glasses and a crew cut and skin red from sun who screamed and pumped his fist and cigarette in the air. Percy moved to avoid him but the man jumped forward and caused Percy to dart to the left behind the man and step on another farmer's foot who kicked at him. He dashed on ahead. He did not look back or raise his eyes to see, but kept his fast path toward the scent, looking for the largest opening he could find through the crowd to the roasting hog.

He soon found his way out of the mass of people and to the food tents by the river where a big drum was covered with a lid and smoke poured out of it. There were trays, all covered with cloth or metal lids, lined up beside the smoker. Percy smelled warm cornbread, the buttery odor intermingling with the strong scent of smoke from the hickory fire over which the hog had roasted.

He watched two fat-faced men and three women behind the tables, the men tending to the big drum with the meat, the women to the bread and the metal trays and paper cups of sweetened ice tea. They would stop and listen to the speaker for a while and then they would turn their attention back to the food, speaking quietly to one another while the rest of the audience focused on the man at the stage with the mellifluous voice.

Percy trotted behind the tents, along the edge of the river, and leaned over the water. The river smelled fresh and wet, and a cool breeze gently came off of it. He lapped up a cold drink, detecting a funny taste, almost like sand or chalk had gotten into the water. He stopped drinking and looked at the river and to the concrete wall built across it, under which the water now flowed, the surface smooth and flat down this far.

A waft of smoke drifted by, and another hunger pang came over him. He turned and looked back up at the tents where the food waited, and he moved back and forth, watching the barbecue pit and the big sideways drum with smoke. He scanned the ground for scraps or a bone or even a few bread crumbs but there was nothing to be had.

He started making gradual lateral moves toward the food tents, sneaking in until he was only about five feet behind the men working over the smoking drum. When one of them opened the lid of the big cooker, Percy ran to it and stood on his back legs and grabbed at the whole hog roasting there, his teeth ripping loose a hunk of hot pork. The man shouted at him and kicked him in the ribs. The other man grabbed a broom and whacked Percy across his shoulders, knocking him on his side. The blows hurt and most of the meat fell out of his mouth. He scurried to his feet and snarled at the man who had kicked him but the other man raised the broom again so he ran off south down the river away from the crowd. He ran as hard as he could for about a hundred yards before he looked back to see if anyone was chasing him, but they were not.

It had grown darker and was very dim where he stopped, beyond the lights of the stage. He rested cautiously and licked his chops to taste the remnants of the pork on his tongue. Atop the big concrete wall there were enormous spotlights shining down, and the wall itself was also bathed in light. He listened to the crowd roar with cheers as the man at the microphone spoke passionately and louder. The sky was falling to black and the man speaking was illuminated in a powerful, round light. Percy panted, trying to catch his breath, and sat on his side. His ribs and shoulders hurt and he was tired enough to take a nap but was scared to do so with this many people around. His eyes eased shut but he forced them open and kept his head held up. He waited there while the man spoke, becoming more and more passionate with each shouted word. The man carried on for a long time.

The man speaking then slowed down and began talking low, repeating a phrase, before ratcheting back up in intensity. He was drowned out by the cheers, but then the crowd quieted down again and the man returned to the fervent tones in a gasping rhythm. The people *oohed* and *aahhed* and applauded, some shouting affirmations as the man spoke.

The man ended with a fiery flourish and the crowd yelled and the music started to play again. Percy heard a strange hiss and raised his head with a tinge of fear. Above the new concrete wall a red streaming line of fire rocketed into the sky and exploded like a gun shot, and then a big round pattern of red and white and blue appeared high overhead where birds flew. Percy rose to his feet as another line of fire crossed into the heavens, and it exploded even louder and then others followed. The flashes of fire in the sky scared him and he began to whimper, and then as more red fire lines raced up he started running as fast as he could, going the long way around the crowd and past the cars and up the artificial hill and to the other side of the big white concrete wall that straddled the river. He sprinted as hard as he could go.

Soon he was safely in the darkness of the brush line, beneath a few remaining trees, on the other side of the dam. All he could see from there were the burning lights in the night, exploding and booming as the music played and the delirious people all screamed with strange joy. He paused and panted, catching his breath some, before running on back toward the junkyard and the shack along the river that was his home.

ELMER PULLED UP INTO the yard in front of his childhood homeplace. The house, tucked in between three old oak trees and a pecan tree, had been vacant since his mama died and grass and weeds had grown up in the dirt driveway. He occasionally had come out to do a little maintenance, clean up the yard and such, but he had been lax in the past several years, and hadn't set foot inside the house in more than two.

The white, one-story farmhouse had three gables all covered in rusty tin, a piece of which over the front was loose and threatened to slide off, exposing the beams through a gaping hole. He didn't want to think about the leak that must be inside, water pouring down through the ceiling and onto the hardwood floors planed smooth back when his great-grandfather had built the place out of oak and pine. Although it had been a dry fall, it had been a very rainy summer, and he was certain that part of the house must be ruined. Beneath the roof was a big wraparound porch supported on short, unadorned columns that rose from the edge of the floor. The paint was peeling badly from the clapboards, warped and deep with water stains.

He got out of the truck and slammed the door. He started walking toward the porch but then stood still to hear better the commotion from the dam. A half-mile to the south he could faintly make out the pomp and circumstance of the ceremonies, the clatter and honk of the high school band running through that patriotic song again, the seal-like beating of palms by the thousands gathered there, gratuitous applause like the sound of a distant rain, and then the hoots and the hollers of the voices, haint-like as they wafted across the border of the Coastal Plain and up into the Piedmont. He thought of the long-gone Indians and what their chants must have been like.

He walked on through the high, dry grass of the yard. The azaleas in front of the porch had gone untrimmed for years, so long he couldn't remember when he did it last. The bushes grew high and in unseemly shapes so that some of the branches were dying with brown leaves but others were healthy green and thick. His mama had loved those azaleas, had bought them from the Sears, Roebuck and Co. catalogue and had planted them herself in the years his daddy had first run off, working the ground and ignoring the criticisms of Lloyd and neighbors that she shouldn't be wasting her time on a non-food bearing, city slicker plant. She never argued, never even raised her voice, but kept right on digging and pruning and watering and throwing food scraps and cow manure on the roots. In late March and early April, the rather mundane looking shrubs took on a whole new existence, blooming white and red and pink, a bouquet of warm hues enshrouding the house, as though the porch were floating atop a cloud of fiery colors. On spring days she would sit out there and drink iced tea or lemonade or coffee and enjoy her flowering plants. She encouraged Elmer and Lloyd to join her, which they had done occasionally to humor her, but both had short patience for such trivialities and did not appreciate flowers like she had.

He stepped onto the porch and grasped the front doorknob, looking through the window into the front hall and at the door to her bedroom. He stalled as memory came up and grasped him like a strong pair of hands around his throat.

HE HAD GOTTEN A call on his police radio the afternoon that his mama had fainted at the high school lunchroom. He had been all the way across the county, down near the women's prison, and it took him twenty minutes to get there. By the time he arrived, they had put her in a hearse—a hearse because the county had no ambulance—and carried her to the hospital.

In the year prior to her collapse, she had begun losing weight and tiring easily, complaining some to Elmer that she was getting stiff from standing, serving up teenagers for six hours a day, or that stirring the big pots of food hurt her shoulders. Elmer just figured that she was getting old, and told her so. He knew now that he should have paid more attention to her, gone to church with her, stopped by to see her when he was out on his rounds.

When he got to the hospital, they were taking her out of the hearse and she was unconscious and so pale she looked dead.

She still had the hairnet on her head. If he had known then what she was about to go through, he would have wished her dead on the spot. They operated on her and kept her about two weeks before sending her home, removing a tumor as big as a loaf of bread from her back. She never did sit up straight again and Elmer, still married at the time, took to staying with her a few nights a week, napping in an armchair while she tried to sleep. But she didn't sleep much, instead she moaned and cried and gasped for air. Sometimes she would ask Elmer to hold her hand and she would tell him he was a good boy and that she had always been proud of him, never more than that day he was in his Navy whites and the town honored him with a parade. She would ask about her azaleas. Other times she would just lie quiet with wild eyes, chewing her lips and gnashing her teeth. A thousand times Elmer tried to tell her that she should go to the doctor and maybe they could do something for her pain, but she refused, said she didn't want to die in that hospital. It was getting "full of nigras," and she wanted to be at home, under her own roof, in her own bed, that the doctors "didn't know nothing," that it was God's will. He tried to tell her that the colored folks had their own hospital, but she didn't listen. That went on for weeks, Elmer sitting up with her, and then she started getting better, eating solid food, not sitting all the way up, but turning on her side so she could at least turn her head to look at the world upright, not from flat on her back. She even got cheerful for a while, talking about getting back to work, how she missed the children and her friends down at the school. An occasional visit by one of the lunchroom ladies or the pastor boosted her spirits.

But then she would regress, start feeling bad again, the moaning and crying and staying up all night, still refusing to go to the hospital. This cycle of mild recovery and agony repeated for about six months. And then one hot August morning she died and soon after they put her in the ground. The last time he saw her she was only fifty-one years old, shined up with funeral home makeup in her coffin, her eyelids shut and her hands crossed.

ELMER PUSHED OPEN THE weathered poplar door to the home where he had lived until he turned eighteen and went off to war, twelve years ago this month. The door creaked but opened easily, the hinges cracking as it swung loose. He stepped into the front hall and dust rose up around his shoes and he smelled the sour scent of mildew. He left the door open and moved into the hallway and stopped and looked in the living room immediately to his left. The windows were shut but varmints had gotten inside through the chimney and had gnawed on the doors and the molding. Pea-sized turds littered the bricks and hardwoods around the fireplace.

He stepped back out into the hallway, becoming aware of the sound of his cowboy boots on the hardwood planks. He noticed that the interior doors to the dining room were missing. Lloyd must have sold the doors to that man in Macon who bought all the furniture and hauled it away. Greedy bastard. Lloyd had split the $150 profit with Elmer even after Elmer had told him he didn't want any part of it, that he didn't care if the furniture went down in the flood. That had been shortly after Elmer had lost his job as a deputy. He had objected, but ultimately spent the money.

Elmer walked down to where the hallway ended at the kitchen and dining room. The rooms seemed huge without the small kitchen table and the massive oak dining set that had been made from the same trees that had been used to make the floors. The wood-burning stove also was gone from the kitchen. The only stick of furniture left behind was a broken chair leaning precariously against a wall.

A leak in the dining room had burst through the ceiling at the back wall and water had warped the floorboards, moldy despite the dry weather of late. Weeds that had grown up through the floor were withering with the coolness of the season, but had clearly bloomed heavy in the dining room in the summer. Elmer's face reddened with shame at not having been a better keeper of this house. He was sure his great-grandfather was cursing him from the grave, that freshly dug hole of his down there near the dump where all of Elmer's ancestors now rested.

He was breathing hard and his elbow began to hurt from the beating he had taken earlier and his knee felt tender, two crosswise joint pains shooting through his body. His bad tooth ached and his jaw was sore where he had been punched. He lost himself in his ailments for a moment until he heard the marching bands again, distant and wispy on the wind a half-mile away, the music only as loud as his breathing.

A clear thought rose in his muddled mind. Why do I give a goddamn about a roof leak if they are going to flood the land? *We don't even own this house.* He tried to picture the house under water, boats and water skiers overhead and fish swimming through the doorways and over the transoms, water snakes in the chimney and turtles on the roof as it succumbed to the dammed—the *damned*—river. He thought about the sunken battleships on the bottom of the Pacific, the ones attacked at Pearl Harbor and then the Jap ones the U.S. Navy fighter planes had sunk. He had never dreamed that his own homeplace would be submerged like those ships half-a-world away. The Navy always stressed how the globe was three-quarters water and that they had the largest area to cover of any of the military branches. So why in the Sam Hill had he come home to more drowning of the earth, more territory for the goddamned water? What was so bad about being landlocked?

Elmer stormed up the hallway toward the front door but before going out he stopped and looked back. He reached beneath his coat and pulled the .38-.44 from his shoulder holster and stepped into the living room. He took aim at the wall above the fireplace mantel and pulled the trigger. The gun sounded like a cannon in the house, the bullet an invisible force ripping through the wall, the metal slug burying deep in the soft-red bricks of the chimney. He fired twice more and poofs of red dust drifted out of the bullet holes and onto the dirty floor.

He turned and stormed out of the house and into the yard and stood by his truck, holding the revolver by his side. A cool was settling in as the waning daylight relinquished its hold on the night. From the direction of the dam he again heard the sound of distant applause and cheering and he could make out the smooth rhythm of Aubrey Terrell speaking, his melodic sentences rolling across the fields with the aid of a loudspeaker. Elmer could not make out the words but he heard the fervency in the old man's voice, the cult of personality that he had banked on for all of these years. He knew what Terrell's words meant without hearing them. "Bull . . . shit," Elmer said, and spat on the ground.

After a while, Terrell's voice ended in a huge round of applause with the most intense screaming yet, then the sound of the band playing, and then something Elmer had seen only once in his life, had seen that distant happy day when the war in the Pacific was over and his ship returned to port in California: fireworks, red and white and blue, sparks shooting across the dark evening sky. He watched the colored lines form shapes of huge flower blooms above the horizon to the south, clinging close to the tree line, but high enough that he could clearly see even from a half-mile away. He knew that if he were up close and under those fireworks, like he had been on that ship that night for VJ day, the big balls of rockets on the bluish canvas of the coming night sky would be enormous, the biggest fireball he'd ever seen, like it must have been for those Japs in Hiroshima and Nagasaki. He preferred this perspective. He was old enough to know that things were always less painful the further you were away from them. He wished he was far away from Finley Shoals, but he wasn't. He knew he never could be far away, even when it would be under water.

Elmer raised the gun over his head and fired three rounds into the sky, echoing across the valley where the Oogasula River flowed for the last time. He doubted the gunshots even registered with the slaphappy idiots celebrating the destruction of the river. Another screaming red line was drawn across the sky, exploded like a bomb, and formed an enormous flower shape of red and white before fading out to wisps of smoke.

He decided to give them some fireworks of his own. He got six cartridges from beneath his truck seat and reloaded the revolver. He stomped back into the house and found an old lantern, half full of kerosene, in a closet off the kitchen. He carried it to the dining room and smashed it on the floor next to a wall, the globe shattering and the pinkish coal oil spreading out in a circle amongst glimmering glass shards. The pungency of the accelerant rose in nostrils. He ripped a gray curtain from the window and tossed it onto the spilled oil and then took the wooden kitchen chair and raised it over his head and flung it across the room and up against the wall. The legs of the chair broke loose from the backrest as it fell to the floor in pieces on the oil-stained drapes.

He lifted the .38-.44 and fired it across the room into the

busted chair and ragged curtain. The chair legs jolted and a hole in the baseboard appeared. He studied on the target and fired again, shooting five more shots, the entire cylinder, into the pile. Sparks had flown but the flames he wanted had not started. He opened up the cylinder and hit the ejector rod and the shells fell loose on the floor at his feet, clattering on the warped hardwoods. He put the warm gun back into the leather shoulder holster. He bent and picked up a spent casing and held it to his nose, inhaling, and then stuck it in his left nostril. It hung there and he enjoyed the scent of warm ammunition. He stood there breathing in until the smell of the fired casing faded. He flicked it loose and it clinked dully on the floor when it fell.

Elmer took his Lucky Strikes from the right front pocket of his jacket and tapped one loose from the near empty pack into his mouth and put the cigarettes back into the pocket opposite the heavy gun in the shoulder holster. He reached into his left pants pocket and got out his Zippo and sparked the wheel and watched the small tight flame come up. He lit the cigarette and inhaled deep, the nicotine mixing with the faint smell of the fired bullet casing and the whiff of kerosene from the floor and the mildew stink of the leak and the fresh air blowing in the front door carrying that far away scent of the river in its final day on Earth. He could hear the fireworks exploding, could hear the band starting up that same damned patriotic song again.

He sucked in on the shrinking cigarette and then flicked it across the room toward the chair and curtain and kerosene. The butt landed on the grimy cloth and rolled into a crevice and smoldered there until smoke began to increase. A small flame kicked up and grew until the curtain was consumed, and then the old chair began to burn like kindling. The fire took up the ridged molding on the doorframe to the hallway, the paint there bubbling as it retreated from the wood, and then the floorboards began to blacken and curl and smoke in the hissing anticipation of a full-on fire.

He watched the flames spread up the wall and across the hardwood floors, a fast-scurrying ball, flickering blue and red and orange dancing. Elmer saw all this like it was taken by a stroboscopic camera, fast-moving images of flame flickered out into still photographs before him. He couldn't express it in words, but he knew he wasn't right in the head and that he never would be again.

The fireball grew and the room got hot and he began to sweat. He stepped back into the open doorway, watching the flames race to the walls of the kitchen and the dining room, but also moving forward toward the door and the porch. The flames were a foot from him when he turned and hurried out of the house. He ran down the steps and turned as the front wall and porch was enveloped in flames, the tin roof buckling with heat under the burning ceiling. He undid the top button on his dress shirt and took off his tie and wadded it up and tossed it toward the burning porch where it festooned before it was gone, vanished into the smoke rising from the fire.

Elmer stepped farther away from the house to observe the immersion. The wind was blowing toward the river, and the blaze spread into the azaleas beneath the side of the wraparound porch, the bushes beginning to crackle. He saw the flames above shooting from the roof move hard and to the east with a gust of wind. Sparks floated into the trees behind the right corner of the house, and then the old oak there exploded in flames, torching the remaining brown leaves and beginning the slow burn of the hardwood branches and trunk. The heat was warm on Elmer's skin, a dry but comforting balm.

The fire moved rapidly through the dry winter grass, high and abandoned since early spring, faster than a man could run, about the clip of a coon dog hightailing it after a squirrel. The barn to the west of the house was safe but the outhouse behind the home was soon engulfed in flames, the old wood privy burning fast. The fire moved with the wind from his family's land toward the main intersection of Finley Shoals, only a quarter of a mile away, scorching a small patch of cedar trees, the wispy needles burning in an instant, almost like each red cedar was a light or a firecracker going off. He stood by his truck on what he would have called the windward side of the house when he was in the Navy and watched the blaze that he had started scurry across the ground, bound for the Finley Shoals crossroads.

He got into the truck and cranked it up and drove out the driveway and onto the short stretch of Sills Road toward the intersection, coming up behind the big general store and P.O. He had thought that perhaps the fire wouldn't be able to cross the road and would just die in the dirt, but enough weeds and grass had sprung up in the unkempt two-lane that the flame passed over in a few places, little dancing rivulets of orange and red, spreading to the grassy dry ditches of the other side like a snake slithering across the roadway in the summertime.

Elmer drove through the two-foot high strips of fire across Sills Road and turned on Finley Shoals Road where he stopped in a safe spot in front of the remains of the church and the exhumed graveyard. He got out and watched as the three shot-gun houses on the corner closest to his homeplace burned, the old pine wood smelling sweet. The hiss of boiling resin cried out faintly from the narrow homes as they disappeared into smoke and ash. Next was the general store across Sills Roads, the two-story warehouse-sized building rickety from the day

Elmer was born. Its weathered dark boards had loosened and spat out more flat nails every year, but it still stood defiantly. The fire came at it from behind in the ditch, first burning an outbuilding used to store tools, then the two community out-houses, shared by the homes along the crossroads. The flames eerily lit the half moons cut into the doors of the jakes. The wind picked up, and within seconds the flames rushed around the smaller structures and leapt from the ditch and climbed up to the top and licked the tin into a curl until the roof fell in and the fire was free to dance high above the general store from the edge of the oak cross beams. The fire reached high into the night sky, and smoke billowed up, the wind blowing it toward the river. Elmer stood in the middle of the abandoned intersection that had been the heart of Finley Shoals, feeling the fireball's warmth on his skin from twenty yards away.

The wind blew the flames catty-corner from the shotgun houses to the long row of dogtrot homes across from the general store, the fire crossing the intersection within ten feet of Elmer, tumbleweed-like balls of leaves and grass carrying sparks to the row of homes that ignited with the help of the dry shrubs and leaf piles that the early winter winds had pushed against the foundation. He watched the dogtrots burn and the passageways between the interconnected homes spew out rolling clouds of gray smoke. The wind's northeast direction caused the fire to spare the corner where the church had been and the cemetery once was, leaving it to lie fallow unlike the singed black of the rest of Finley Shoals' charred remains. It was just west of this fire line where Elmer sat, watching the flames race away, down and along the easternmost stretch of Finley Shoals Road toward the Oogasula, blackening the ditches and cleansing by flame the rocky macadam filled with potholes.

Elmer watched as the fire scaled three high wooden poles,

each hung with four crossbars that dangled more than a dozen dried gourds cut with holes for martins. The flames scurried along the two-by-fours and set the gourds to sizzling like demonic Christmas ornaments hung on burning crosses in the dark field.

Beyond the stand of burning gourds, the woods had been cut and pine straw covered the ground and burned like tissue paper, fast and with a resigned *poof*, but the stumps there caught slowly, smoldering and sizzling, before burning with the bubbling smell of resin and wasted creosote.

Elmer climbed into the bed of his pickup and watched from a distance as the fire moved east and consumed the old mill, the high roof engulfed and the big river oak near it like a huge red sparkler, a cremation ceremony that would do proud the old hermit from Tennessee, the long-bearded loner whose only companion had been a goat.

Everything between Elmer and the river a quarter of a mile away was scorched, black or still burning, but he could see that the fire would not be able to get across the water without a stronger wind. He strained to see the pulpwood truck he had driven into the river that afternoon, but it was not visible beneath the riverbank in the evening darkness. He watched as drifts of flame floated over the water, but before reaching the other side, the sparks were extinguished by the cool wet Oogasula. He could see that the breeze was pushing the fire up against the banks and north, up the edge of the river and in the direction of the boulders and the fall line, beyond which lay Mrs. McNulty's house.

Elmer got back in the truck and revved the engine, heading out for Junkyard Road and Mrs. McNulty, to see if the fire would cross the boulders and get up that far. The river to the north wound back slightly to the west, and he worried she would be in the path of the fire if it could get a lift over the boulders that made up the low cliff between Finley Shoals and her home. He didn't think that the fire would be able to reach her, but he also had not expected to set the woods on fire.

The sky was black and the air was much cooler and smelled of burning wood, the scent of rust and flame, that smell of the winter when fireplaces burn and chimneys spew out smoke, but the smell was hundreds of times stronger, permeating his clothes and his truck and all the air he breathed. He continued to sweat despite the cool of the evening settling all around him in the darkness of the country road at nighttime.

He mashed down the gas pedal and shifted into high gear, and the truck raced along the macadam of Finley Shoals Road for Junkyard Road. He imagined the flames moving up the river and somehow getting up and through the boulders and to the ramshackle shotgun house that was Mrs. McNulty's home. He pictured it burning like a tinderbox with her in it, her flesh singed like those hogs the Witcher brothers had been roasting, her hair gone and her bathtub blackened in the heat of the fire. He wondered if she had sense enough to get out of the path of the flames.

He turned right on Drowning Creek Road and the truck slid in the dry dirt. He sped up as fast as he could push it to Junkyard Road and turned sharp for the McNulty place, his eyes scanning the woods to the right for the fire but seeing only darkness of the brush and the hardwoods on down and smelling only the distant drift of smoke. The truck's headlights moved across the tall river oak near her home that stood forlornly with its leaves gone in the new dark of night. That old tree would burn up fast as a match if the fire got up here. But the dirt cliff and the granite boulders had not allowed the fire to pass, to move up to Mrs. McNulty's home by the kudzu-covered junkyard that would soon be at the bottom of the lake.

He drove by her house and turned around. She was not outside, and there were no indications of candle or lantern light. He figured she was like all the old country women, like his mama had been, getting into bed at dusk in order to get up before the dawn. He knew that he should wake her, force her to go into town, maybe leave her at the bus station or on the doorstep of the hospital or the old folks home. But he was weary, and a heavy dread came over him. He stopped the truck and sat there, unable to even bring himself to set the parking brake. A tiredness rushed over him like it often did these days that just flat-out took the life from him for a while. He sat there, staring vacantly at the faded dashboard.

After a while he roused himself and looked at Mrs. Mc-Nulty's house. He decided that she was gone. Must have been one of her daughters had come out and gotten her. He didn't see that old dog of hers around anywhere. He was an old country dog that barked at everyone who came down the road, the good kind of dog who looked out for his master. He would come out barking if he and Mrs. McNulty were still here.

Percy, Elmer recalled, Percy was the name she had called him.

PERCY RAN NORTH THROUGH the dark brush along the river's edge. He smelled woodsmoke wafting from the direction of the crossroad houses and the graveyard and the old church and gristmill. He moved cautiously, his eyes darting around, checking behind him toward the concrete blocking the river where the people and music and the strange fiery explosions in the sky had been, the place still abuzz with noise and emitting a warm glow that bathed the surrounding countryside. He was hungry and scared and confused, anxious to get back to normal behavior and comforts of home.

The further north he went, the darker and smokier the air became. His familiar path that ran along the edge of the river and beneath the brush and small trees with each step became stranger and more unfamiliar as the smoke got thicker. He oscillated his nostrils, sniffing hard. The smoke was not the straight product of burning hickory or oak or pine logs. It was a different scent that included hardwoods, but also the odor of paints and stains and manmade contrivances used in homes and buildings and automobiles. His wet nose smelled it again and twitched, and he tried to make sense of it. He pushed ahead, deeper in the billowing smoke with each step.

All of his training in fire, like all that he knew in life, had come from the old man whom he had accompanied on trips into the woods. The old man, armed with axe and saw, would fell a tree or two and drag it back near the house with a rope and then cut it into sections and stack it on or beneath the porch, depending on the season. The old man had made sure to keep the wood plentiful because the burning of it in the fireplace would be what would keep them—the old man and old lady and Percy—warm in the short but sometimes cold winters of Middle Georgia. When the old lady would agree to let him in the house, Percy had slept on the bricks at the front edge of the fireplace, soaking all of its heat into his thick black fur and warming himself to the point where he sweated, but still he loved the heat on his muscles and skin. If it was very cold the old lady would sit in a chair and slide her feet under his thick coat of fur and they kept each other warm on those winter nights.

Once when he was a puppy Percy had leaned too far into the fire and the red flicker caught on his black fur, causing him to yelp and run across the room. The old man opened the door and dragged Percy to the river's edge and splashed water on his neck where he had been singed. He talked to him in a sweet voice and he felt better. The wound scabbed up and healed in a few days. He stayed a few inches farther from the flames in subsequent wintertime warming sessions. But since the old man had died, the old lady had let Percy in the house very few times, only on the coldest of nights.

Percy had seen the old man with his small device that clicked and made a short flame that he had used to light the cigarettes he had rolled himself and occasionally the old pipe that the man stuffed with whatever tobacco he could muster up. Percy had learned to like the smell of the old man's smoke, sitting at his feet while it drifted around the house or on the porch. He used the floating swirls of tobacco in the air as a touchstone to find the old man in the yard when he would come home from a run in the woods or along the river.

Percy ran toward the shack and the junkyard north of Finley Shoals. When he cleared a stand of brush, he saw about a quarter of a mile ahead the distinct shape and color of flames. This wide-ranging fire seemed to be uncontained. From this distance, he was unsure of what he was seeing and stopped and studied on it, trying to figure how big the fire was that he was looking at over the softly sloping ground that led up to the crossroads.

He saw great flames, red and orange and faintly blue, flickering across the ground and amongst the trees, dancing high and lively in the old wooden buildings, the mill violently aflame. The fire was burning or had singed all of the ground between where he stood and the river and west to the crossroads of Finley Shoals where the old lady had gone to church and where the old man had been buried and then dug up. Trees

burned and smoldered like planted embers. The fire was bright
as it covered the earth in streaks along the path that he had
planned to use to get back home. But he knew the land here,
had been running it all his life and knew other routes to get
back to the old lady's shack. He cut a path away from the river
toward what had been a pine forest but was now stumps, and
then up to what had been a cow pasture but as of late had no
cows. There was an old house there where he remembered a
woman who had lived alone and spent much time in her yard
digging in her azaleas around the porch. She would sometimes
feed him and pet him when he came around until she began
looking frail and then stayed inside the house. Sometimes in
the morning he would come down that way when heading over
to chase the cows and he would see her coal oil light in the
window or her making it slowly to the outhouse with a white
porcelain chamber pot in her hand, limping along. In her last
year, he remembered the spitting-scratching man coming out
to stay with her, back when the man had walked with more
warmth instead of his angry posture that he now carried and
which Percy innately feared.

The sky was dark and the smoke was thick and Percy followed the path by memory and instinct. He could see only the
ground beneath his feet and all he could go by was the slope of
the land. All familiar smells were blocked out or burned up by
the raging flames that covered this patch of ground. He came
to a field that had long been cleared, once for cotton and then
for vegetables but had lain fallow the past few seasons. The
ground was loose and soft under his paws. The smoke in the
field thinned out and he could see that the house surrounded
by azaleas had burned, reduced to a stand of smoking embers.
He ran around to the front yard so the house and the fire
was downwind of him. The trees to the right side and behind

the house were blackened scars of wood where the wind had pushed the flames, but the trees in front escaped burning. The fire line, sculpted by the wind, ran from the house to Finley Shoals' crossroads and to the gristmill.

He hightailed it further inland and away from the river and cut north where the fire ended. The smell of smoke was still distinct, but he could see here because the wind was blowing the smoke in the direction of the river. He crossed through a stand of brush and over the road and along the edge of the old cemetery where they had dug up the old man's box and carried him away with all of the others buried there. He paused and looked over near the spot where the old man had rested in the ground and hesitated, then ran over to it. He stood at the edge of the hole and looked down into it and let out a little cry, longing for the old man and his delicious treats and warm hands. He sat back on his haunches and rested his front legs straight out and laid his head on his forepaws and looked at the dark hole as the smell of smoke drifted through the air. He whimpered gently.

Percy rested there a few moments before another hunger pang hit him and he thought of the old lady and the shack up by the junkyard on the river and he hopped to his feet and began running on north. He crossed through a field of stumps on a hill that had been cut only in the past few weeks, the smell of sap still strong, and then up to the small cliff of boulders, cutting through them on a path treaded by deer through two large stones.

He looked east toward the river and saw that the fire seemed to be stalling at the boulders and was not moving further north. He ran along the line where the earth rose to a slight hill and hardwood trees amongst a blanket of leaves, the crunch of photosynthesized death beneath his feet, toward the fire. There he saw it burning out up against the rock line. Down at the riverbank the flames had not been able to cross the Oogasula. The singed smell of earth and wood and grass was still strong in the air, and the hiss of pine stumps burning sizzled in the night.

He turned and ran on up the hill through the hardwood trees, the yellow poplars and oaks and red maples on top of the low hill. He ran down the other side toward the junkyard and started barking when he got in view of the shack, the junkyard and the old leaning house with the bathtub on the front porch. The windows were dark. He barked, dashing sideways back and forth across the yard as he approached the shack.

He dashed up the steps, past the overturned bathtub and the claw feet that lay there like dead quail. He rushed to the door and stood on his hind legs and scratched at the solid pine, running his claws down and then standing back up as he barked with fury and pushed with all of his might. The old lady didn't respond and he pushed on the door with his paws and then he thrust his body against it, barreling into it with his right shoulder only to fall back at the sturdiness of it, shoving it only a slight crack.

He hurled himself against the front door a few more times in panic and then began to pant, whimpering some and growling low, angry at he knew not what, angered by the fire in the sky and across the ground and being hungry and isolated here at the home where he had lived all of his life. He slumped and panted on the porch.

He lay there for a while, but then heard footsteps in the house and he jumped to his feet and began to bark, his gruff voice loud but tired and fading, and he started scratching the door again. He could feel the vibrations of footsteps getting closer and he heard the latch click. The old lady opened the door and called his name. She spoke to him in a sleepy voice and walked out onto the porch. She moved from one end to the other, looking around, sniffing the air and mumbling. He barked again and ran to her and she patted him on the head and said his name a few more times and then said, "Wait, hold on, wait, hold on."

She turned and went back into the door, and he followed her inside. She yelled at him, her voice screechy and high, and he backed out. It had always been their rule that he was never to go into the house except on the coldest of nights when the fireplace was lit.

He waited at the threshold. She shuffled around in the dark kitchen and came back with a dry piece of bread and set it on the porch. He snatched it up and ate ravenously like a wild pack dog, holding the hard bread in his teeth and putting his front paws on it to rip smaller pieces loose that he could chew.

She sat down on the top step of the porch next to the old tub and looked out through the dark at the junkyard and the river and talked aloud to herself, wisps of smoke drifting up from the woods. He finished the bread and then ran to the creek's edge for a drink of cold water to wash it down. The night had come on full and there was no moon. The river's surface glimmered a glossy black in the absence of fire and light.

NIGHT

Elmer was slowed getting home by traffic on North Highway after the fireworks. Along the dark shoulders people walked back to their vehicles, illuminated only by the moving beams of headlights. The sky was clear and black with stars beginning to appear. He could smell the smoke on his clothes, his hair, and his skin, and the inside of his truck was tinged with the odor of burning wood and leafsmoke, but when he rolled down the window the breeze that rushed in was of a fresh early winter night. The wind was blowing the smoke east, across the river. They probably could smell it all the way to Taliaferro County but they couldn't at the dam, only half a mile away, because of the wind direction and with their line of sight blocked down below the giant concrete mass. There a whole mess of fools were yukking it up while, unbeknownst to them, a large nearby swath of the land burned, trees and earth and even houses scorched flat to a crisp.

Elmer hung his head and stared at the two-lane road and the taillights in front of him. He hadn't slept much the night before, perhaps only half an hour or so. He had gotten out of bed at three o'clock and read a day-old newspaper until he left the house before dawn to ride out into the country. His eyes drooped with the need for sleep and his stomach growled, having had no nourishment since the bag of peanuts he bought from the Witcher boy. Some barbecue from the dam sounded mighty good, but he wasn't about to go back there and put up with all those folks laughing and cutting up.

In town the streets were moderately busy, but he hit both traffic lights green and sped on to the southeast side of town where he lived in the mill village. He pulled into his side yard and parked his truck in the spot where the tires had worn down a smooth path in the grass. The *Macon News* had come that afternoon but he didn't bother to read the headlines. He threw the newspaper down on his small square kitchen table and took the .38-.44 out of the shoulder holster and set it down on top of the paper. He removed his suit coat and threw it over a chair and then slipped out of the shoulder holster and set it down on the table. In his bedroom, he took off his dress shirt and tossed it onto the floor in the corner and sat on the edge of the mattress and pulled off his cowboy boots and let them lay where they fell. His dress pants came next, then his gray hunting socks. He reached into the closet and pulled on the tattered bathrobe that Sherry had given him their first Christmas. In the bottom of the closet he found the bedroom shoes that she also had given him, and he slipped those onto his feet.

In the kitchen Elmer took down two of the big black skillets that hung on wall hooks and set them on the stove, and then he picked three eggs from the refrigerator and a couple of sausage patties from the ice chest. The sausage went into one skillet; he cracked eggs into the other. The yokes and whites ran together, and he used a dull knife to cut about an inch off the end of a stick of butter that he let drop into the raw eggs. He mashed the butter into smaller pieces with the tip of a spatula.

He lit the burners and then when he had the stove going, he leaned over and fired a cigarette on a gas flame and inhaled deeply. The sausage meat began to hiss. He held the cigarette between his lips and got two buttermilk biscuits out of the ice chest and warmed the oven and put the biscuits in on a cookie sheet. He had taken to freezing leftover biscuits and reheating them, something his mama would have never abided. He then lit another eye on the stove and put on the coffee pot to percolate. With everything in the kitchen underway, he went into the den and put a disc on the record player. The needle skipped and popped and hit a buzz of static before it got into the song and an electrified guitar cut through the room with a jerky tune and then Ernest Tubb's deep voice sang: *I'm walking the floor over you, I can't sleep a wink that is true . . .*

Elmer went back to the kitchen and stirred the eggs with a fork and scraped a spot where they had started to stick to the black cast iron. He turned the eggs to low and flipped the sizzling sausage patties. The biscuits still looked cold, so he turned up the oven to 400, and he heard the whoosh of the gas.

He stood in the kitchen and listened to Ernest Tubb, but his song brought Elmer no solace or joy. He stubbed out his cigarette in an ashtray on the counter and flipped the sausage patties again and wished that he could have some grits, but cooking them took half an hour and he was too hungry to wait that long. He got a plate from the cabinet and dumped the eggs on it, and then he picked up the two sausage patties with a fork and dropped the meat next to the eggs. He reached in the oven and lifted out the two buttermilk biscuits. They were still a touch cold, but he put them on his plate. He set the plate next to the newspaper and revolver. The warm smell of the eggs and sausage rose up on him. He sat in his kitchen chair and began to eat, head down, eyes focused on the food. He ate about half of the eggs and a sausage patty and he stood and poured a cup of coffee and sipped it slow and then sat back down and cleaned the plate, mopping up with a piece of biscuit. He paid no mind to Ernest Tubb.

The record ended about the time he took his last bite. He slid the plate to the side and took a big drink of coffee and lit another cigarette and leaned forward on his elbows and stared without focusing at the busy specks of the Formica tabletop. He finished the coffee and smoked the cigarette down to the butt, tapping the ashes on the dirty plate. The cigarette burned out and he mashed the stub in the greasy residue of his meal.

He left the dishes on the table with the newspaper, but took the revolver and went to his bedroom where he put it on the nightstand. He kicked off his slippers and crawled under the old blanket still in his robe. He lay back and closed his eyes and sleep was on him fast.

His dream was not the sensible, describable kind like the one he had a few days ago where he saw an enormous Holstein get hit by a pulpwood truck, but instead was a hodgepodge of images: flames climbing up hills and through buildings intermingled with waterfalls and lakes of blue water, deep and serene above trees and roads, and then he would see the fire again. Lloyd and Aubrey Terrell were in his dreams, and so was Sherry, and his daddy too. The dream had no story to it, only waves of water and fire amidst the people who tortured him the most. One minute Sherry would be sunbathing in the back of a new convertible with Terrell driving, and the next Lloyd would be holding the door open for Elmer at the sawmill, his daddy in there, sweaty and dirty, pushing a log along a big table saw that was cutting the giant pine trunk into boards, the saw spinning and hissing and kicking up sawdust. The old hermit and his goat walked down the road, and Po' Baby sang a song and tap-danced on a vaudeville stage. Mrs. McNulty and her dog tried in vain to swim across the river.

These images flowed through his head, repeating in no logical order, but always repeating.

He woke up with a flinch, his eyes wide open in the half-dark, a shaft of light from the kitchen shining through the open bedroom door. He turned his head to the left to look at his alarm clock on the nightstand next to the gun and saw that it was only eight o'clock. He'd slept less than an hour. He lay on his back and shut his eyes, but his mind was charged with thoughts darting about like water bugs on the Oogasula. He stayed there maybe ten minutes with his eyes closed, hoping to sleep, but he knew that he never would. He got up and walked into the kitchen and poured himself a cup of lukewarm black coffee. He sat at the table and started to read the newspaper. There had been a time when he had a great interest in sports, baseball in particular, and would look forward to getting home from work and reading the accounts of the games from the day before, but these days he wasn't interested in much of anything.

He unfolded the paper and looked at the broadsheet. Lymanville rarely made the *Macon News*, but today's lead story was an article that featured a photo of Aubrey Terrell's smiling face and his dam. Aside from a different headline, it seemed to be the same story they had run a few weeks before, the same article the local paper ran every week, a celebratory retelling of the glorious new lake with nary a mention of anyone who might be even remotely displeased with it.

He set the paper down. He took a cigarette out of his robe pocket and lit it. He smoked it and stared at the pots and pans and skillets on the wall next to the refrigerator. He finished the cigarette and got up and flipped over the Ernest Tubb record and started it playing and sat down in his armchair in the den. He lit another cigarette and listened to the twang and the thud of the music, Ernest singing about mean women—*There's lots of mean women on almost any street*—a fact Elmer knew to be true right here in Lymanville, but he wondered why Ernest didn't have any songs about the legions of conniving sumbitches that roamed the Earth. Elmer studied the record cover photo of Ernest Tubb in his blue rhinestone suit. He was probably a mean old sumbitch who had screwed over plenty to get to the top and get his face on a record. He was smiling big just like all those politicians and Uncle Lloyd had been out at the dam. Elmer let the cover fall to the floor.

He glanced into the bedroom and saw the revolver on the nightstand. Something Lloyd once told him popped into his mind: A pistol was good to carry in case you got caught screwing somebody's wife and needed a weapon fast. It was portable and easy to handle and good for a deputy to have with him at all times. But a shotgun loaded with buckshot is what you wanted when you had to go on the offensive and take somebody down.

He picked his 20-gauge Stevens pump out of the back of his closet and unloaded the shells, the red cartridges popping from the chamber, the carriage clicking as they kicked out. With it empty, he worked the forestock forward and then back, that unmistakable contact of metal when the chamber was readied to fire. He carried the long gun in his right hand and went to the closet and took out his shoebox with his cleaning kit. He carried the shotgun and the shoebox and shells into the kitchen and set them down on the tabletop, the barrel extending past the edge. He took a small piece of cheesecloth from the box and doused it with the clear solvent from a small bottle and put it on the end of the thin metal rod. He put the bore swab in the barrel and ran it up almost all the way to the breech and pulled it out, the cloth giving a slight resistance. He removed the swab from the barrel and examined it. The gun had last been cleaned about a year ago and had not fired since, so there was very little residue. He rubbed around the breech with a large piece of cheesecloth near where the pin hit the shell, and then he rubbed down the trigger and then the stock. He put some oil on another rag from the box and polished the gunmetal until it glimmered.

He loaded three shells into the shotgun and leaned it by the kitchen door. He went into his bedroom and took off his robe and put on a clean pair of pants and a flannel shirt and slipped back into his cowboy boots. He would have worn his brogans, but they were filthy from the muddy struggle in the grave with the pulpwooder, as was his favorite pair of britches.

He took the revolver and the shotgun and headed out the door. He didn't bother to turn out the light or even stop the record player from spinning, the needle at the end of the disk just riding in the smooth groove, emitting a low static sound. He let the door slam, leaving it unlocked. He paused, wishing that he could get in the bed and sleep and wake up tomorrow morning and feel better, but he knew there was no way.

Elmer walked through the yard to his truck and opened the driver's door and slid the shotgun behind the seat back. He put the .38-.44 beneath his seat, wedged in under the springs so it would not slide around. He turned the key, pressed the starter button on the floor and the engine warmed to life. He popped it into reverse and rolled back out into the street. There he moved the column into first gear and drove off, shifting into second smoothly. He was relieved that the linkage didn't stick. He was in no mood to get the axe handle and force the gear shifter loose.

His street was quiet, the few children who lived on the

block in for the night, the old folks already in bed with their lights off. In the early morning the old ladies of the neighborhood would get up and put on their flowered housedresses and white cotton bonnets to sweep their porches and sidewalks in the creeping predawn light. Every morning save Sunday they were out, sweeping the borders of the yards clean, the walkways spotless, sidewalks that no one walked down for days at a time, but were always clean. You didn't see that kind of thing in the fancy neighborhood, where Elmer was headed, around Coach Hilliard's house. People there could afford servants to clean up after them.

He got on the main road north into Lymanville and the homes began to get finer with each block. His house was only a mile away from Coach Hilliard's mansion, but a century away in architecture and generations apart in Achena County status. He turned right on Washington Street and went a block past the library at the women's college with its lights all lit up and then turned left up Oglethorpe Street, the homes becoming larger and more-columned as he went. Everyone had their lights turned on and their shutters open. Most of the homes had large Christmas trees in the front windows and giant wreaths, the circles of tightly wrapped pine boughs and holly adorned with red ribbons, hanging from their stately doors.

At Federal Street he turned right and noticed that cars lined both sides of the usually empty street; fancy cars too—Cadillacs, Buicks, Thunderbirds—many with Fulton County tag numbers. He saw Lloyd's patrol car and the Coggins boy's car, too, as well as the state trooper's Ford coupe. There was only one lane to get down the street through the parallel-parked vehicles, most of them wide and black. He saw only one pickup truck.

Elmer eased down the street and saw the two Coca-Cola men walking down the sidewalk, checking out his truck, the

New York man even rude enough to point. He pulled up in front of Coach Hilliard's and paused to look, the house lit up bright. The two-story antebellum home had a sign announcing its name: The Claphourne House, built in 1818. Two high white columns held the giant portico on the front, the house's most distinguishing feature, looming above the large yard. Through giant windowpanes above the door he could see an enormous crystal chandelier shining brightly in the foyer. Smoke puffed from the two brick chimneys on each side of the roof, and Elmer could smell hickory burning.

The yard beneath its two towering oak trees on either side of the walkway was alive with men smoking, many of them puffing on cigars. He saw Lloyd off to the side talking with the state patrolman, both with stogies and drinks in their hands. Parked just beyond the front of the walkway between two brick pillars at the edge of the sidewalk was Congressman Vinson's Buick with his driver waiting for him. Elmer stopped the truck in the street, to the side and behind the black sedan, so he would not attract the driver's attention. He checked his rearview mirror and the street behind him was clear.

He took another glance at the house. On the top step of the porch, above the azaleas and wisteria and manicured boxwood gardens, he saw Aubrey Terrell and Coach Hilliard, both smiling and holding drinks, shaking hands and greeting guests as they made their way up the steps. Beyond them, the door was wide open, and Elmer saw Coach Hilliard's wife, Lucretia. She was a Claphourne and the house had been in her family along with much land in the north part of the county, some of that soon to be lake bottom and other parts lakefront. Her crooked old daddy had been a legendary pinhooker in these parts, the first to buy timber from local landowners and then resell it to the sawmills at a much higher price. All the Claphourne land had fallen into the Hilliard name when she married the coach. She was standing inside the door, and Elmer could see the red-carpeted steps that wound up high behind her. She was directing two servants in white shirts and bow ties who were running about with silver trays of food and drink.

He gazed on this for a minute when he heard a car behind him honk its horn. He looked into the rearview to see a Cadillac driven by a fat bald man, the Coca-Cola president Lloyd had pointed out. The man honked again and raised his hands as if to ask was Elmer deaf or dumb and why didn't he get the hell out of the way.

Elmer had been sitting in second gear with the clutch depressed. He tried to downshift into first gear but the linkage stuck and he couldn't get it moving. He didn't want to open the hood and get the axe handle out with everyone around watching him like he was a show, so he revved the gas and eased off on the clutch, but too quickly and it went dead. He mashed the clutch back down and hit the starter button again and the engine roared to life. The man honked a third time, and Elmer revved the gas harder and eased off on the clutch again until he got rolling in second gear and then he took off down the smooth black asphalt of Federal Street.

He sped off toward Glascock Street and bolted through the stop sign without touching the brakes and turned left up the hill and then right on Taliaferro Street toward the bottoms where he could hide under the rising girders of the steel river bridge over the Oogasula's southern bend near town. He pulled off behind the elementary school and drove down to the footings of the bridge, checking to make sure that no one had followed him and there was no one watching from the school playground or from the mill on the other side of the river or on the high bridge that loomed ominous and dark over the water. He shut off the engine and got out and took the axe handle and opened the hood. He knocked the linkage loose, then slammed the hood and slid the axe handle down in its spot and got back into the truck. He started out in first and shifted into second smoothly and pulled out from under the darkness of the bridge over the river here where it was wide with dirty brown water beneath the steel trestle.

HE GOT ON NORTH Highway and shifted into third as he drove toward the dam. Elmer pushed his truck hard, and it shot along the dark road into the country, much of it soon to be lakeside. It was about nine o'clock and there was no traffic going north and only a smattering of cars going south, stragglers from the dam dedication heading home. His headlights panned across the shoulders of the road and he could see the impressions of tire marks in the crushed dry grass.

He zoomed past Dam Road and went on up to Finley Shoals Road. The night sky was black, and the almost bare trees waved ghostlike over the roadside as he sped along the narrow macadam two-lane. He didn't see a single car, not that the roads ever had much traffic this late, but usually driving around out here at night he passed at least a few coloreds coming home from the Ridleyville juke joint or a few redneck boys spotlighting possums and squirrels and shooting at signs and liquor bottles they tossed up into the air. And there was always at least one or two of the old town alcoholics out drinking and driving slow, waving at everyone they passed. But nary a soul was out tonight.

He followed the roads until he made the curve at Mrs. McNulty's house. His headlight beams hit her sitting in a rocking chair on her porch next to her dog, the tub's four claw feet lined up beside them. He pulled in front of her house

onto her dirt yard and parked. The old black chow bristled
and barked and showed his teeth. Mrs. McNulty did not
acknowledge Elmer.

He cut the truck lights and couldn't see a thing and he waited
for his eyes to get used to the dark. He got out of the pickup
when he could finally see the silhouettes of Mrs. McNulty and
her dog. It was a clear, moonless night and the stars twinkled
bright overhead. The air was cooler and the wind was picking
up, rustling the trees and the leaves that clung to the old cars
in the junkyard. The wind blew in the direction of the river and
the singe of woodsmoke from the evening wildfire was only
faintly detectable. He could smell the fresh river water and
hear its flow. He walked gingerly toward the house, keeping
an eye on her dog, his murky black shape shifting around in
the darkness.

"Hey, Mrs. McNulty," he said. "What you still doing out
here? You gonna get washed away."

"Who's that? What you want? I got a gun. I ain't got nothing to steal."

"It's me . . . Elmer Blizzard." He stopped about thirty feet
from her.

"You ain't a deputy no more, is you?"

"No, ma'am."

"Well, what are you doing out here? Sneaking around in
the dark? At this hour? I'm an old woman . . . but I ain't that
old. I ain't scared to shoot you."

"I believe you." He spat. "Mrs. McNulty, I was just checking
up on you. You know they damming up the river—tonight.
It's gonna flood you out pretty soon. Probably sometime in
the early morning. Maybe tomorrow. Ain't you got no plans
to leave?"

She didn't answer. Elmer stepped closer and the dog took

to barking again, this time coming down to the bottom step, growling low. He scanned the ground for a rock to throw in case it charged him.

"Percy!" she said. "*Percy.*" The dog calmed. "That's a good boy. You don't bite him lest I tell you to."

"Mrs. McNulty, I done knowed you all my life. I mean well. I'm just making sure you get out of here before the flood."

"You ain't no Christian," she said. "You just trying to act like one."

This hurt him. He hadn't been to church in the six years since his mama died of the cancer. He had always gone to church to make his mama happy. He had a good mind to get in his pickup and drive back to town and let Mrs. McNulty drown with that damn dog.

"If you such a good Christian," she said, "why you pull your thing out and befoul the river today where I could see you?"

"Ma'am, I'm sorry." His cheeks flushed. "I . . . I didn't think you could see me."

"You coulda used my outhouse."

He stepped up closer. Her skin looked pale and wrinkled in the almost dark. She had on the same gray robe and housedress as she did that afternoon. She still hadn't combed her hair.

"Why don't you let me give you a ride into town? I can put you on the bus to Atlanta to go to your daughter, Sarah. She's probably got an extra bedroom you can use, ain't she?"

"I ain't going back up there. They all highfalutin, act like they don't know me anymore." She raised her voice high and prissy. "'*Grandma*, don't say that in front of the children. *Grandma*, we don't eat that kind of food anymore.'"

"Well, what about your other girl? Rhonda? She'd help you out, wouldn't she? Where is she living?"

"She's over in Augusta. But I don't want no help from her

neither. She's worse. She ain't got that much money, but acts like she does. She ain't nothing but a sow carrying a silk purse."

He stepped up on the first step so he could see her better. She was staring in his direction, but he couldn't tell if she saw him or not, her face frazzled and angry as hell at the same time, a desperation he had seen in the eyes of prisoners.

"Well, what about your church folks? They's some of them'll take you in, won't they?"

"Ssss," was all she said.

"Won't somebody from the Finley Shoals church'll help you out?"

She just shook her head and her expression softened, turning sad.

"They ain't no more Finley Shoals church," she said, her voice almost a sob. She looked down at the porch floor for a few moments, staring at the rough-hewn boards. Then she raised her head and smiled.

"Hey look, Elmer. I got all them feet off the tub."

"Yes, ma'am," he said. "That's good."

She nodded happily, and her dog began wagging his tail.

Elmer scratched his neck, thinking. He couldn't see the river in the darkness but he could smell the water. He listened closely and heard it rushing like it was backing up and running over its banks. He studied the low land around her house. She would be underwater pretty soon if the lake filled up like the power company said. He spat lightly into the hydrangeas. He stepped up another two feet, closer to her.

"Mrs. McNulty, why don't you bring them feet and get your clothes and anything else you want . . . let me take you into town? You don't wanna end up at the bottom of the lake. Maybe . . ." and here he had his doubts, paused and almost quit talking, but said it anyway, "maybe we can even bring the tub with us in my truck. I know a feller that could sandblast it, put a new coat of enamel on it, screw them feet back on and it'd be just like new."

"You mean it?" she said.

"Yeah," he said. "You got any lights in the house?"

"My candles is all burned out. I got some kerosene I can put in the lantern."

"Naw, that's all right. I'll flip on my truck lights. And I got a flashlight. You got anything inside?"

"I just need to get some clothes. And Ralph's gun. I can get 'em together right quick. None of the rest of this stuff's worth keeping. My daughters got the furniture they wanted long ago. And I need to get the check from the power company out from under my mattress."

"You mean you ain't cashed it yet?"

"Nope, not yet."

"Well, make sure you get that." Again he spat into the hydrangeas. "Let me get my flashlight. I'm gonna take a look at the river first."

She went into the house, and Elmer walked back to his pickup. He flipped on the headlights, casting two beams that merged into one light upon the shack. He retrieved his flashlight from the passenger's seat and clicked it on and walked past the bumper of the truck down across the road toward the river. He walked beyond the junkyard and shone the light at the Oogasula only about ten feet away. The water was brown with white frothy streaks, at least two feet higher than it had been that afternoon, the banks reminding him of a full cup of coffee threatening to spill over the brim.

He realized then that the current was going the wrong way, a reversal of the stream that had always gone south. He flipped off the flashlight and looked up to the stars and listened to the soft sounds of the river water, rushing northward.

After standing there a while, he went into the house. The truck headlights cut into the windows. She was shuffling around the piles of junk, her clothes in an old pillow case.

"C'mon, Mrs. McNulty. The river is coming up. They done shut the flood gates. Let's get that tub in my truck."

She followed him onto the porch and put the clothes-stuffed pillow case on the top step.

"Did you get your gun?"

"It's wrapped up in the clothes. Percy gets upset if he sees a gun. I got the check, too."

In the light of the high-beams they slid the cast iron tub across the porch and bumped it down the steps, Elmer going backwards and straining mightily to control it. They pushed and pulled it through the yard until they reached the truck, where they rested for a minute. He opened the tailgate and they both lifted one end and got part of it up into the back, and then pressed with all their might to slide the tub into the truck bed. It was a tight fit and he worried that his tailgate might not hold if the tub slid around. He had dropped things out of a truck before—most memorably, a standup piano he offered to move for a neighbor that ended up busted to pieces in the street.

"I need to tie this thing down. You got any rope?"

"I got a whole coil of twine," she said, huffing hard from moving the tub. "In the bedroom. Over in the corner. You can't miss it."

He took his flashlight and went into the house. He walked carefully through the auto parts strewn around the front room and went into her bedroom. The coil was right where she had said it would be, beneath a hoe and a rake that leaned against the wall, threads dangling loose from the yellow-wrapped cord.

He took the coil out to the yard and tied the tub to the truck bed and threaded the twine through the drain hole for traction and then battened it down on the stanchion holes. He knotted the twine and gave the tub a strong shove to see if it would stay once the truck started bumping along the roads. It was in there tight.

"This thing ain't going nowhere," he said. "You ready? Want to take one last look around?"

"I got to get my dawg," she said. She called out loudly, "Here boy, here boy, here boy." The dog didn't come.

She walked around the truck and continued to call Percy's name, the two syllables distinct, the second drawn out and echoing. "*Purse—eee*! Percy, here boy, *Percy*. Percy!"

She walked around the back side of her house and up toward the old oak tree.

Elmer took the flashlight and went down along the river's edge the opposite way Mrs. McNulty was going, cutting through the vine-strangled wrecks that were rusting in the junkyard. Beyond the husks of the cars and old trucks, he found the dog hiding in the brush line, its black thick chow fur curled in a crouching, defensive posture, his teeth bared. Elmer heard the dog growl low as he moved slowly to it.

"C'mon, boy," he said, nervous, thinking about how when he was little an old chow had pinned him on the ground and bit into the side of his face and gnawed on his ear. He was only four years old then, but he could still vividly see that dog biting him. He could see the color of his own blood in his eyes and taste it in his mouth. That was his earliest memory, getting mauled by a dog. Of all names, they had called the dog Elmer. That dog had been older than he was, so they never said but he figured out later in life that he had been named after the dog that eventually tried to kill him. The dog had been his father's, but his mama made him kill it, and he shot it dead with a load of 20-gauge buckshot. From the same gun Elmer had with him tonight. Elmer remembered seeing the dog dead out in the field nearest the river. The dog had trusted his daddy and had come right up to him and he had held the gun to his head and blasted. His daddy had tossed the black dog's body into the Oogasula after he laid it low. It was the only time he had ever seen his daddy cry. But there was nothing else to do with a mean-ass dog than to shoot it. To this day Elmer had no time for mean dogs.

Mrs. McNulty's dog growled at him. Elmer wondered how he was supposed to corral this angry black mutt and haul it into town in his truck and let it stay at his house, of all places, until he could get Mrs. McNulty settled. This dog was wild and mean and lived by its wits in the woods. It was not a town dog and would not last two days on his street, chasing cars and people and trying to eat children.

Elmer took a few steps back from the dog and turned and shouted.

"Mrs. McNulty, down here. He's down here. By the river."

But she was not even in sight and Elmer was certain she didn't hear him, up there behind the old oak tree or further along the river in the dark. He kept an eye on the dog and walked backward, sort of sideways, with one eye on the dog and one on the oak tree about fifty yards away, near where the old woman had wandered into the darkness. He could still hear her calling her dog's name, her voice starting to tire.

"Mrs. McNulty," Elmer yelled, as loud as he could when she came into sight. He waggled the flashlight beam in her direction. She started walking his way. He shined the light up at her again. "He's down here, in the brush. By the river."

The old woman made her way over and stopped for a moment to study the rising water, swirling in the dark. Elmer shined the light where she was looking and she stared, confused, moving her lips as though talking to herself, before coming on down toward him.

"Over here," Elmer shouted. "There," and he pointed the light at the dog. Canine eyes flashed from deep inside the sockets like a pair of metallic yellow dishes inside his skull. The dog seemed stunned and did not move, even after Elmer took the light off him. She called his name a few more times, repeating it.

"Percy ... *Percy* ... Percy." Her inflections changed with each repetition, alternating tender, and then scolding mildly, and then loving, and then firm again. "Come, here, boy, come here. That's a good boy. You are a good boy. Percy is a good dog. A good boy."

Elmer took the light off Percy and shone it on the ground between the part-chow and Mrs. McNulty. The dog relaxed a little and Elmer could see the mutt's gentler nature. The mutt in him was just an old yard dog that wanted to be loved and petted and scratched and fed, unlike the chow blood that was angry and would bite in a minute for no good reason. The dog came out of its crouch and trotted to Mrs. McNulty who petted him and rubbed the scruff of fur under his chin.

"Let's go, now boy, we got to leave this place," she said, her voice cracking. She leaned down and put her head to Percy's neck as though she was crying on his shoulder. The dog raised his head and pressed himself to her affectionately.

Elmer turned. "C'mon, you can hold onto him in the front seat with me."

Elmer walked ahead of them and got in the truck and turned the key in the ignition and hit the floor starter button. The engine turned over but didn't crank right away. He panicked for a moment about what he would have to do way out here in the boondocks with the flood coming up and his battery dead and she without a car, but then after he gave it more gas the engine sputtered to life and roared on its own and the lights beamed a little stronger when they started getting juice from the generator. He let it down into neutral where it idled smoothly. He looked back at the old woman and the dog slowly coming up from the river through the junkyard, lit against the red taillights of his truck amongst the withering kudzu leaves, stopping periodically as she bent down and petted the dog who nuzzled up to her at her touch.

Elmer left the truck in neutral and set the emergency brake and walked up to the step and got her clothes in the pillow case. He could feel the weight of the handgun in the bunch, probably an old .44. He tucked it into the front of the truck bed between the bathtub and the cab. He then went back for the four claw feet and set them in the bed next to the bag of clothes. He walked down to her and the dog who had stopped again. They were looking back at the river.

"Is there anything else you need?" he asked. "We need to get on the road pretty soon."

She shook her head no. Elmer went to the passenger door and held it open, waiting for her and Percy.

"Get him in first," he said. "Then you get in and get a hold of him. He can ride in between us. Just hold him tight so he stays off me."

The dog bristled as she got near the truck. She pulled him by the scruff of the neck to get him to jump up into the seat.

"All right, boy," she said. She looked up at Elmer, "He ain't ridden in a truck since Ralph died." She turned back to the dog and coddled him. "All right boy, hop on in here."

The dog lunged into the truck and slid on the floor board, scuffling to get all four paws up on the seat. Mrs. McNulty climbed in and pushed him in farther and the dog turned around where his head was facing her and his butt was against the steering wheel, his bushy tail wagging. Elmer said, "Look out, now," and shut her door. He came around to the driver's side where the dog was taking up all of the seat not used by Mrs. McNulty.

"Can you hold him?" he asked, and tried to push the dog's rear back across the seat, hoping he would sit up on his haunches and take the middle and give Elmer enough room to slide in behind the wheel. It was going to be a long ride into town like this.

The big black dog didn't budge, and he resisted when Elmer tried to move him. He was licking Mrs. McNulty's face and she was talking sweet to him, petting his head.

"C'mon, now, he's got to move over a little here," Elmer said, and pushed the dog's rear a little harder. The dog moved and slipped off the seat and then scuffled back up in Mrs. McNulty's lap, causing her to groan. Elmer crawled up in the cab and grabbed him with both his arms and set him down how he wanted him to sit. The dog squirmed and whined a little but went along with it.

"That's it, that's a good boy," he said. As the dog settled Elmer could see behind the back seat that the shotgun was lying flat with the trigger guard and the pump wedged against the frame.

He reached to adjust the shotgun and lifted it up where the barrel rose above the top of the seat. The dog turned his head and saw the glint of gunmetal and bolted for the door with all his might, his paws shoving Elmer's chest, pushing him out of the truck and down, flat on his back in the dirt.

The dog dashed over him and then off. Elmer rolled over and watched as the dog hightailed it down through the darkness and into the junkyard, his thick black coat only a faint flicker vanishing into the shadowy brush.

He stood and Mrs. McNulty got out of the truck and came around next to him. They peered into the black night and could detect only a faint rustling in the brush well past the junk cars, a sound that was fading as the dog ran farther away.

"*Percy*," she shouted, her voice tired and dry. "Percy, boy," and then she went into the ritual of calling his name over and over in alternating inflections, becoming more hoarse as she did. Elmer got the flashlight out of the truck and flipped on the beam and pointed it down toward the shrubs where the dog had run. There was no sign of Percy, and Elmer feared they would not see him again tonight, maybe ever.

When she stopped calling out the dog's name down the riverbank, he said, "Mrs. McNulty, let's go on into town and get you settled. I'll come out and look for him later. He ain't coming with us now."

Mrs. McNulty didn't say anything for about a minute, then she sighed and said, "I told you that dog don't take to guns . . . I ain't leaving without Ralph's dog, *my* dog. That dog's all I got in this world . . . and all that that dog's got in this world is me."

Elmer had been looking along the brush line but turned and saw Mrs. McNulty's face sad and drawn and wrinkled in the faint side glow of the truck lights. He stared down at the ground and pawed his toe in the dirt.

"But I bet he ain't coming back here tonight, not anytime soon. He's smart, he's a dog, he's not going to just drown. He's lived out here a long time. I bet someone will find him and bring him into town. Or I can find him in the morning for you."

"My foot," she said. "They'll shoot him just as quick as

anything, that's what'll happen if we leave him out here. They don't care about the people 'round here, much less a dog."

"I promise you I'll come back with my truck and get him and tie him in the cab. I can catch him. I won't let him see my guns."

Mrs. McNulty either didn't hear or acted like she didn't and turned and trudged up to the house. She climbed the steps slowly and walked onto the porch and surveyed the yard with a long look. Then she sat down in the far rocking chair on the right front side.

She began to rock there, the chair creaking forward and back. Elmer considered leaving her there to fend for herself when the water came. He couldn't blame her for wanting to stay here and ride out the flood, risking drowning if she had to. It would be better to go down here where she had lived all her life than to be forced to live somewhere she didn't want to be. But his mama's ghost would never let him rest if he went off and left Mrs. McNulty here to die.

He turned off the truck engine and cut the headlights. He took his flashlight from the floorboard and turned on the beam and lit his way. He paused after a few steps and turned the light toward the river. The water was churning, brown with specks of white. It had risen higher and was about to start leaking over the banks. He panned the light down the edge and found a low spot where the water had come up and was pooling on the low ground bordering the river, the once dry grass there wet and falling to the side.

"Mrs. McNulty, you see that?" He yelled at her, and he shone the beam on the river where it had broken through the bank.

"You think I ain't never seen the river flood before?" she said, her voice with a newfound strength that surprised him. She was rocking fast in the chair like she had a purpose.

"Yes ma'am, I'm sure you have. But this one is different. It's to make a lake. This flood ain't going down."

She shook her head from side to side and rocked faster. He moved toward the porch and could see that her eyes were alight, her face intense.

"That ain't nothin'," she said. "That flood ain't nothin'. I've seen it get all the way up to the steps of this house. Me and Ralph thought we was going to float away. He was upset because the water filled up the junkyard. High as the rooftops on most of the cars. He didn't have many cars in there then, but he did have an old Stanley Steamer that he could get running from time to time. Until the flood ruined it. We drove that old car all the way to Savannah once. That was the car that got Ralph started. He would collect any old piece of junk he could get his hands on. But he never did find one he liked as a much as that old steamer. *Steam.* Can you believe that?"

Elmer walked up on the steps and sat down in the rocking chair next to her. He flipped off the flashlight. The cane-woven seat creaked even under his light frame but held him. He rocked forward lightly in a rhythm much slower than she was moving. He started to speak, but she spoke first and with surprising vigor.

"Yes, sir, I was born in this house and have lived here all of my life. I was born in 1880. I had two brothers and three sisters. We was sometimes crowded in this here house. We was spread out over twenty-four years, so the most kids living in the house at one time was three. Mama and Daddy had a bedroom. The rest of us kids shared the other room. We all slept in the same bed. Kept you warm in the winter. That's the truth."

She smiled at the recollection. He had never heard Mrs. McNulty talk this fast and with such enthusiasm. She was taciturn like most country folks out this way, like he was. The old folks especially were quiet, holding onto their words like they were worth money, saying only what needed to be said, afraid to say more as though it might cost them a penny per word. The only time Elmer had heard old country folks talk like this was right before they died, letting loose for once, a last reminiscing before going on to meet their maker. His mama had gone on a storytelling jag a few days before she passed, talking of her childhood and the cotton picking and of Finley Shoals back like it used to be. Her memories had bubbled up from her mind and off her tongue and through her lips, stories that had been locked away for a long time. Three days later she was dead.

"My daddy didn't need a farm," Mrs. McNulty said. "He made a living off of this river for all of us. Some folks called him a river rat, and I reckon he was, but he worked hard. When I was a little girl, he and granddaddy pulled eels out of the river. They'd catch them in nets and string them up on a clothesline until they were dead and then we'd tear the skin right off and clean 'em. He'd sell the skins in town and Mama would fry up the meat as white and flaky as any fish. They ain't been any eels in this water since the thirties. Young people today don't believe they were eels, tell us we are crazy and that we were catching cottonmouths and water snakes. But I got sense enough to know the difference between an eel and a snake."

It was dark under the porch awning and Elmer couldn't see her face, but just listened to her dry voice next to him, steady in a light patter.

"They pulled pearls out of the river, too. Them mussels with pearls in 'em were really something. My granddaddy and daddy would drag the river with a brail that scraped the bottom, picking up those mussels by the armload. They had me and my brothers and my younger sisters crack open the shells and look for the pearls. Those shiny white jewels were gifts from God. Daddy would give us each a nickel for every one we found. A nickel a pearl. I'm telling you, that was a lot of money for a child back in them days. I was the best at finding 'em. I saved me up two dollars worth of nickels and bought a porcelain doll out of the Montgomery Ward's catalogue. My two older brothers were scofflaws at an early age and would take my doll and hide it from me until daddy would come around. I would tell him and he would beat them with his belt something fierce and make them give it back and apologize. Then a few weeks would pass and they'd be at it again and daddy would beat them until they cried. Then it would repeat all over again in a few weeks . . . One day the boys just broke it into smithereens." She shook her head. "Lord, the beatin' they got that time."

Elmer's eyes adjusted to the dark and he looked up at the night and the bright stars and the formation of the Milky Way, a cloudlike apparition subdividing the sky with its fuzzy whiteness. He glanced at her face, alive with telling.

"Only time daddy ever beat any of us any harder was if we threw a shell away with a pearl still in it. My brothers sometimes were lazy and didn't look close enough. Daddy beat us good. I didn't get beaten that often 'cause I was thorough . . . but our granddaddy, Lord have mercy, when he set to beating he wasn't holding nothing back. Once he beat my older brother with a board with a nail in it until he was unconscious. Granddaddy had been in the war and didn't have but one arm and he walked with a limp. He never smiled unless you found him in the evening when he had a jug of corn liquor."

She sighed, and took a deep breath.

"Mama was a quiet woman. She kept her mouth shut and worked hard day and night keeping the house up and all of us fed. She kept a garden and tended to the hogs and the chickens and the cow. She would take our clothes in a big tin bucket over to the river and wash them with lye and slap the clothes on the boulders out in the river. She always said God set them rocks there so we could go out into the river and wash our clothes. I was the oldest girl, so I'd go out there and help her, and in the summers I'd swim in the cool water. I been washing my clothes, and Ralph's too before he passed, all my life in that river . . . where am I going to wash my clothes when the river is gone?"

She was silent for a few moments. He did not try to answer her because he didn't know how to say what he felt. He watched her face, and even in the dim starlight he could see a fire in her old gray eyes. She took a deep breath and went on.

"Ralph found me out here. He married me when I was only fourteen. He told my daddy he was only twenty-one but really he was twenty-eight, double my age at that time. Ralph also told my daddy that he was hunting for arrowheads along the riverbanks. He said he'd heard there once was a Creek settlement near the shoals. Men from the university who came down to study the rock mounds north of here told him about it. I knew Ralph was hunting for me, but he told my daddy that anything he found on or around our land he'd split with daddy, fifty-fifty. Daddy by that time was sick and broke and would always agree to something if there was a little money in it for him. And Ralph, dang his hide, if he didn't find an arrowhead that very first day he and I went walking, just north of the big boulders, right where he said it might be. He was so excited, spitting on that old sharp piece of flint and rubbing it on his britches. We sat there on the riverbank, and he speculated on the story of that arrowhead. He imagined some Creek brave out hunting for food and shooting it at a deer, or maybe he decided it was part of a battle between different tribes of Creeks. He described a pack of braves coming down the river in canoes and another pack on the bank firing arrows at them and the ones in the river shooting arrows back, the points sticking in the buckskin that was thick and heavy and wet. Ralph loved finding things . . . and could make up a story to go with anything he could find. He told me his tales, and then he kissed me, sitting right there on the edge of that river. I knew I shouldn't, but I let him. It was nice."

She smiled and paused for a minute, catching her breath.

"Ralph thought the arrowhead might be worth ten dollars. Of course he didn't get but fifty cents for it, although old man Goldstein enjoyed hearing his stories about it. Ralph was smart enough to give all fifty cents to my daddy. Daddy didn't believe him, thought he was getting cheated, and cussed Ralph out and even threatened him with his old rifle. The next day Daddy went down and talked to old man Goldstein who verified what he had paid Ralph for it. After that, Daddy agreed to let me marry Ralph as long as we lived in the house with him and mama and my younger sisters. I loved Ralph, but . . . I was only fourteen and didn't really know anything then. I was just a little girl although I was tall for my age and had matured early. By then all my brothers were gone and daddy was sick, sick as a dog. We never knew exactly what he had. The doctor who came out and looked at daddy figured it was cancer, but said he couldn't be sure unless daddy went up to the hospital in Atlanta for tests. He said he might have to stay there a few weeks, maybe even a month, and then they still might not know what was wrong with him. Daddy said he'd rather stay home and die than spend a month in Atlanta and be cured. I think he knew what was coming . . . whatever it was inside Daddy that made him hurt and moan and cry got him in the end. He got to where he couldn't eat, and then he couldn't even drink a glass of water. He just withered up and passed. This was only about a month after Ralph had first come around, and only a week after he had moved in with us. We had been planning to go down to the courthouse and make it official but mama wouldn't let us go while Daddy was so sick. Mama had a fit when Ralph wanted to sleep in the bed with me. She made him take to a pallet out on the porch until we got married with our hands on the Bible. Daddy died, and the next morning we buried him down at the church.

"That very afternoon after we ate and cleared people out of the house, Ralph hitched up his wagon and drove us into town to see the Justice of the Peace. Lucien Andrews was a funny old man, cracking a joke a minute while we filled out the paperwork. He made us put our hands on the Bible, like Mama wanted, winking at Ralph in a dirty old man smile as he did it. I didn't even have a wedding dress or nothing, just a makeshift veil that mama had cut out of these linen curtains that had hung in the front of the house for all of my life. I repeated back to Lucien what he wanted me to say until Ralph flicked back the veil and kissed me.

"Ralph was sweet to me then. He smiled like he was the luckiest man in the world, and I suppose he was. I didn't learn 'til about a year later that he had been married before. His wife ran off on him and took their three kids with her only six months before he met me. It was too late to care anyway . . . I was taking care of a baby by then. Ralph was trying to earn a living fishing mussels out of the river and cracking them open for pearls. When the river pearl business all but died out, he tried farming—you've never seen a sorrier farmer in your life. The man couldn't grow a thing. But he was always good at scavenging. When the cold season came on that year he starting tinkering with automobiles and engine parts. He got that old car I told you about that had been abandoned. He got it running, a steam engine in that booger if you can believe that. *Steam*, just like the trains. He had to feed that boiler kerosene and crank the handle . . . it would chug along. That kept him going.

"He sold just enough car parts for us to get by. We were poor, but I'll tell you the truth . . . I enjoyed life. He got excited every time he found something, believing that it would bring a huge price tag, that we would be rich before the sun set on us. I knew in my head that it would never happen, and I think he did too, but we never said that. Playing along like we were going to get rich kept us young and in love in spite of our troubles, especially the fates that befell our young'uns. I guess the two youngest girls are doing all right, it's just they don't like to admit where they came from, like they are too good for their own mama."

She paused and Elmer spoke. "I ain't seen those girls around town in a long time. Years, I guess. They was a few years ahead of me in school."

"Them two won't have nothing to do with me anymore. And my oldest girl is down in the state hospital. They say she ain't never getting out and there's no point in visiting her 'cause she don't recognize anybody . . . My boys is another sad story. There's six of them—that's not counting the two died as babies, bless their hearts. Ralph Jr. was the meanest of them all, but I loved him. He was my first. I don't believe those things they said he did to that woman in Alabama were true. They hung him down there in Montgomery one morning a long time ago. He said they did him wrong, and I believe him. I'm his mama—I would know. That liked to about have killed me. I ain't been the same since. The second boy, Eustis, was a good boy, too, but he got himself killed in a hunting accident, one week before he was supposed to go off to the Great War. And Richard, the third boy . . . he was plain sorry. He got to drinking and gambling and running around over there in Phenix City. The twins, Sonny and Carl, grew up and went to *Dee-troit*. They making money like it's running out of style, I hear. They don't never write their mama or come back home. They Yankees now . . . long gone. Walter, the baby, had the head troubles, like his sister, and just up and disappeared . . . most likely dead somewhere.

"Nine young'uns. *Nine.* I just wish that one of the sane ones would have stayed around here . . . would have come out to see their mama every now and then and take her for who she is and not try to change her. Nine children raised on the river and not a one of 'em here to see it perish, to see its last days. Not a one of 'em that's still alive and still has sense gives a flip. That's the truth."

She shook her head and sighed. Elmer said nothing, remembering the faces of her children he had known. She continued.

"It has been mighty lonely out here since Ralph died. Percy's a good dog but he ain't got much to say. I talk to him a lot but he don't never talk back. I ain't got a way to even know if I'm sane or not, nobody to tell me."

Elmer started to tell her she sounded as sane as anyone he knew, but she kept talking.

"Ralph always said the head troubles runs in my family, that something about our brains ain't right. He would waggle his finger at me and say that I got some of it, too, that I didn't think straight. He said thinking crooked would get me one day, sooner or later. I know he was right part-ways. I can feel it in my mind now, that craziness working around in there, making me shaky, forgetful. I get out my Bible and pray when I feel the crazies coming on. I don't think it's my brain . . . it's the devil messing with me. But the Lord gave me his word he'd keep me safe. Ralph never went to church but he was a good man nonetheless. He said a lot of cross words to me over the years, but Lord knows I said 'em back, and sometimes said 'em first. But he never hit me . . . he said as least as many nice things as he did mean ones, or close to it. I miss him."

Elmer waited to see if she was going to continue talking a blue streak, but she got quiet. He let a minute or two pass.

"You can't stay out here anymore, Mrs. McNulty," Elmer said. "It's going to flood you out before morning. I bet one of your girls would take you in, wouldn't they?"

"Shoot," she said, her voice got loud and she leaned forward and raised her finger. "You know what? They sorry. They the ones that act like white trash. They let their dogs run around *inside* the house. I tell 'em dogs ain't meant to be inside. They is animals just like pigs and cows and chickens. They dirty and they smell. They ain't no sense in an animal sharing the roof where humans live. That's the truth."

She calmed a little and continued.

"Ralph would let Percy in the house sometimes when it was really cold, let him warm by the fire. Ralph knew how I felt about a dog in the house. Percy is a good dog. I let Ralph bring him in when it was freezing outside. But I would never let him get in the bed like Ralph wanted. I love that dog too, but ain't no telling where he has been. His thick fur can get to stinking, although it ain't that bad in the wintertime. I just can't stand for dogs in the house. All my people were like that, my mama especially. If there was one rule mama had, that was it, no dogs in the house. Sarah near had a fit when she took me in to see them in Atlanta . . . while she was cooking, you see,

I opened up the front door and let those pesky little varmints out. I ain't been invited back and that suits me just fine.

"The day our last young'un left home, Ralph found that puppy. I don't know why he named him Percy, but he did. Somebody had dumped him out on the road, so small his eyes hadn't been open long. I think Ralph must've been the first thing that he ever laid eyes on. Ralph went to town for milk and a bottle. He built a fire and warmed up the milk and suckled that old pup like a baby. That cute little pup grew up pretty and black . . . and he worshipped that man . . . yes, sir, a dog's more grateful than a child is every day of the week.

"Poor old Percy moped for months after Ralph died. I took care of him, but I guess I wasn't ever the same master. I wonder today what that old dog thinks about Ralph. I bet he thinks Ralph might still come walking down the road as bright as day . . . ain't no telling what's on that dog's mind. I have always been good to that dog but sometimes lately when the troubles get on me I forget to feed him. Ralph said he would come back and haunt me if I didn't take care of Percy. I guess he's planning to return any old time now 'cause I just can't remember to keep him fed. Seems like the only time I remember to do it is when I'm lying in the bed . . . sometimes I'll remember it in my sleep . . . then when I get up, I get into another project like getting the legs off this here bathtub. I can't think about nothing else until it's done."

She looked out at the truck and pointed. "This old bathtub here Ralph got for free. We never turned down anything, 'specially if it was a car or a truck or if it was made of iron, like the tub. That thing is *cast* iron. I just know it's got to be worth something. It's a rich person's tub. I know it . . . I might be old and a little crazy in the head, but I know what I'm talking about. I know where I came from and I know who I am. I told my daughter up there in Atlanta that it's a bad curse awaits those who forget where they came from. It's a *bad* curse ... that's the God's honest truth."

Her voice trailed off. They sat quietly, listening to the wind rustle the almost bare trees and the leaves flopping across the ground, the murmuring sound of the water chugging in the river.

THEY SAT LIKE THAT a long time. He didn't realize that she had quit rocking until he stopped rocking himself. He looked at her face, wrinkled and fixed in a tight-lipped scowl, her eyes closed. He listened closer and her breathing was raspy, and then her face changed and her head relaxed and her mouth opened and she began to snore softly.

Elmer stood and stepped lightly off the porch and down into the yard with his flashlight. His knee ached as he walked down the steps and he turned his foot to the side as he descended to ease the pressure on it. He kept the flashlight turned off and walked behind the oak tree where he had peed in the river that morning. He got near the river and heard a splash and was surprised to look down and see he had stepped in an inch of water. He flipped on the light and shone it on the ground. All along the bank was wet, almost an inch deep, the water gathering into puddles.

He walked from the shallow water and sat down on the bumper of a kudzu-enmeshed truck on the edge of the junk-yard. He looked skyward and saw the first cloud he'd seen all day, a black mass on the otherwise clear sky. He looked at the water's surface again, the bulging river brown and sinister and disrupted. He flipped off the flashlight and fished a cigarette from his pocket and lit it. He sat there a good long while, smoking one cigarette after another, until the red smolder showed the hands of his watch approaching midnight.

He shined the light around the junkyard and then walked down south of it and checked the brush line where he'd found Mrs. McNulty's dog earlier. There were no signs of the black half-chow. He went back up onto the porch and approached Mrs. McNulty, but she did not awake. He gently touched her on the shoulder. She opened her eyes and looked at him like she had never seen him before.

"C'mon, Mrs. McNulty, we need to go. I'm going to come out and get your dog tomorrow. He ain't coming back tonight, and we can't stay here."

She looked about, her eyes glazed and nervous. He supported her as she stood and led her down the steps, holding tight to her upper arm. She was shaky as he guided her to his truck. She said nothing, moving along like a zombie, her eyes narrowed and thin.

He got her situated in the passenger side, and then he put his flashlight on the floorboard. He turned the key and pressed the starter button with his foot and the engine rolled over slowly but started, much to his relief. He dropped it into first and pulled onto the road and then put it into second and then third gear. This time it shifted smoothly. He drove off toward town and neither one of them looked back.

PERCY RAN FARTHER FROM the house, dashing through the brush and down the river's edge until he could no longer hear the old lady calling his name, toward the land that had burned and where the concrete wall blocked the river's flow. He scrambled through a briar patch and slowed some as he got far enough away where he knew the gun could not reach.

He trotted along, toward the boulders, and here he could smell the remnants of the fire that had burned that night. A person would wonder why he ran toward the dam, to the spot where fire had been launched into the sky and spread across the ground, but he was seeking safety across the river where there were no homes or people, just stumps and some hardwoods left behind by the pulpwood men.

He came to the boulders that traversed the river and was unable to comprehend what he saw. The water had multiplied and grown. The river was bigger. It rose out of its banks, high water like when he remembered heavy rains, the floods of late spring and summer when the sky was gray and moist and thick, the air so wet and heavy he could feel it, the times when the river would spill over its banks and form ponds on the low ground where it normally did not flow. It had not rained in days and days, and the earth he ran on was dry and dusty and the leaves blew and crunched beneath his paws, but here he was trotting up on a flood. A dry weather flood? His paws were wet although the sky was clear. His eyebrows fidgeted as he studied the riverbank and its many breaches.

He never had understood people but had learned to rely on their routines and rituals: the meal times and the sleeping and the early rising of the old lady, and when he was alive, the old man. But the old man had died and death Percy understood instinctively. It was a ritual to which all animals and people would succumb. He had seen it in dogs and cows and other creatures of the woods. He himself had brought death upon snakes shaken lifeless, chipmunks crunched in his teeth, and rabbits chased down and mauled. The floppy-eared cottontails were the easiest of the prey, and he often thought about them. He craved meat and blood and sinewy tissue.

But Percy could no longer rely on routine. He traipsed through paw-deep water and then up a dry rise that led to the top of the rock path across the river, up on the first high boulder. Stars provided the only light, but his eyes were keen for an old dog. From this perch he studied what he could see downstream, the water level high beneath the boulders, the granite that once had risen well above the water's surface now like a sidewalk of stones someone had laid across the river, barely jutting above the channel. He could see the water below the fall line had already started to fan out from the river, forming a wide and flat sheen. What was left of the river was churning and spewing back in the opposite direction of the way it had always flowed, but today was the day where nothing made any sense, so the river flowing backward should come as no surprise after the fire in the sky and the fire on the ground and the old lady and the spitting-scratching man trying to get him into the truck, reaching for his gun. He had seen what men did with guns, had been fired at and grazed a time or two by angry farmers with lightweight shotguns, and he would have no part of it as long as he could run. He was an old dog, but he could still run.

He moved with some trepidation across the stones that no longer seemed to stand above the river but instead floated in it, the water black and sinister and cold. He stepped across the first three rocks and measured his leap over the wide gap in the middle of the rising river with care and jumped, but he slipped and didn't get a full push off and landed with only his front half on the next boulder, his forepaws scratching on the rock, his back half splashing in the river. His legs flailed, his forepaws grasping at the granite while his hind legs kicked in a demented dog paddle until he lunged forward and scrambled with all of his wet fur onto the boulder. As soon as he was back on all four paws, he dashed to the other side like he was being chased, running across the wet stones as fast as he could and then through a wide pool where the river was out of its banks and up to his haunches before he reached dry ground. He stopped there and shook his fur and river water flew from him in all directions, a fine mist enshrouding him as he convulsed.

The night had not seemed cold until the river had soaked deep into his fur and clung to his skin. After shaking off the water and adjusting as well as he could to the chill, he sensed an uncommon nighttime commotion of the creatures of the low ground. All of the varmints were on the move, flushed out of their holes burrowed beneath the stumps and brush crowding the riverbanks.

His eyes came alive at the prospect of something warm and fleshy to eat. A chipmunk scooted past into the high grass. He chased, but it disappeared back into the watery brush, and he could not find it even though he could smell it. His eyes darted back toward the creeping pools of water and he saw a squirrel emerge, running and screeching from beneath a small tree along the edge of the river, its long fluffy tail straight and high and agitated behind him. Percy chased after the squirrel and it streaked down the edge of the water line and climbed up a lone sycamore tree with mottled brown bark, the squirrel's claws scraping on the skin of the tree that had peeled away in puzzle-like pieces to reveal a smooth, whitish yellow trunk.

Percy stood on his hind legs and scratched the tree with his front paws as high as he could reach, his guttural growl at the squirrel threatening but useless. The squirrel skittered about in the high branches and looked down at him with bulging eyes.

Percy barked a few more times, but gave up the pursuit and trotted farther up from the river to try and get a better view of the water and make sure he was safe from it. He meandered about, watching the black wetness moving, higher than he had ever seen as it pooled beyond its banks. The water lapped out from the river in shallow waves. He could smell the water churning and the new mud it was making. His nostrils shifted, sniffing for the cottontail rabbits that populated this woodland. This side of the river had always been rich with the bewhiskered herbivores.

He watched like this for a long time, occasionally turning his stare to the old sycamore. The squirrel in the branches taunted him with its bug eyes and occasional laughing cry. He wished the old man was here with his shotgun, the only man the dog had ever trusted with a long barrel of gun metal.

He heard a scuffling in the privet down south along the riverbank. He trotted in that direction and saw a briar patch where the water seemed to have begun arriving in sheets. He saw two silvery-gray bunnies hopping from the safety of the dense thicket into a more open space of grass, hunting for dry ground.

He charged the rabbits who hopped as fast as they could away from the coming pools of water and into the dry grass of the abandoned cow pasture, heading for a briar patch on the other side of the field. Percy caught up to them and hit the slower and fatter of the two cottontails with a snarling slash of fangs, but he stumbled as he tried to make the kill. He fell, rolling onto his side while the stricken rabbit charged off behind the lead rabbit, of which Percy could see only a poof of tail bobbing up and down across the grass pasture. He got back on his feet and resumed his chase, the taste of fur and a drop of rabbit blood on his tongue whetting his appetite.

He homed in on the bigger and slower of the two rabbits, the injured straggler pushing hard. He caught up to it at the edge of the field as it dove into a patch of dried honeysuckle and pokeweed along an overgrown fence line. He surged at the rabbit again, but it was a step ahead of him and went through a low hole in the hogwire fence that was too small for Percy. He charged into the hole in the weeds and rusted wire and was stuck for a moment. He had once seen an abandoned town dog get caught in a fence and die there, whining and crying until it breathed its last breath. Percy, determined not to suffer such a fate, pulled back with all his might and broke loose.

Freed, he leapt onto the sagging fence and climbed over, landing in the thicket of dry honeysuckle and kept going, his nose on the trail of the rabbits running for the patch of hardwood trees that offered a warren of holes amongst the gnarled roots in the red clay. Percy knew if they reached the hardwoods, the rabbits would be gone, plunged deep into the ground where his barking and clawing and digging would do him no good. But to get there, the rabbits would have to cross the field of pine stumps that offered no protection. It was a maze of dying trunks, the pines like legs that had been hacked off at the ankles.

Between the weeds and the fence lay a mess of dry pokeweed. The first rabbit had stretched out his lead over the slower rabbit and was practically out of sight in the dark. Percy set his eyes on the second rabbit, the fat one with the gray fluffy tail that he saw dart onto the pine straw. Percy was able to get good footing on the solid earth where the pokeweed grew and bolted into the pine stump field at full speed just as the rabbit hopped too far and tripped into a stump that it was trying to maneuver around. Percy hurled himself onto the rabbit and bit down on its neck and collided with the stump, holding the rabbit briefly in his jaws until it flung loose like he had tossed it, the wounded animal terrified and flinging its legs in flight until it landed on its feet and rolled over once and ended upright. The stunned rabbit ran the way it was facing, back toward the river from whence it had come, too bloodied to think but still full of a vigorous instinct to survive. Percy, confused by the change of directions, paused, looking where the first rabbit had gone while the wounded fat one ran back the opposite way. He followed the hurt cottontail and he almost got to it in the pokeweed patch, but lost sight of it in the briars and honeysuckle vine on the fence, the rabbit going through another low hole in the wire. This time Percy leapt over the sagging fence and landed firmly on his feet as he chased the delirious rabbit into the cow pasture. The rabbit had slowed and Percy ran with confidence as he sighted down the bobbing cottontail, hitting it in stride right at the edge of the field where the river had begun encroaching. He snatched the panting rabbit in his jaws, holding on tight, rabbit bones cracking as Percy fell and rolled into an inch of water that was beginning to smother the field.

He got to his feet, the rabbit still in his clutches, and trotted to a dry spot where he collapsed in the grass and let the disabled prey drop onto the ground before him, watching as the rabbit struggled to hop its last step. Percy panted, his long tongue hanging, until he caught his breath.

Once he was breathing more normally he carried the limp rabbit to the base of the lone sycamore where the squirrel still clung to the branches and looked down warily. Percy dropped the rabbit on the leaf-covered ground at the base of the trunk. From this spot he could keep an eye on the rising river water pouring steadily over the bank. He was a safe distance from it, the water yet unable to climb the short hill where the sycamore stood. He sat down with the dying rabbit at his forepaws. It was trying to breathe and was still warm with a beating heart and futile twitching of muscles beneath its fur that was wet with blood where it had been torn across its abdomen.

He pawed at the wounded varmint and sniffed, its smells

a convoluted mixture of fur and damp earth and water and blood, the unmistakable scent of rabbit. He nuzzled his nose to the hare as its troubled inhalations and exhalations stopped. He detected it immediately start to stiffen, get colder. He bit down into the fur of the fat belly and held the bunny's head with his front paws as his fangs slashed through the cotton lining and into the soft sweet innards. Its insides were warm. A steamy, stinky waft came up as Percy bit off a hunk of guts and fat and meat and ground it in his teeth and swallowed. There was no easy way to eat a raw varmint other than to gnaw on it, crunching up the bones until they could be swallowed, masticating the fur until it was like goo. He ate the rabbit's underbelly, slurping up the warm entrails. He then began to crunch and gnaw on the backbone, getting his black snout wet with blood and rabbit slime. The spinal bones were tasty, coated with small globs of jelly in between the crooked, tiny bones. The eating of a rabbit took a long time, the effort to chew the moist bones until they could be swallowed.

After the spine he went for the head, crunching the skull and the moist eyeballs popping in his mouth like muscadines, and then after the skullcap gave way, the sweet taste of the brain that sprayed juice in his mouth when it cracked open under the force of his molars. He gnawed the fur and crushed the bones to small digestible bites. The sinew of the furry ears was difficult to chew so he just swallowed whole the long pointy appendages, tickling his throat as they went down.

All that was left were the feet, the toughest part. Had he been eating better, he might have left the toes with the hard nails alone, but he was still ravenous and began gnawing on the long, bony pods. He remembered the old man carried a dried rabbit foot in his pocket and would sometimes take it out and rub it and say a few words as though in a trance when he went fishing or hunting. The rabbit feet were tough, but his fangs were tougher, and the sharp incisors shattered the bones and he swallowed down first the front feet and then the back feet in a fury of biting and growling and smacking. With the ingestion of the last foot there was nothing left of the rabbit but blood on his nose.

Satiated for the first time in days, he reclined on his side in the pile of leaves and nestled there. His belly was warm with digestion, and the water in his fur had dried in the chase. He kept his eyes turned toward the dark water but his lids began to droop. He tried to keep them open to watch the water closely, but it only lapped in slow waves rolling out toward him. He snuggled deeper into the leaves and burrowed down and enjoyed the warmth of his own being, the rush of blood to his full stomach. He began to doze and then would snap awake and raise his head. Sleeping was how he spent two-thirds of most days, but he hadn't slept in a long time, since the many hours before in the early afternoon. His mind rested and he fell into a deep slumber, his paws beginning to twitch with dreams as the river lapped and churned next to him, cool water spilling up from the riverbed and out over its banks.

THEY RODE WITHOUT SPEAKING. Elmer drove and Mrs. McNulty gazed forlornly out the window. She wept, starting when they pulled off Junkyard Road until they got to the smooth, fresh asphalt of North Highway. She dabbed her eyes with the sleeve of her robe, and got silent again as they approached Lymanville.

It was after midnight and the roads were empty except for a big black Buick with Fulton County tags and a silver Cadillac from Bibb County. He veered off the main road through town and went east and then past Coach Hilliard's street. He coasted for a moment and took a look down the block, still busy with parked cars at this late hour, although it had thinned out considerably from earlier in the evening. He saw Lloyd's patrol car there, and the Coggins boy's car too, as well as Aubrey Terrell's Crown Victoria Skyliner.

He didn't linger, but gunned the engine and headed on the last mile to his home. Elmer parked his truck in his yard, pulling up far on the grass, as close as he could get to the kitchen door since they had the tub to carry.

"You go on in the house, Mrs. McNulty," he said. "Make yourself at home."

She did not move from the truck seat. He got out and walked around and opened the passenger door.

"C'mon, now," he said. "You can sleep in my guest bedroom, get you some rest. You need it."

He got her pillow case holding her clothes and gun from the bed of the truck. She moved with her head down and her shoulders stooped, her face sleepy. He walked ahead of her and opened the kitchen door and she followed him in and stood there.

"In here," he said. He turned on the overhead light and set her clothes down on the desk in the small bedroom. He folded back the covers of the twin bed. The bed had never been used except by Sherry's mama, the last time six years ago. He still thought of this as Sherry's mama's room, if he ever thought of it at all. He went into it only once or twice a year if he needed a pencil from the stash in the desk drawer. Sherry had used the desk to write letters and pay bills, and there was still some stationery that she had left behind. He had always done his limited business at the kitchen table and still did so.

Mrs. McNulty stood in the doorway of the small room. He pointed down the hall. "The bathroom is right here." He walked to the open door and flipped on the light. It occurred to him that she may have never used electric lights and indoor plumbing, or at the most only a few times when seeing her daughters. He started to explain how these worked, but then decided he didn't want to insult her.

"All right. You need anything?"

She shook her head no.

"Well, then, get on to bed. I'm going to be outside if you need me."

Elmer went out the kitchen door and sat on his stoop and took a cigarette from the pack in his front pocket. He lit it and inhaled, thinking about Aubrey Terrell and Coach Hilliard's party.

He finished the cigarette and stubbed it in the ashy dirt in the old urn by the door that Sherry had once planted with flowers. He took his pocketknife from his jeans and walked over to his truck and cut the twine loose. He pulled the tub out of the truck bed and slid it through the grass to the side of his house. He gathered up the claw feet and set them in the bathtub, and then he closed the gate of his pickup truck.

He retrieved the shotgun from behind his truck seat and worked the pump, chambering a shell. He clicked the safety button off and then back on again. He then flicked the release lever and kicked the shell out of the breech and put it in his pocket. He set the butt of the shotgun on the floorboard with the barrel leaning back and the muzzle just beneath the window. He reached under the driver's seat and got the .38-.44. He opened up the chamber, spinning the cylinder and studying the bullets as they rotated. He clicked the cylinder back into place and put the revolver on the passenger seat and left the truck door open.

He went in the house to see about Mrs. McNulty. He walked

quietly to the door of the small bedroom. The overhead light was still lit. Mrs. McNulty lay flat on her back on top of the covers, still wearing her robe over her house dress. She had not taken her shoes off. Her hands were folded over her stomach like she was waiting for something. He stepped nearer to see if she was awake, but her eyes were closed and he could hear her breathing, a raspy low snore that came from her partly opened mouth. He turned out the light and went to his truck.

ELMER DROVE DOWNTOWN AND parked in one of the angled spots on Main Street in front of the jewelry store, a few doors down from the Magnolia Restaurant. There was only one other vehicle on the street, an old International pickup truck near the Feed-and-Seed. Terrell lived in a room above the office of his small loan business at the corner of Lyman Avenue. Word had it that he owned a house where his wife lived in Atlanta, less than a mile from the governor's mansion.

"Close as he's going to get to the Guvnah's mansion," Elmer said, and spat out the window.

Elmer looked around for Terrell's fancy new car but it was not here. He stared up at the dark second-story window. The man owned thousands of acres of Achena County land that had belonged to the Finley family, as well as a dozen other rural family farms that had not survived the combination of the boll weevil and the Big One. The old sumbitch had all the land a man could want or need, acres of farmland, hills, a river, trees by the hundreds of thousands, but he chose to live in this attic room above his office. He was a man who did not appreciate what he had or where he came from. Some politicians were the fervent, angry demagogue types, their eyes bulging and their fingers pointing and their voice damning and quivering like a fire-and-brimstone preacher, spewing sulfur and castigating

any and all who got in the way. But that had never been Aubrey
Terrell's style. Some speculated that is why he could never win
statewide office, that he just wasn't mean enough. But mean
has different forms and for Elmer's purposes, Terrell was as
sinister as they come, a charming Judas Iscariot smiling to
your face but conniving and crooked as all get out when you
turned your back.

Elmer waited about an hour in the dark street until he
decided he didn't like sitting out in the open for anyone to
see him, so he cranked up the engine and drove back toward
Federal Street, pausing under the oaks at the intersection near
Coach Hilliard's house. He drove past the house and thought
he saw Lloyd on the porch talking to Terrell, a hint of recogni-
tion in Lloyd's face, his broad visage under the bright porch
light. As soon as Lloyd made eye contact, Elmer turned his
head, breaking away from that gaze that he felt like had been
on him all of his life, the face that shared his mama's short
but stout set jaw, the knobby chin and wide, deep-set eyes.
The faces of Lloyd and his mama had always haunted him,
much like Sherry's fine brow and smooth forehead and blue
eyes and blond hair were with him always. It was a shame how
someone gone for so long from your life could stay in it like
a goddamn ghost.

Elmer looped around and went east on Washington Street
toward the other end of Federal Street. He parked at the corner
of Federal and Glascock, on the side where the Nelligans had
a big brick wall that surrounded their home. It gave him a
good spot to hide his truck and spy on Coach Hilliard's house
eight doors away.

He sat for a minute until he decided he wanted to get closer.
He took the handgun and got out of the truck, sticking the
.38-.44 in the back of his britches, and walked along the brick

side wall. From here, he could hear the rise and fall of their foolish voices in the dead of night. Elmer paused and listened. He could make out Terrell's distinct tone, the charming jokester spinning another story, his drawl slurring loose with liquor. Elmer walked around the Nelligan house in the alleyway behind houses fronting Federal Street and Washington Street, a gravel path barely wide enough for one car, a roadway manicured and graded much better than the roads Finley Shoals had ever had. The alley was protected on both sides by a six-foot hedge, and Elmer hoped there were no yard dogs to upset. He stepped softly to avoid crunching the clean gravel.

He snuck up in the alleyway behind the Hilliard house and paused, listening to the voices, mainly Terrell's, carrying on. He looked at his watch and saw it was almost two o'clock. He reached back for the gun and was about to make a move to the yard and hide on the side of the Hilliard's carriage house when he heard someone say "goodnight," and then a chorus of goodnights, and then footsteps on the sidewalk and the opening of car doors and starting of engines. Porch lights flicked off, and he saw the Hilliard's servants starting to pull closed the red thick curtains on the side of the big house.

Elmer turned and ran back down the alley and onto Glascock Street and to his truck. He cranked it but kept the headlights off and drove back one block and parked under the branches of an old pecan tree near the main outlet to Federal Street where everyone would pass.

He pulled up close to the curb and crouched down, waiting there with his engine running but his lights turned off. He watched as Lloyd drove slowly past, clearly inebriated, the car listing to the middle of the street.

Lloyd's taillights disappeared around the corner and then two Cadillacs raced away. Behind them Terrell's Crown Victoria Skyliner pulled steady up to the stop sign. Elmer peered over his dashboard and saw a Negro he didn't recognize in the driver's seat and Terrell sitting in the passenger seat, talking and gesturing. The driver wore a bowtie and a black cap.

Elmer was surprised when the car turned toward him and not in the direction of Terrell's street. The headlights raked over Elmer's truck. He slid down low to avoid the glare as they went past. Elmer watched in his side mirror as the sleek pink-and-white car headed up to the stop sign and took a right.

Elmer put his truck into gear and took a U-turn and followed. He kept his lights off and trailed about a block behind Terrell's Crown Vic, following its long loop around the women's college and past the courthouse. He could see Terrell gesturing and his head bobbing as he talked, telling the driver yet another story. They drove through downtown and up the hill to the intersection where Terrell lived. They parked outside Terrell's door, but they stayed in the car, Terrell still talking. Elmer figured the old man would talk to a bug in the bushes if there was no one else around to listen.

Elmer waited for what seemed an interminable time, Terrell's gestures and talking steady while the driver—*who was this uppity-looking nigger?*—sat still, his head turned only halfway to Terrell, as though he was only partially listening to the lying politician's stories.

Elmer held the pistol while he waited, putting his index finger on the trigger and then rubbing it over the cylinder. He hefted the gun with a cock of his wrist just to measure the weight of it. Wasn't nothing else heavy like a big-barreled pistol, the kind that would blow someone away in a minute.

Terrell and the man got out of the car and stood there on the sidewalk, talking some more. Terrell rambled on while the man listened, his face without emotion, a mask that black folks sometimes put on where Elmer couldn't tell what they were thinking, one of those expressions where he didn't know if they loved him or wanted to slit his throat. Terrell stopped talking for a moment and fiddled with his key chain, pulling one off and handing it to the man. Then he pointed up at his window on the second floor, then to the door on the street that was back by the alley, and then back at the window. The man's eyes followed Terrell's gestures, looking hesitant. Terrell put his arm around his shoulders and squeezed him. He patted the Negro on the backside and shook his hand one more time.

Terrell walked around to the Crown Vic's driver's side and got in and slammed the door and cranked the engine and turned on the lights and started to drive off with the passenger door wide open. The man waved at him and called out— Elmer hadn't been able to hear their talking at this distance, but he could hear him holler. Terrell hit the brakes and the car screeched and the door slung open wider on the force of the sudden stop. The man ran up to the car and slammed the door shut and then Terrell waved and sped off, the sectional taillights bright on the empty street of shadowy awnings and dark window fronts.

Elmer watched as he drove to the stop sign at the top of the hill at Taliaferro Street and turned right. Elmer dropped the truck into gear and sped through the light and past the man who stood there on the street corner. The man had been watching Terrell drive away, but now turned to see Elmer's truck barreling through town with his lights off. Elmer looked over at him and glared. The man returned his stare with no expression, but Elmer guessed that if he offered him the chance, this Negro would be glad to go with him and help him shoot Terrell square between the eyes.

Elmer turned right on Taliaferro Street and stomped the

gas pedal and roared down the hill toward the river bridge. He could see Terrell's taillights in the distance ahead of him speeding along the street that marked the north city limits, a dingy stretch of repair shops and low-rent merchants. *The old sumbitch just never quit.* Elmer figured Terrell must be headed to the bridge, but the politician surprised him again and turned on Toomsboro Street and then down Deepstep Lane, the narrow street where Woody Garrett kept his used car lot.

Elmer turned and stopped on Toomsboro Street where he could see that Terrell had parked next to Garrett's lot and three big garages. Cars and trucks were all marked with shoe polish messages on the windshields that reflected bright floodlights. A GREAT DEAL $350. YOU CAN'T GO WRONG AT THIS PRICE $150. A squat black guard dog with a thick neck barked ferociously, yanking at its heavy chain.

Terrell parked and got out and a young woman in a frilly white dress ran over and hugged him. Elmer could tell even from this distance that it was Raynelle Watson, the high school majorette. He had not seen where she had come from, but it must have been one of the old Buicks parked near the street. She cut a curvaceous shadow beneath the streetlights.

Terrell held her and Elmer could see the old lecher reach down and lift up her white dress and grab a handful of her small round rump. They separated and he fumbled in his pocket before holding a giant key ring up to the streetlight and studying it, the little flecks of metal glimmering in the near darkness of the street.

Terrell unlocked the padlock on the heavy chain stretched across the entrance to the car lot. He handed her the end of the chain to hold and he went to an oversized Studebaker pickup truck with a green-painted wooden camper built onto the back, a truck Elmer remembered had been retired after years of hauling milk from the dairies into town. Terrell got in and turned on the lights and started the engine. He drove it off the lot and left it running out on the street and got out and took the chain from the girl and locked it across the entrance. Elmer backed up a little, pulling out of the line of the Studebaker's headlights. Terrell pointed at the girl and said something to her and she got in the cab. He got in the driver's side and she slid over next to him as he drove, sitting upright in that posture of which he was so damned proud. Elmer ducked as the truck passed but Terrell seemed oblivious to the road around him as he drove away.

Elmer watched the truck go by and turn back west on Taliaferro Street, the same direction from which they had just come. He turned around and drove up to the intersection and watched the taillights driving away, pausing for about thirty seconds before pulling out to follow. The Studebaker with the high-riding camper on the back moved ponderously along the road. Elmer had to keep easing off the gas and hitting the brake to avoid getting too close. At North Highway Terrell turned right, heading up in the direction of the dam.

"That sumbitch," Elmer said. "That old sumbitch." He followed along slowly as the state senator and the majorette made their way up the new road in the middle of the night. It was almost three o'clock.

Elmer had expected him to turn on Dam Road so he could show her all he had done for Achena County, but the Studebaker truck kept on, passing the sign for the dam without even slowing down. Elmer bristled at the idea that the old man was about to go screw the lead high school majorette in Finley Shoals.

The Studebaker seemed to coast along North Highway until it reached the macadam of Finley Shoals Road where

Terrell turned without turning on the blinker. Elmer still had his lights off and stayed closer once Terrell was on the dark road ensconced in brush and wild privet. He drove along for two miles, past Drowning Creek Road, went another mile and turned on the narrow unnamed logging road. The big truck lurched up the track for pulpwood trucks, wobbling like a circus wagon as it made the sharp turn. This was the same road where Elmer had run into his cousin Warren this morning. Elmer figured the lascivious sumbitches must have carved a spot out back in here where they went to violate their concubines.

Elmer stopped on Finley Shoals Road to let Terrell get a lead up into the logging road where in the swales it was grown heavy with young oaks and yellow poplars. The low growth was so thick that he couldn't see the truck for a while but Elmer knew there was no other outlet. He shut the engine and sat there and snapped open his Zippo and lit another cigarette and smoked, looking down the road, not far from the Finley Shoals crossroads. He wondered if it was getting water yet. He imagined it was but he resisted the urge to go look. Seeing it burn had been enough. The heavy scent of woodsmoke had faded.

Elmer got out of his truck and stood in the road and leaned back against his grille. There was something about being out in the woods alone at night that was infinite and free, yet the dark closed in on him like coffin walls, especially on moonless nights like this one. The only way out of this wrapped feeling was to look up and hope that clouds had not blotted out the twinkling stars. He looked up at the sky and could tell that the Milky Way had shifted and the Big Dipper had dropped near the horizon, that a few more clouds were beginning to drift in from the west, a covering of the strip of sky above the distant tree line that would probably bring rain in the next day or two.

Elmer could hear the Studebaker truck climbing up the low hill that the logging road cut through the boulders and then along it to the river, the gears gnashing as the old drunk sumbitch shifted up and down and the engine groaned. He listened as the truck got farther away and parked, near the river where the road ended, and the engine turned off. Elmer guessed he was about a mile away.

Elmer walked around to the passenger side of his truck and opened the door and took the shotgun out and held it. He was tempted to fire a round into the sky, to put Terrell on notice that his time had come, that it was time to meet his maker and die like the sumbitch that he was.

But he figured that the old sumbitch was packing some weaponry himself, probably a Colt .45 like the ones used back in the Great War over in France, fighting those Krauts down in the trenches. Lloyd always said that Terrell's stories about his time in the war in France were true, but Elmer didn't believe them. But he did believe that the old sumbitch would be crafty enough to carry a gun with him. And despite his proclaimed love for his fellow Achena County man, Elmer knew the old bastard would shoot quick to save his own hide. He had done himself proud in taking care of it through his sixty-five years. His war stories might even be true, Elmer figured, because Terrell was sneaky tough in his own way.

Elmer started the truck and parked it so it blocked the entrance to the logging road. He shut the engine and put the keys in his pocket and slid the revolver far up under the seat. He took the shotgun and five extra shells and shut the door and got out and started walking slowly. He took his time, stepping carefully in the ruts of the scraped clay. It was dark in the swales through the thicket of hardwoods before the land started to rise and open up where the pine trees had been cut.

He could see better in the open fields of stumps although the gradations between the dark of the land and the sky were very thin—the earth on which he walked a solid black while the horizon was a misty line and the heavens above lighter with stars. Occasionally he stepped off the road into a ditch. In a few places it was so rutted it seemed that the ditch was in the middle of the road where it began to climb up the hill. He knew this land well enough to know that the road would soon cut through the line of six-foot high stones that stood atop the ridge.

He trudged on and came to the boulders, the road angling through a bare spot in the line of giant rocks. The row of granite was ominous like enormous tombstones in the dark of night, and Elmer walked up the road and ran his hand over the cold boulders.

The pulpwood trail cut through the pass and then curved around behind the rock line and ran along the bluff parallel toward the river. Although it was too dark to see much of anything, in his mind he could imagine what he knew was there because he had seen it before and his eyes gave life to the shapes that he could only faintly make out.

He began walking cautiously with the gun out in front of him ready to fire in case he came up on the old sumbitch. He walked and walked, surprised that he was not to the end of the road by now. He moved to the edge, along the boulders, and began to sneak up ambush style. That truck had to be along here somewhere. He began having panic attacks, fearing that he was lost, that he had gotten off the road and was down away from the boulders, but then he would move to his right and feel the boulders and knew that he was on the right path.

Could the truck have gone off somewhere else? He shook his head. There was no way that truck could have gotten down off the logging road, that behemoth Studebaker and huge camper, the old man's mobile sex room. Elmer had never been more disgusted. The old sumbitch had a specially arranged truck for screwing majorettes. *Lord God almighty*, Elmer's mama would pull the trigger herself if she knew.

Elmer crept along, squatting low against the boulders, when he began to hear the river, that powerful yet gentle rushing of water, its barely perceptible movement along the banks. He stopped and tried to focus as hard as he could on the end of the road, but he saw nothing but the hulking shapes of the boulders. He did not see anything as high as the truck should be, but then again it was full dark and he was still maybe thirty yards to the river, farther than he could see in the blackness.

He started moving again and soon neared the end of the road where he stopped suddenly. He had almost walked right into the grille of the Studebaker, parked up against the end boulder in the darkest of shadows. It was backed in atop the bluff under an old oak, before the land sloped down about thirty feet from the river. Elmer had forgotten how far back this logging road had gone and he hadn't thought it possible to get a truck, much less this cumbersome vehicle, in here this far.

He ducked down fast and pressed himself against the boulder near the left front tire of the Studebaker. He could hear Terrell talking and the high-pitched giggles of Raynelle from the camper, the back window of it open so they could look down on the water from the high ground. She was baby-talking to Terrell, cooing softly, and the old man was smooth-talking in return.

Elmer gritted his teeth and fought the urge to shoot them both right then and there. But he could not bring himself to kill the girl. He sat down near the passenger door of the truck and pressed his back into the ancient granite boulder.

He closed his eyes and told himself to be patient. At some point the old man would have to come out of that camper and take a piss while that young girl was sleeping. A few hours here in the dark woods, waiting on the dawn, wouldn't cost Elmer anything. He had been waiting it seemed all his life to gut-shoot this old sumbitch.

PERCY WOKE UP WHEN he sensed the dawn coming. The sky that had been black along the eastern horizon was now a navy bluish purple, the colors banding out in ribbons from the edge of the earth. He looked at the sky and then at the river, and it was easier to see in the very faint light that water was beginning to filter out over the land. What he saw of the river panicked him. It was well out of its banks, and the pool that had been just beyond the edge of the river had expanded and was almost up to him under the sycamore tree where he had been sleeping.

The water lapped with waves that seemed to expand its dominion over the dirt. The river and the land were in a chase much like he and the rabbit had been, and the river was winning. He stood and felt queasy with the rabbit still digesting, its fur and bones and flesh sitting heavy on his stomach.

Percy wanted to go back to the house, hoping that the old lady would be there and the spitting-scratching man would be gone. He could go under the porch and sleep the rest of the day, or maybe in the sun if it was too cool for him, the rays warming his black fur that was thickening in preparation for winter.

He trotted by the sycamore tree to the higher rise near where the line of boulders cut across the river, but there was no sight of the granite in the water anymore. The path on which he had crossed the river and that had been there all his life was gone.

His fur bristled and his eyes darted about. He ran along the river, barking, panting, whining some, his eyes searching for the boulders. Not even the spring and summertime floods had brought such high waters.

He dashed around the flooding, some spots as far as fifty feet back from the river's original banks, splashing in the seeping water and mud. He ran up the river almost a quarter of a mile, hunting for the boulders. He stopped and looked at the rising water and to the other side, the land there and the few hardwoods that remained beginning to appear in the predawn light. He saw an old oak tree across the river that he recognized, light beginning to filter through the darkness enough that he could see its outline on the wet horizon, a faint pale of light on the gray bark.

He looked about at the dark water and he started to whimper, a high pitched almost moan-like hum . . . *bowwwww* . . . *bowwwww*. He cried for a while and then he barked, not an angry, threatening bark, but an almost questioning growl, a growl grew into a full-blown howl and then repeated.

He howled at the river for a while, standing on its eastern edge to which he seemed exiled, away from his home with the old lady. He barked some more in the direction of the familiar tree. As the sky to the east began to lighten, he saw a quarter rind of the moon rise, slipping up above the horizon and glowing luminescent and thin and curved above the faraway hills. He continued to bark as though his rough voice crying in the wilderness might change the world before him.

He ran one more time up the river's edge about a quarter of a mile, seeing where the water cascaded in sheets across the low ground, and then he turned and ran toward the dam where the flood was higher and spreading farther from the original riverbed and submerging the land, reaching as far as the field of stumps on the east side.

He continued that way and heard the abandoned pups he had seen earlier in the day. He went over and saw them squirming in a ditch in an inch of water, their eyes still closed and their thin coats wet with mud along the edge of the logging road, their cries mournful as they splashed about but their starved little bodies too weak and clumsy to escape. He looked at them, but then turned back and looked to the river where the boulders had been, focusing on the old oak on the other side, and then back to the helpless pups. He hovered over them for a few minutes, staring at the shivering dogs until finally he barked angrily and ran away toward the river.

He stood at the Oogasula's edge. The only way to get home to the house and the old lady was to swim. He was hesitant to go into the river water because his experiences at swimming had been bad, the past dealings with the strong currents and the boulders etched in his mind. He had not tried to swim in several years, since he last chased a snake into the water in a futile effort to catch it and kill it in a shaking and slashing fury. Now that he was an old dog, he knew that his life was easier if he stayed out of the water. He was not built for swimming like beavers or snakes or water rats.

But he wanted to get back to the only home he had ever known, so into the dark river he plunged. He ran into the shallow pools of water and kept his head up and focused on the distant rising branches of the oak tree becoming more visible in the light. It was his beacon on the west side of the river. He waded deeper into the water, up to his haunches. When he moved to where the original edge of the riverbank had been, the footing fell away from him and he plunged deeper, his body splashing fully under. He lost sight of the tree.

He slashed with his paws, paddling and forcing his head above the surface. Beneath him the deep currents were stronger, pulling and pushing in opposite directions. When he would get under control, the current again would spin him and twist him the opposite direction of where he thought he was. He desperately paddled toward the tree but the swirling water turned him and faced him down toward the dam. His head bobbed above and below the surface as he fought to stay afloat. He could see the wide channel that flowed down to the enormous concrete wall that was illuminated with unnatural lights. He spun himself in the water and paddled furiously, his body seemingly helpless and somewhat lethargic in the water, unable to take foot and run like he could on the earth. Here he was held by the river itself, the water enveloping him, a great cold grasp that he could not overpower. He plunged below and blinked his eyes rapidly in the cold, wet blackness.

He rose back up and kicked and splashed and fought against a wave that tried to spin him back toward the dam. He panicked then, convinced the enormous machine would shred his carcass. He kicked harder until he found a shallow spot and got his paws in the mud and felt footing under him. His feet took over and he ran away from the deep and into a shallower pool and he splashed up out of it. He ran by the sycamore and did not stop until he reached the pine tree stumps spread out in the east field. He panted heavily, safely on dry land again. He turned and stared downriver at the giant concrete wall from which he had escaped.

In the east, he saw a prism of colors rising up above the horizon, the coming of dawn, and he turned and looked west across the river, glistening silver in the early morning light. He saw the oak tree in the morning sun, and he knew that he was still on the wrong side and would never get back across to his home. His instinct was clear: If he tried to swim again he would not survive. He had crossed the river for good.

AUBREY WAS SLEEPING WHEN Raynelle's voice woke him.

"Guvnah," she said, leaning over him. "Guvnah. Wake up. You tol' me to wake you up before it got light. It's about done there."

Raynelle was his all-time favorite. She was sixteen and had red hair that burned in his heart like a pine-knot fire. And here he was an old man, sixty-five, and something like this in his heart, stronger than him. He usually had better sense than to feel this way about a woman. He was hungover, but not too bad considering all he had drunk over the course of the dedication. Raynelle softened the blow of too much liquor. She softened everything for him.

He didn't open his eyes even though she kept shaking him, shouting, "Guvnah" in that high school girl squeal of hers. He told her months ago when he started driving her in Woody Garrett's old milk-truck turned camper out here to the river to call him by his first name, but she wouldn't ever do it. She would do just about anything else for him, but not that.

Raynelle kept trying to wake him, even though he was not asleep, just playing dead, stretched out naked on an old sleeping bag. The camper was cozy, just enough room for them to lie down.

"Guvnah," she said, leaning down on him, her hands on his shoulder, her naked parts rubbing on his chest. "Guvnah."

It made a man happy. He was happier to be himself more than any man could be, getting aroused as she tried to wake him, her smoothness brushing his skin.

This was the first time she had ever tried to wake him up,

and she wasn't ready for the rolled-back eyes, a trick he could do without even his hands. He'd learned it in the Army from a boy who claimed that his daddy had been a circus carnival clown who got run over by a train, the same boy who had taught him card tricks.

Raynelle continued trying to shake him awake, worried that she had a dead Guvnah on her hands. He kept as still as he could, only his member slowly rising to attention. She didn't see that one rather large sign of life. She was hovering over his face, trying to determine if he was breathing, when he did his famous trick—opened his eyelids while keeping his eye balls rolled backwards, exposing only white, glassy flesh in the dim morning light.

She screamed, jumped up, hitting her delicate noggin on the low ceiling, and fell down to him, thrashing, hysterical, tears opening up like a faucet.

"Honey pie, honey pie," he said, catching her in his arms. She trembled violently, and he wrapped his arms around tight. "Old Aubrey ain't gone yet. Although you got something so good it'll make a man die right on the spot. I ain't ready to go."

She continued to cry, still trembling, her skin cold and sleek against his, her pink nipples hard and wet from tears. He rolled her over—"let Uncle Aubrey take care of you, you sweet little baby chicken, let Uncle Aubrey make it all right."

After he finished, she napped and he climbed out of the camper and walked naked out into the brush in the cool morning dawn and looked out where the river was rising high beyond its banks and creeping up the hill. The hill to the south looked charred, as though it had burned, but he figured it was simply fog on the land in early light.

He walked to the edge of the water, a shallow pool on this side where it had risen out of its banks, and held his penis away from his body and peed. The stream trickled for a long while. When he was done he felt a tingling in his loins—doing it twice in one night at his age. He hadn't done it twice in the same day in ten years or more. He rubbed his flaccid pecker and his old wrinkled sack and stood there watching the water rise so slowly he could hardly tell it was moving. But it was moving, acquiring land for lake bottom, moving into the swales and up the low hills, inch-by-inch, turning from farmland and forest into Lake Terrell. He stood there, touching himself, wondering if there was any chance to get it up again.

He was lost in this thought when the clack of a pump-action shotgun startled him. Before he could turn, he felt a cold steel barrel jab him in the back of his neck.

ELMER HAD WAITED THERE all night, snoozing only moments at a time, his back up against the boulder at the end of the low cliff. The sky was beginning to lighten from navy blue to purple when he opened his eyes and saw Terrell climbing out of the camper. The old fool was naked except for his horn-rimmed glasses. He climbed over the truck gate and got both bare feet on the bumper, his bare ass sagging, and then stepped backwards onto the ground.

Elmer watched as Terrell turned and squinted, trying to make out the river. The land was dark with shadows but the surface of the river began to gleam with a silver sheen from the first rays of the sunlight climbing above the eastern horizon. He was so close that Elmer could have jammed the barrel right up his ass and fired.

But Elmer held still and let him go. His white skin was so pale that it seemed to suck up almost all of the light beneath the old oak tree, leaving everything else there in a state of pitch black while his old wrinkled body glowed like a snowman. His chest sagged and was covered in a tangle of gray hairs and he walked much more stooped over here, where he thought he was alone, than he usually did when strutting for the good people of Achena County.

Elmer let him get about ten yards ahead and then he stood and followed, the 20-gauge out in front of him, his hand on the stock ready to pump it and fire if the sumbitch turned around. The old man was heading down the bluff to the river, which Elmer could see had risen high and far and wide, spreading like a new aquatic cover on the old earth.

Elmer tried to step as lightly as he could so the old man would not hear his boots. The sun was below the horizon but coming up fast as the light increased with each minute. Elmer paused at the back of the open truck camper and listened. He could hear soft breathing sounds, not really snoring but sleepy and deep inhalations and exhalations. He was tempted to look in on Raynelle, to see her naked, but he was afraid she would scream and he didn't want any noise until the shotgun pump worked a shell into the chamber.

The old man walked down to the water and stood there, hunched over, looking out across the expanding river. He held his hand to his eyes and gazed at the churning surface, the frothy white specks amongst the silvery brownness of the water and mud and tree bark and all else in the river, the detritus of leaves and pine needles all washed together into what was becoming Lake Terrell. Elmer watched as he walked down the short hill to the edge of the water, where it had risen, and took a piss, the stream dribbling from him into the new lake bearing his name. He peed for a long time.

Elmer crept up slowly, the shotgun at the ready, until he was only five feet behind the buck-naked old man, close enough to get a sniff of his aftershave. Terrell had finished peeing but was now touching himself, his right hand down on his genitals like he was scratching his balls, his face forward and occasionally turning to pan along the bloated river. The water was spreading far out across the opposite bank, but hadn't climbed up as high on the hilly side where Terrell stood, the low slant of the bluff where Elmer waited behind him with the shotgun.

They stood that way for a long minute, until the old man finally stopped rubbing his balls. Elmer worked the pump forward, that unmistakable sound of metal on metal and of the shell being fed into the chamber as the breech closed up tight and the pin got ready to hit the brass. Terrell began to turn but before he could, Elmer jabbed the muzzle against the back of his sleek old neck and poked him hard at the base of his skull.

"Mornin', you old sumbitch."

The old man gasped and let out sort of a low scream, a shocked sound, and reached his arms out to balance himself and avoid falling forward into the water. He got his feet steady and tried to turn but Elmer shoved with the end of the gun again. "Keep your eyes on the river, goddammit. Don't turn around or I'll shoot your ass right here. You'll die without knowing who kilt you."

"Who ... *who* is that?" Terrell's voice was higher, panicked.

"You mean you don't know my voice? You oughta be able to recognize your constituents, 'specially the ones you screwed out of their land."

The old man paused and then said softly, "Elmer?"

"That's me, Guvnah," Elmer said, spitting out the fake honorary title as he jabbed the gun into the old man's neck, a little lower this time, where it joined on with the spine between the shoulder blades. The old man stumbled again and threw his arms out to catch his balance as he bent over.

"Stand up straight, you old sumbitch," Elmer said.

The old man stood up straight. He was at least eight inches taller than Elmer.

"Elmer, son, why do you want to do this?" Terrell's voice was panicked but still had a little of that familiar confidence in it. "What would Lloyd say?"

"Lloyd would say I ought to kiss your ass like everybody else in this damn county. But I'd tell him I ain't going to do it."

"Son, you ain't thinking straight."

Elmer smacked the old man across the shoulder blades with the butt of the shotgun. Terrell fell forward onto his hands and knees into the dirt and cowered there.

"Don't you never call me *son*," Elmer said. "How you like my daddy's old 20-gauge?"

He held the gun crossways for Terrell to see, the way that rifles were presented in military processions. The old man was gasping to catch his breath and started to stand, but while he was bent over on the ground, Elmer kicked him hard in the ass and he fell prostrate next to the river.

He glared down at the old man and said, "I'm the only one thinking straight around here. The only goddamn one. But ain't nobody ever listen to me. And I ain't got the gift of bullshit like you. But you gonna listen to me now. I'm gonna speak the last words you hear before you go on down to hell."

The old man lifted up on his hands and was trying to stand, shakily. Elmer stepped back and let him get to his feet. Terrell again tried to turn and this time Elmer let him face him. In the creeping morning light Elmer could see that his face was red and his normally coiffed gray hair was a mess. His black horn-rimmed glasses were crooked.

"Elmer, you don't want to do this. Let me go and I won't say a thing. We both got a lot to live for. You are just hitting a bad spell. This ain't your nature."

Terrell had stepped forward and was beginning to gesture with his hands but Elmer raised the shotgun up and softly jabbed the muzzle into the old man's belly.

"How you know what my nature is? You knew my daddy. You think he's got a good nature?"

The old man kept his hands at his sides. "I knew your mama. She was a fine woman, as fine as any."

"I'm sure you think she's a fine woman as cheap as she let you have all our farm, land that had been in my family more than a hundred years."

The old man shook his head fast side-to-side, despite the shotgun pressing his belly.

"It wasn't like that, son. The bank was going to foreclose, to take everything from your mama. It was hard times, the big'un. I bought it and let them stay on their farm. Your mama would have been kicked out of that house if it wasn't for me."

Elmer swung the butt of the gun up at the old man's head and hit him in the jaw and knocked him to the ground. Terrell's glasses fell off and he stumbled and tried to keep his feet but couldn't hold, landing on his right side in the dirt.

"I told you not to call me son. Only my mama and daddy can do that. Now get your sorry ass up again."

Elmer nudged him with his boot. "Get up, now." The old man was starting to whine and his mouth was bleeding. "Get your ass on up. I got to talk to you, serious like."

The tall old man struggled but stood, his back to the glistening river, his front in shadows. The sunlight was increasing and Elmer could see the old man's chest was covered with dirt and mud and was red and blotchy. His belly was big but his legs were skinny and his penis and scrotum withered beneath a wild swirl of gray hair.

Elmer jabbed at Terrell's midsection with the shotgun. "Mama told me that you were going to give her a chance to buy it back. To take back the farm, but you never did allow that."

"I would have gladly sold it back to her." His voice had weakened. "But she never had the money. And then she took sick. There was nothing I could do."

"That's bullshit, Guvnah. You wanted that land for the lake. And you made a fortune selling it to the government, to Georgia Power, didn't you?"

The old man didn't say anything. He reached his hand up and rubbed his jaw and wiped blood away from his lower lip. The sky had shifted from dark blue to purple and was getting lighter. A fluffy cloud high in the sky was showing traces of pink and red in its billowing folds, while along the western horizon dark clouds bunched and thickened. The river water was lighter with a silvery gleam, but also visible were the white suds of froth where it churned in the brown muddy water.

"C'mon you old sumbitch. Tell me how much money you made off my land. Tell me how rich the Finleys made you."

Elmer prodded him with the gun again. He pushed him back a few steps so that Terrell stepped into six inches of cold water where the river had begun to pool.

"C'mon, goddamn it," Elmer said. "Tell me."

"I only did it for the good of Achena County. That's all I was thinking about. This lake here will be the best thing that ever happened to this area."

"Shit," Elmer said, and raised the butt and smashed Terrell across the side of his head, knocking him down and further into the shallow water.

Elmer looked down the river toward the dam, the morning

light bright enough to see the other side of the river where the water had spread far beyond the banks, maybe one hundred yards or so, to the field of pine stumps. It was no longer a river, it was becoming a lake, and it was happening fast, the water churning and flowing backwards. The old man crawled from the shallow water to a dry spot beyond the water line and lay curled on his side, moaning.

Elmer saw his glasses lying in the dirt. He went over and crunched them with the stamp of a boot heel, the plastic and glass cracking. The old man cried out when he heard his glasses shatter. "Elmer, goddamn you. Why you want to do this to me, boy?"

He gasped and tried to stand but couldn't, and rolled back onto his side, looking up at Elmer. He was wet and his skin red with exertion and his eyes were crazy.

"You oughtn't do this to me, son. I kept you from going to jail for what you did to that woman at the prison farm. Don't you know that?"

Elmer raised the gun and put his finger on the trigger and pointed it at the old man, sighting it on his forehead. He tensed to pull the trigger but yanked up on the barrel and fired into the air, the gun kicking back firm into his shoulder and the echo of buckshot filling the river valley and drowning out the slush of the water for a moment.

The shot silenced the old man's whimper. Elmer stepped over to him as though to kick him but held off, getting up close to his face.

"We both know that ain't true. You could have kept me in my job if you wanted. But that's not what I'm upset about. I'm upset about my land, my family's land. That's what this is about. It's about the Finley land that you took. And what you are doing to it."

Elmer looked around and gestured to the flooding river with his shotgun. He poked the old man in the side with the barrel. "Tell me you are sorry, you old sumbitch. Tell me you are wrong for what you have done and that you are sorry for it."

The old man looked away and then at the ground but didn't say anything. Elmer again prodded him in the gut with the muzzle.

"C'mon, you old sumbitch. You conniving old bastard. Tell me the truth. You was wrong and you are sorry."

Elmer continued prodding him as he lay on his side, until all of a sudden the old man pushed at Elmer and rose up halfway on his knees and yelled, "I ain't done nothing wrong, goddamn you."

He flailed his long arms in Elmer's direction. Elmer let him take a few futile swings before he took his boot and planted the heel square in the old naked man's chest and kicked him into the water. Terrell fell splashing and hollering and moaning and jibbering. He came back up faster than Elmer expected and surprised him by getting to his feet and charging, like some wild prehistoric reptile cracked open from his shell. He was on Elmer quick, but Elmer simply stepped back and slammed the butt of the gun into his gut and knocked him down again.

Elmer waded after him into the edge of the shallow pool along what had been the riverbanks. He put his boot on Terrell's throat and pressed him down under the water.

"You gonna drown in your own goddamn lake, boy. You gonna drown in your own goddamn lake. How you like that?"

He pressed some more and the old man began to gurgle. Terrell began to fight harder and Elmer grew tired of hassling with him. He worked the pump back and the empty red shell popped out the right side of the breech into the water and

floated there a moment before it sunk. Elmer watched the
shell submerge under the water of Lake Terrell. He worked the
pump forward and another shell slid into the chamber and he
turned the gun on Terrell's head and snuggled the muzzle up
close to his brow, the old man half-conscious and on his side
in two-feet of cold lapping water.

Elmer didn't blink when he pulled the trigger. The muzzle
flashed and Terrell's head splashed red and his body went limp,
receding in the shallows, blood gushing from his ruined eye
sockets. Elmer kicked at Terrell, pushing him out toward the
deeper water, and then turned and walked back to the shore
and set his gun down on the dry ground. He waded back to
where Terrell's blood and brain matter swirled like oil amidst
the brown water and white froth.

Elmer grabbed the corpse by the feet and dragged him
through the shallow water to the old riverbank. Elmer felt for
the edge with his water-filled boots until the bottom gave way.
He stopped there and pulled Terrell's legs and propelled him
into the deep over the river channel. He watched the body
float in the current but then submerge into the roiling waters,
plummeting shoulders first below the Oogasula. Aubrey Terrell's bare white feet were the last to go under. Elmer suspected
the body would float back to the surface, or perhaps be ground
up in the machinery beneath the dam's generators. He turned
and waded back toward the bank.

Elmer was almost to dry land when he looked up and saw
Raynelle Watson standing beside the river's edge, naked as
a jaybird, a polished silver Colt .45 automatic in her hands
pointed at him, only about thirty feet away. The morning sun at
his back shone straight onto her sleek white body that glowed
in the light. She was easily the prettiest woman he had ever
seen naked or dressed, soft and white and curvy and smooth,

the hair between her legs as fiery red as that on her head. All he could do was smile.

Someone had taught her how to shoot because she held the .45 with both hands, her thin arms steady despite the weight of the shiny silver gun. Majorettes are remarkable athletes, he remembered his Uncle Lloyd telling him breathily during a halftime show.

She aimed the pistol at his chest and pulled back on the trigger. An explosion flamed from the barrel and the gun lifted up in a kick. He felt a thud in his sternum and his blood warm on his skin and he staggered backward. He looked at her and could see that her face was twisted up in tears. His vision blurred and he thought he saw a golden halo appear over her head and white, feathery wings sprout from her back, but she still cried mournfully, anguish in her eyes. He stayed on his feet for a moment, wishing he could go to her and take her in his arms and comfort her, but instead he fell back into Lake Terrell's Oogasula River-fed waters and sank beneath its surface forever.

PERCY HEARD A GUNSHOT from far across the river. It was distant but nonetheless he could tell it was not the old lady's handgun. The heavy explosion sounded like a deer hunter's shot echoing through the low valley that was filling up with water. He was certain it was the long gun that belonged to the spitting-scratching man who had scared him away earlier. He began to run away from the river east through the pine stumps on the far edge of the open field, the part of that forest graveyard nearest the river already beginning to submerge, the water about halfway up the low height of the stumps left behind. He darted through the maze of pine stumps, the needles under his feet soft like he was running across an enormous brown bed.

He could have stopped and slept at any place and been very comfortable. He was very tired, weary in his legs and back, but he kept going.

He ran straight into the rising sun, riffles of fire jutting above the horizon amidst the clouds that were bunched low and flat there. He was running farther away from his touchstones, his house, running against the desire to go home that pulled on him like a harness.

But he continued on. He crossed halfway through the pine stumps, the long expanse of wood tops like stools exposed to the sun and sky and rain. The field of stumps was enormous, and he ran until he was dead tired, only partway across the decimated forest east of the river. He paused to rest and looked back in the direction of the house where he had lived with the old lady and again thought of going back there. He wheezed trying to catch his breath, his tongue hanging. He heard another gunshot, this time more distant, but he could tell it was from the same weapon.

He paused and turned around and ran slowly toward the river again. He worried the old lady might be in trouble and he turned and headed back through the pine stumps, backtracking his trail, forcing his tired body along against his fears.

He ran for a long time until he approached the water and cut north where the land rose. The flood had widened and was taking more of the pine stump field and was sloshing around the sycamore where he had slept. The water had submerged the base of the sycamore's thick trunk. The squirrel he had chased into the tree was still up there screeching, running a circling path from branch to branch to branch, nervous eyes watching the rising water surrounding him.

He heard another gunshot, this one also in the distance across the river and north. It was not a shotgun this time, but a report from a handgun. It sounded too heavy to be the old lady's pistol, but maybe it was her gun. Percy worried about the old lady and thought about how the old man had loved her. He thought about diving into the river again and trying to swim across, but he knew that doing so would be the end of him. He pawed at the dirt and began to bark, his gruff call rapid and fast until he worked it up into a howl, a rueful and deep cry.

He howled and paused and howled again. He continued to howl until his lungs began to tire, and he rested longer stretches between each mournful wail. He could hear the cawing of crows from down the river and the skittering squirrel in the sycamore tree that was slowly drowning in the river that had gone mad.

He let out a last long howl and then stood in silence, panting, his big black tongue hanging loose from his mouth. He listened for the old lady's call, but it did not come. He feared another gunshot, but it did not come either. He feared more exploding lines of fire in the sky like he had seen last night, a night that seemed like years away if it had ever happened at all, but the streaks of flame did not appear. All he heard were the subterranean animals on the move through the brush, chipmunks and squirrels and rabbits all screaming about being forced out of their holes by the flood. In the few remaining treetops he heard the cries and squawks of birds as they flew from tree to tree. He looked up and saw three hawks circling above the river's expanding edges.

Percy grew so tired he could barely stand. The sun rose higher, propelled above the clouds that clung to the distant line of pines far from the river and the pooling lake. The sunlight was not blue or silvery on the water, but it was the color of shiny mud, wet and luminescent in the new day. He turned and again trotted slowly east, the only direction he could go, away from his home and the river he had once known but could no longer understand.

He moved wearily back down the other side of the bluff and into the field where the pine trees were cut and found a dry spot in the pine straw in the sun. He was so tired he began to stumble, and then he just lay where he fell. The sunlight on his still damp black fur felt good. He was exhausted and helpless. He gave up the fight to keep his eyes open.

PERCY AWOKE MANY HOURS later, the sun high overhead, and lay there feeling the warmth of the rays in his black fur. He was sore and tired from the exertion of chasing the rabbit and swimming for his life in the river. Despite the long sleep, he did not feel good. His bones were weary still and his breathing was labored. A strange taste permeated his mouth.

He lay there with his head flat against the ground. After a long while, he raised up and looked toward the lower stretch of the field to see that more of the pine stumps sat in water, the stumps nearest the river almost completely submerged. He couldn't get anywhere close to the old riverbank, the water spread out far from it. The sycamore tree where he had chased the squirrel was in deeper, the waterline high up on the trunk. The squirrel was running wild circles in the tree, its cries more hectic as the water reached for the low-hanging branches.

He rolled over onto his other side and looked down at the ditch where he had seen the puppies and saw that the water had covered that spot. He listened, but heard no yelps. Above, the hawks still sailed in tight loops over the river. He watched as one dived, its claws bared to snag some confused prey.

Percy put his head back down on the ground and lay there for a while, warming in the sun. He contemplated going back to the river, but he was too tired to move. And despite increasing clouds over the western horizon that smelled of rain, the sun had shifted behind him, shining along his back, warming his spine through his black coat. He felt as old and tired as he ever had in his life, the sun on his muscles comforting but not rejuvenating. His eyes began to droop, and he fell into a deep, dark sleep.

AFTER

Percy opens his eyes and sees a bright blue sky, all of the clouds gone. He stands easily and feels younger in his legs, his muscles strong and his lungs alive with the soft air of the river valley. He had fallen asleep in pine needles under an open sky, but now stands on lush grass beneath the sycamore tree, its leaves full and vibrant in the warm sunlight. He looks around at the pastures bathed in green and the pine forest majestic and uncut behind him. Birds sing happy songs in the crowns of the trees.

Down the hill the river is blue and sparkling and flowing south without impediment beneath the hanging branches of the willow trees. The sound of the current trickling is clear and the water smells fresh splashing over the granite boulders that bisect the river and offer him a path back to the other side.

He runs friskily to the bank and studies the boulders for only a moment before crossing, his paws firm on the rocks and his nails clicking as he runs over the river, jumping the three-foot gap with ease. He stops on a stone for a tongue-full of water, the drink crisp and pristine and as good as anything he has ever tasted. He laps up more of the fresh water until quenched, and then runs off the boulders and onto the other side of the riverbank toward home.

The brush is bright and green and the sun's rays disperse amongst the perfumed honeysuckle vines, and the blackberries smell fresh and fruity and ripe in the briar patch, but no thorns stick him. He runs on through the brush and into the junkyard where the cars are shiny and the tires a crisp black, the kudzu there like a decorative drapery. The oak tree to the side of the house is as full as he has ever seen, thick with leaves and squirrels and cardinals and blue jays, the birds singing their songs back and forth to one another.

The bathtub is gone, only the two rocking chairs adorn the porch. He runs up the path and climbs the porch steps, his eyes alive with excitement, feeling like a puppy again. He hears footsteps inside the house. The door opens and the old man comes out and smiles and calls to him, repeating his name, calling him "good boy, sweet boy," and reaches down and strokes his head and then takes both of his hands and rubs firmly on his neck. "You are a good boy, Percy. Percy's a good boy."

The old man pets him for a while and then reaches into the pocket of his overalls and pulls out a biscuit and a piece of a hot dog and feeds it to him. He eats, the bread flaky and warm and the hot dog juicy and satiating. Percy then flops over on his back and the old man crouches and rubs his belly, causing his back right paw to twitch in the happy rhythm of the old man's affectionate scratching.

After a while, the old man stands up and lights his pipe and sits in the rocking chair. The smoke smells sweet as it drifts down to Percy and he watches the puffs float through the yard and dissipate. The old man tilts back and then forward and then back again, that familiar creaking of the rockers on the hardwood porch floor. He rocks there looking out at the junkyard, studying the cars, all of which gleam with color and silvery chrome and clear glass windows. Percy sits on the floor next to him. The old man periodically reaches over and scratches his head, speaking again in the smooth tones, repeating his name and calling him a good boy.

They sit there a good long while when Percy begins to wonder about the old lady, where she is, if she is okay. He barks a low bark, softly, hoping that the old man can understand. The old man laughs and strokes his head and the back of his neck. "Don't you worry, boy. She'll be here with us before too long, boy. Don't worry. It won't be too long. She'll be here soon enough."

Percy licks his hand and the old man reaches down and puts his arm around his neck and hugs him so that Percy's head rests on his knee. The old man rubs the top of his skull and scratches softly behind his ears. They sit that way on the front porch, waiting on the old lady to come home for good, watching the river, the clear blue waters of the Oogasula flowing down through the riverbanks, southbound for the endless ocean, very cold and very far away from here.

ACKNOWLEDGMENTS

Writing a novel alone in a room with the door closed is mostly a solitary act, but I am indebted to so many who have opened doors for me along the way. I've been blessed with parents—Eddie and Jo Anne—who early in life showed me the joys of reading and storytelling, bosses who kept me gainfully employed and made being in an office or classroom a pleasant experience, teachers who inspired me to read and write and revise my work, friends who encouraged me (including many who read flawed drafts), agents who championed my work, and editors who made it better. Without all of this encouragement and support, I'd never have come close to finishing even a short story.

A lifetime of teachers from the first grade through grad school and beyond to whom I'm greatly indebted to include, but are not limited to, Tony Grooms, Conrad Fink, Kent Middleton, Leslie T. Sharpe, Tara McCarthy Altebrando, Alice Elliott Dark, Fran Bartkowski, Rachel Hadas, Jack Lynch, John Casey, Barry Hannah, Sam Frew, Darrell Sorrells, Fay Elliott, Milton Honeycutt, Steve Terry, Dave Brown, Don Davis, Marian Williams, Lynn Green, Patty Lee Rogers, and Avelyn Fort. I also want to thank everyone at the Sewanee Writers' Conference (and in particular Greg Williamson, who happily granted me permission to partially plagiarize two lines from his poem "Man").

A small selection of friends include my brother Dan Starnes, Lee Allen Wells, Tenaya Darlington, Mark Williams, Cecil Bentley, Ken Dowell, Dana Jennings, Jessica Handler, Jerry Mitchell, Chuck Spencer, Jeff Veasey, David Stevens, Ryan Lynch, Greg Gillespie, Roger Petersen, Tom Coyne, Mark Russell, Doug Landrum Jr., Brian Robinson, and my numerous buddies at the Green Valley Tennis Club.

Agents and editors include Scott Miller, Ellen Geiger and Arlene Prunkl. I am especially grateful to all the folks at NewSouth Books who made this publication possible, most notably Randall Williams and Suzanne La Rosa, but also Katharine Freeman who assisted with editing.

I want to thank two men in particular. My friend and marvelous writer Kevin Catalano read drafts of this novel and provided extremely insightful and encouraging feedback. Putnam County Sheriff Howard Sills, a storied lawman and detective of rare intelligence, integrity, and wit who exceeds in full any character the finest of our crime fiction writers can concoct, told me fascinating stories and answered numerous questions about weaponry, cars, trucks, law enforcement, politics, and the distinct details of the Middle Georgia region he has served and protected for more than thirty years.

Most importantly, I want to thank my wife, Amy, for her unwavering love and support, not to mention being a very perceptive reader and editor.